SEX AND DEATH
ON THE BEACH

Also by Elaine Viets

The Angela Richman, Death Investigator mysteries

BRAIN STORM
FIRE AND ASHES
A STAR IS DEAD *
DEATH GRIP *
LIFE WITHOUT PAROLE *
LATE FOR HIS OWN FUNERAL *
THE DEAD OF NIGHT *
A SCARLET DEATH *

The Dead-End Job mysteries

FINAL SAIL
BOARD STIFF
CATNAPPED!
CHECKED OUT
THE ART OF MURDER

The Josie Marcus, Mystery Shopper series

DYING IN STYLE
HIGH HEELS ARE MURDER
ACCESSORY TO MURDER
MURDER WITH ALL THE TRIMMINGS
THE FASHION HOUND MURDERS
AN UPLIFTING MURDER
DEATH ON A PLATTER
MURDER IS A PIECE OF CAKE
FIXING TO DIE
A DOG GONE MURDER

* available from Severn House

SEX AND DEATH ON THE BEACH

Elaine Viets

SEVERN
HOUSE

First world edition published in Great Britain and the USA in 2025
by Severn House, an imprint of Canongate Books Ltd,
14 High Street, Edinburgh EH1 1TE.

severnhouse.com

British Library Cataloguing-in-Publication Data
A CIP catalogue record for this title is available from the British Library.

ISBN-13: 978-1-4483-1479-9 (cased)
ISBN-13: 978-1-4483-1680-9 (e-book)

All Severn House titles are printed on acid-free paper.

Typeset by Palimpsest Book Production Ltd., Falkirk, Stirlingshire, Scotland.
Printed and bound in Great Britain by TJ Books, Padstow, Cornwall.

The manufacturer's authorised representative in the EU for product safety is
Authorised Rep Compliance Ltd, 71 Lower Baggot Street, Dublin D02 P593
Ireland (arccompliance.com)

Praise for Elaine Viets

"Multiple puzzles keep up the suspense"
Kirkus Reviews on *A Scarlet Death*

"Enjoyable . . . Plenty to like"
Publishers Weekly on *The Dead of Night*

"Will appeal to fans of Patricia Cornwell and Kathy Reichs"
Booklist on *Late for His Own Funeral*

"Angela's usual snark and fondness for wine help propel the twisty plot"
Publishers Weekly on *Late for His Own Funeral*

"A fascinating exploration of sex workers, high society, and the ways in which they feed off of one another"
Kings River Life on *Late for His Own Funeral*

"Viets consistently entertains"
Publishers Weekly on *Life Without Parole*

About the author

Elaine Viets is the author of the Angela Richman, Death Investigator series as well as the novella *Ice Blonde*. She has over thirty-five bestselling mysteries in four series. A St. Louis native, Elaine took the Medicolegal Death Investigator Training Course for forensic professionals at St. Louis University, and has won the Agatha, Anthony and Lefty Awards. Elaine received the Lifetime Achievement Award from the Malice Domestic mystery convention. *Sex and Death on the Beach* is the first title in the Florida Beach mystery series. Elaine lives in Fort Lauderdale with her husband, writer Don Crinklaw.

www.elaineviets.com

For Sara Porter, with thanks from Norah and me.

Acknowledgments

I've missed writing about my quirky adopted home, Florida, so it's good to be back. Mythical Peerless Point is similar to many beach towns, and its light-hearted exterior hides dark secrets.

I've brought some of these out into the sunlight for your enjoyment, and introduced you to more benign examples of the storied Florida Man and Woman. And yes, there really is an After School Satan Club.

In Florida, you can't make this stuff up.

It took a team to edit and produce this book, and I want to thank them.

Detective R.C. White, Fort Lauderdale Police Department (retired) and licensed private eye, and Synae White gave me many hours of advice and help. Thank you to death investigator Krysten Addison and Harold R. Messler, retired manager-criminalistics, St. Louis Police Laboratory. Gregg E. Brickman, author of *Imperfect Friends*, helped me kill off my characters. These experts did their best to make this novel accurate.

Many other people helped with this first Florida Beach mystery, including my husband, Don Crinklaw, first reader and critiquer.

Thanks also to my agent, Joshua Bilmes, president of JABberwocky Literary Agency, and the entire JABberwocky team. Joshua reads my novels and gives detailed suggestions to improve them. He also asked for many rewrites to perfect them.

Thanks to the Severn House staff, especially editor Sara Porter, who worked hard to polish this mystery and bring Norah to life. I also appreciate the sharp eyes of copyeditor Anna Harrisson. Cover artist Piers Tilbury perfectly captured my new mystery.

I'm grateful to Alan Portman, Jinny Gender, Alison McMahan and mystery writer Marcia Talley, author of *Circles of Death*. Thank you to the Summit Book Club for your helpful advice and direction and to Stephanie Nuria Sabato for your encouragement.

Special thanks to the many librarians, including those at the

Broward County, St. Louis, and St. Louis County libraries, who answered my questions, no matter how strange they seemed. I could not survive without the help and encouragement of librarians.

I hope I haven't missed anyone. I also hope you'll enjoy Norah McCarthy's first Florida adventure.

Remember, all mistakes are mine. I hope they won't spoil your reading enjoyment.

Email me at eviets@aol.com

ONE

My name is Norah McCarthy, and I own the most exclusive apartment building in Peerless Point, Florida. The Florodora is more than a hundred years old, the first apartment building in this south Florida beach town between Fort Lauderdale and Miami.

You don't need money or social status to rent an apartment at the Florodora. You must be a member of a more exclusive group. You have to be a genuine Florida Man or Woman. You've seen the headlines: 'Florida Man Busted with Meth, Guns and Baby Gator in Truck.' Or: 'Florida Woman Bathes in Mountain Dew in Attempt to Erase DNA after Committing Murder.'

Yes, those are real headlines. So is this one from the morning paper: 'Florida Man Arrested by Coast Guard for Trying to Cross Atlantic in Human-sized Hamster Wheel.'

Florida Men and Women stories often involve alcohol and alligators, although the Florida Man who tossed a live alligator the size of a Labrador through the drive-up window of a burger joint was probably sober.

Seems this Florida Man found a gator by the road and dumped it in the back of his pickup (pickups are Florida Man's favorite vehicle). Then he got out of the truck and chucked the gator through the burger joint drive-up window. *After* he paid for his soft drink.

Unbelievable?

That's the standard reaction to Florida Man. Are there any limits on his (or her) so-called pranks?

Nope. And many of them aren't funny. Including the Miami Cannibal, a naked marauder who attacked an innocent man, chewed off the poor guy's face and left him blind. The cops shot that Florida Man dead.

Webster's Dictionary didn't deign to define the Florida Man, but a slang dictionary says Florida Man 'commits bizarre or idiotic crimes, popularly associated with – and often reported in – Florida.'

Florida Man, known as the 'world's worst superhero,' became nationally famous in 2013 when he was given his own Twitter account. He's inspired a play, two TV series, a song, and more. Like many Floridians, my feelings about Florida Man and Woman are somewhere between appalled and perversely proud. I'm descended from an early Florida Woman, my grandmother, Eleanor Harriman.

Grandma always had a soft spot for scapegraces, since she was one herself. She was a Florodora Girl, a superstar chorus girl a century ago. Grandma was in the 1920 Broadway production of *Florodora*, before she eloped with handsome Johnny Harriman, a millionaire, back when a million was real money. She was married at sixteen and madly in love.

When I was old enough, Grandma told me about poor Johnny's accidental death, which involved a champagne bottle and a chandelier.

'I loved that man,' Grandma said. 'I'm glad he died happy.'

Johnny's death made Grandma a rich widow at seventeen. She moved to Peerless Point and built this apartment building right on the ocean in 1923, on a narrow barrier island.

The building was as quirky as Grandma, with grand rooms, odd hideaways and at least one secret staircase. To her bedroom.

Grandma never married again, but she never lacked for male companionship. In 1941, Grandma left the apartment with a caretaker and went north to New York for six months. She returned in mid-December with a newborn baby girl, Dot, my mother. Grandma said she'd adopted an unmarried cousin's baby.

Was Dot Grandma's biological daughter? No one knows for sure. Grandma raised Dot as her own. Pearl Harbor was bombed December seventh and the US entered World War Two. People had more important things to talk about than Dot's parentage.

I moved in with Grandma when I was four, after my parents were killed by a drunken driver in 1988. The residents became my family, an eccentric collection of honorary uncles and aunts. When Grandma died at age ninety-eight some twenty years ago, she left me the Florodora.

I miss her. Every day. I'm reminded of her constantly. Her life-size portrait dominates the apartment building's office on the first floor. Florodora Girls had to be either brunettes or redheads, weigh no more than 130 pounds and stand five-feet-four-inches tall. Grandma insisted that was 'tall for the time.' I inherited her thick dark hair and hope mine will turn the same shade of white as Grandma's hair when I get older. I'm five feet ten. I got my height from my father.

Grandpa Johnny commissioned the portrait of Grandma in her *Florodora* costume: a black picture hat, pink ruffled dress, long black gloves, and a frilly parasol. She was seventeen, a pink-cheeked brunette beauty. The costume was stunningly modest by today's standards, especially here on the beach.

Next to the portrait, Grandma had framed a newspaper critic's *Florodora* review. Here's my favorite phrase from the show's first run in the US: 'One of the most uncompromisingly filthy plays ever seen in New York.'

There was more, all of it disapproving. 'That review made the Florodora Girls a sensation,' Grandma said. 'Every rich man in New York wanted to see the show. It's how I met your dear grandfather.'

'What was so filthy about the show?' I asked.

'Most of the girls didn't wear pink tights when they danced.'

'That's it?' I laughed.

Grandma gave me a soft reproof. 'I know it seems quaint, dear, but Florodora Girls were in some very modern scandals. Stanford White, the famous architect, was shot and killed by Harry Thaw, the husband of Evelyn Nesbit, for drugging and raping that poor child.'

'Evelyn, the girl in the movie *Ragtime*?'

'Yes. Also, an older movie, *The Girl in the Red Velvet Swing*. The real story was quite different. Evelyn was sixteen when White took up with her. He was married and in his fifties. He drugged and raped her. Terrible man, and yet everyone thinks he's the victim.'

That story tells you a lot about Grandma. So does the apartment building.

The Florodora is a prime example of high-style Spanish Colonial, a white stucco structure with a red barrel-tile roof. The windows in front have elaborate plaster Churrigueresque style, which make the windows look like they're framed in cake frosting.

If you drive past the Florodora on South Ocean Drive, you'll see the old white apartment building looks much the same as it did during the Roaring Twenties. It's shaded by palm trees and surrounded by a coral rock wall with purple bougainvillea spilling over the top. The Florodora is set back from the sidewalk by a courtyard cooled with a jungle of tropical plants.

The courtyard's centerpiece is a swimming pool with a flirty Twenties' bathing beauty in mosaic on the bottom. Most days you'll find the apartment's carefully curated collection of misfits sunning themselves by the pool.

Not today. The plumbers, Liam and Lester Sykes, were digging up the courtyard. Again. Once again, the antique plumbing was a problem.

The Florodora needs constant maintenance. That may be why it's almost the only old Florida building left on Ocean Drive. On either side of the building, and marching relentlessly down to Miami, are high-rise condos. Most look like shoeboxes standing on end. The condo to the north of us, the High Tide, definitely belonged to the shoebox architectural school.

So did the condo to the south, the Crocus. Because the average age of its residents was eighty, the locals called it the Croak Us.

Developers offered Grandma fabulous sums for the Florodora and its five-acre lot, but she stubbornly refused to sell.

Grandma made me promise not to sell the building or the property. I gladly keep that promise. I love the Florodora almost as much as I loved Grandma. Besides, there's no reason to sell it. I have plenty of money. I'm forty-one and love beach life.

What you can't see from the road is the beachfront. The Florodora sits on the edge of the Beachwalk, a wide strip of boardwalk teeming with tourists and vendors selling everything from ice cream and rum-filled pineapples to T-shirts and beach umbrellas. The sea air smells of salt and suntan lotion and the breeze is soft on the hottest days.

I longed to be out there now, but I couldn't lounge on the beach. After I got the bad news from the plumber, I went back inside to finish my work. I needed to find a new resident for the empty apartment. It had been vacant for a year now, after the last resident moved to Seattle. The extra bucks would help pay for the plumbers.

I kept my grandmother's tradition of renting to Florida Men and Women, using my gut feeling. After years of living with Grandma's choices, I thought I could recognize the more benign versions of the breed.

There was no way I could advertise for the resident I wanted. I needed a referral from someone I trusted. Ben the beach cop had found two possible renters. The third one just showed up.

The four-story Florodora has eight apartments. Each floor has only two suites, and they're two thousand square feet. That's huge by beach standards. People will kill for a big, affordable apartment with ocean views.

The special Floridians at the Florodora Apartments have never been in the news – not yet, anyway. Not even Billie, who held up a convenience store with a banana and stole three overdone dogs from its hot dog roller grill.

The empty apartment is on the first floor. Next to it lives Mickey, our artistic saboteur. Kind, gentle Mickey lives alone and works as a freelance artist, but she's been known to vandalize for a good cause.

When posters appeared on the local telephone poles insulting black people, Mickey was horrified. She went around Peerless, covering the offensive posters with her homemade one, which said, 'I covered the ugly racist poster here with a cat photo.'

My favorite prank was what Mickey did in the local gas station bathroom. In the restroom was a wall-mounted infant diaper changing station that pulled down into a changing bed. Mickey put a sign on the plastic baby bed that said, 'Place sacrifice here.'

Right above Mickey, on the second floor, lives Lennox, a Shakespearean actor and my grandmother's last tenant. Somewhere in his seventies, I'm not sure if Lennox is a real Florida Man. Maybe forty-five years ago, when Grandma rented to a flamboyantly gay actor, that was a qualification.

Right now, Lennox is playing Bottom in a local production of *A Midsummer Night's Dream*.

Mickey is helping Lennox run his lines for the Pyramus and Thisbe scene. Lennox has a voice that can be heard in the back of the theater. Without a microphone.

Lennox asked, '"What is Pyramus – a lover or a tyrant?"'

Mickey, reading Quince's part, said in a flat voice, "'A lover that kills himself most gallant for love.'"

Lennox started in bravely on the next line, declaiming, "'That will ask some tears in the true performing of it.'" A long, awkward pause, and then Lennox said, 'Line.'

Mickey prompted, "'If I do it, let the audience look to their . . .'"

"'Eyes!'" Lennox said, and finished the passage.

Next to Lennox on the second floor is a real Florida Woman, Willow. Five years ago, Willow was a successful Manhattan model known as Gorgeous Gwen. Max Devine, a big deal designer, caught her eating a cheeseburger and fries in a diner.

'Stop that, darling.' He tried to take the cheeseburger out of her hand. 'Fast food will make you fat.'

'Not as fat as your head,' Willow said, and broke the plate over his head.

Fortunately, Gwen had saved enough money to retire to Florida. Now she cultivates pot and studies Eastern philosophy.

Willow loves bright flowers and good weed. I can smell what Willow is doing. She's smoking her latest cannabis crop on her back balcony, where she gardens. Willow has long blonde hair and wears loose, floaty clothes. Usually. Last year, Willow grew Godfather OG, supposedly the world's strongest weed strain. When the crop was ready, Willow fixed a fat doobie and sat on her balcony, watching the sunset. About midnight, I got a call from the pastor of the Peerless Point Christian Church. Willow was bathing in the baptismal pool, buck-naked, with flowers in her hair. The pastor promised not to call the cops, if I would pick up Willow and pay for the damages.

The pastor said the font would have to be drained, cleaned and sanitized, then refilled with fresh, purified water. That would cost five hundred dollars. He didn't charge to bless the fountain again. I wrote a check to the pastor, then wrapped Willow in a white robe and drove her home.

Billie the banana bandit lives on the third floor. Since he couldn't hang by the pool today, he retreated to his living room to watch old movies. *Rocky,* by the sound of it. Billie writes retrospectives about movies. His first book was a *New York Times* bestseller.

Billie worries his crime will somehow come to light, even though there was no police report and he ate the evidence.

I live on the top floor, in Grandma's old apartment. Dean the diver lives next door to me. That's convenient, since Dean and I are sometime lovers. I'm sure the whole building knows that. Dean is forty-two, with blond hair and hazel eyes. Smart and funny. A certified hunk. Grandma would have said he was the bee's knees.

I went with a different gut feeling when I saw Dean. I felt the Florodora could use some eye candy. I admired Billie the banana bandit's fine mind, but Billie could turn a person into a pillar of salt when he talked about his latest movie obsession.

Two weeks after moving into the Florodora, Dean proved he was a real Florida Man. He drove through Peerless Lakes, a charming subdivision with a duck pond. A mamma duck was leading a parade of eight fluffy yellow ducklings across the road.

Most locals who took the shortcut through the subdivision were amused by the delay, but a self-important jerk in a Bentley had a fit. He hit the horn, causing the mother duck to squawk and the panicked ducklings scattered on the road. The drivers, including Dean, put their cars in park and began rounding up the ducklings.

Bentley Man got out, captured a duckling hiding by his front tire, and tried to twist its head off. Dean decked the guy, held him by the tie, punched twice more until Bentley Man's nose was bleeding on his bespoke suit. Then Dean delivered the duckling to safety. The bystanders cheered.

Meanwhile the Peerless police were called. A woman showed the uniformed officer a video of the action. The cop studied it and told Bentley Man, 'Well, you can file assault charges against this duck-rescuing gentleman, but then I'd have to cite you for attempted cruelty to animals. You could get up to a five-thousand-dollar fine and a year in jail if you're convicted. And when you're convicted, your name will be on the Animal Cruelty Offender Registry.

'What business are you in?'

'Real estate,' Bentley Man said.

'Not a good look,' the cop said. 'I'll tell you what. If you refuse to file charges against this man, and this nice woman who videoed your attack on a baby duck agrees not to sell the video to the television stations, you can go.'

'I'll go.' Bentley Man started for his car.

The cop stepped in front of Bentley Man. 'Wait a minute, sir. You owe that videographer compensation for lost income. Write her a check for five hundred dollars, right now.'

Bentley Man reluctantly wrote the check.

'And now you'll write another check for five hundred dollars to the Peerless Point Animal Shelter. I'll mail it myself.'

Bentley Man squawked.

'It's tax deductible,' the cop said. 'Think what the bad publicity would cost you.'

By the time Bentley Man wrote the second check, the cop had all the witnesses' names and the ducks were escorted to safety.

That night Dean and Mickey made 'duck crossing' signs and put them up on the spot where the baby ducks were almost squashed.

The signs are still there. Mickey told me the story. Dean would only admit, 'I ducked the assault charges.'

I'm the only one who knows Dean is an ex-cop who went into Witness Protection after he testified against fifteen mobsters who ran online prostitution rings, selling underage girls. The mob put out a contract on Dean while he spent two stressful years testifying against the cyber-pimps. Dean's testimony put fourteen mobsters in prison. Another hanged himself.

A visit to a plastic surgeon changed Dean's looks. Now he lives at the beach, drinking, fishing and diving. It's lobster season, and today he's diving for spiny lobsters.

I like our current residents, though not in the same way as Dean. I was relieved when the live-in staff agreed to stay on after Grandma died. Calypso, the housekeeper, is Bahamian, what the islanders call a 'big-panty woman.' She is proud of her callipygous posterior. Calypso keeps the Florodora shining and cleans the residents' rooms, as she sings spirituals in a pure, clear contralto, a preview of the heavenly choir.

Rafael, a dark, stocky man who knows inventive ways to repair ancient machinery, handles maintenance and takes care of the grounds. He keeps the building one step ahead of the city inspectors, who are determined to shut us down. I figure the inspectors are in the pay of the developers, and will get a hefty bonus if they successfully condemn the Florodora.

Rafael has a bachelor apartment above the garage. Calypso lives rent-free in my parents' old apartment, 302. It's supposed to be haunted. 'I don't believe in ghosts,' the housekeeper said. 'But I do believe in a good deal.'

Calypso is quirky, but too hard-working to be a Florida Woman. The same goes for Rafael. He's definitely not Florida Man material.

So that's the Florodora line-up: a Shakespearean actor my grandmother found, and my four picks: Billie the banana bandit; Mickey the artistic saboteur; Willow, the pot-smoking ex-model; and Dean the duck-saving diver.

I did well picking those four, so you'd think I'd know exactly who'd fit in, but I couldn't find the right person. I sat behind the reception desk, reading through my file of applicants.

One applicant was an accountant. I asked him what was the craziest thing he'd ever done. He confessed to skinny dipping 'but it was dark and I was alone. No one saw me.'

He definitely wasn't a Florida Man. Especially since he wanted 'peace and quiet.'

I could hear Calypso vacuuming the upstairs hall and singing 'What a Friend We Have in Jesus' while the Sykes brothers tore up the courtyard with a mini-excavator. Rafael was trimming the bougainvillea with something that sounded like a dental drill. Drunken college students were playing beach volleyball to cheers and loud Eighties music. Plus Lennox was declaiming Shakespeare and Billie was watching TV at full volume.

No way that accountant would be happy at the Florodora. Sorry, sir, I thought. No peace and quiet here. Application denied. For your own good.

A woman wanted an apartment for herself and her sixteen 'very clean cats.' The craziest thing this woman ever did was make a kitty litter cake for a party. The cake looked like a dirty litter box, using melted Tootsie Rolls. It was served in a real litter box.

Yuck. No thank you.

I still had the three applications from Sammie Lant. Ugh. That woman ignited such a red rage in me, I forgot manners and customer service. About six months ago, she applied for the empty apartment. I told her no. She was the worst kind of Florida Woman.

Sammie was locally famous – make that notorious – for having sex on the beach with a college quarterback during spring break. The beach cop threw a blanket over the copulating couple and hauled them off to jail for indecent exposure. The judge fined them both, but Sammie's partner lost his college scholarship for lascivious behavior.

Sammie thought it was funny that she'd destroyed a young man's promising career.

She was back the next week, offering me double the rent. I still said no. The third time Sammie caught me when I was outside, watering the courtyard plants. Calypso was sweeping. Sammie was dressed formally for Florida, in a red blouse, black pleather skirt, and red heels with rhinestone butterflies. Her blonde hair hung loose and her bulging breasts were nearly falling out of her top. A rhinestone butterfly rested in her décolleté.

This Sammie attempted a hoity-toity accent. 'The Lants are an old Lancaster family,' she said. 'That's Lancaster in England. Your building has nothing but nobodies.' She looked pointedly at Calypso and said, 'And mutts.'

That's when I lost my temper. 'Old families are like potatoes,' I said. 'The best part is underground. And that's where I'd like to put you. If you ever come back and insult me or my residents again, you'll regret it. I will never, ever rent that apartment to you. I will rent it over my dead body. Or better yet, yours.'

We must have been arguing pretty loud, because someone called 911. Jordan DeMille, a Peerless Point cop, showed up. I wasn't sure how much he'd heard.

Sammie cried crocodile tears and said, 'Did you hear that, Officer? She threatened my life.'

'Yeah, yeah, Sammie,' Jordan DeMille said. Like most of the local force, he was sick of Sammie's shenanigans. DeMille marched Sammie out of there, to the cheers of the Florodora residents.

'If that woman moved in here, I would have given notice,' Calypso said. All the other residents had quietly told me the same thing after Sammie's first application. She was universally hated at the Florodora.

That day was the last time I'd seen Sammie. I remembered the date. April nineteenth, five months ago. A bad day all around.

That morning, I'd misplaced the locket my grandmother had given me. The one with the photos of my parents. The clasp broke and I set it on the table by the pool. Calypso and I looked everywhere, but it had disappeared.

'It will turn up,' I told her. 'It couldn't walk away.'

I never found it.

I checked the stack again, but there were no more applicants. I listened to the clock tick and the familiar blend of Florodora noise, when suddenly I heard loud screams. So loud, Calypso switched off her vacuum and pounded outside. I followed her. We were hit by a horrible sight.

A muddy Liam the plumber was pointing into the hole excavated for the pipes and shouting, 'Dead. Real dead.' Lester was throwing up in a potted palm.

I looked over the side of the excavation. Even though the body was reduced to a pile of cartilage, bones and scraps of skin that looked like dirty clothing, I knew who it was.

Sammie Lant. She'd been strangled with a gold bikini top.

I felt like I'd been socked in the stomach. Was one of the Florodora's residents a killer?

TWO

South Florida's humid air was like swimming in warm soup, but it didn't ward off the chill in my body. After I saw the remains, I felt so cold I was shaking, and my teeth chattered. I couldn't stop them.

'You're in shock,' Calypso said, her brown eyes soft with sympathy. Calypso wrapped me in a warm blanket, then wrapped me in her arms. Calypso reminded me of my grandmother, with her pink cotton sundress and her graying hair pulled into a tight bun.

'It will be OK, dear,' she said. 'You'll see.'

'How? A woman is dead. We can't fix that.'

'It's probably that no-good Sammie,' Calypso said. 'Good riddance.'

'Shh,' I said. 'Don't let the police hear you.'

Calypso guided me to a striped deckchair by the pool and said, 'Sit. I'll get you some water.'

'I can get it.'

'Sit.'

It was a command. I sat.

While I waited, I studied the desecrated Florodora courtyard, my favorite spot. The pool with its mosaic on the bottom: the dark-haired Twenties' bathing beauty in a blue one-piece suit and a big polka-dot bow on her bobbed hair. She had a saucy wink and a Japanese sun umbrella.

As a kid, I would swim down and try to touch her face. As an adult, I'd swim laps, barely noticing the flirty charmer below. Then I'd climb out and sun in a striped chair, lulled to sleep by the whispering palms.

Now, that peace was gone. Uniformed Peerless Point police boiled over the place, corralling protesting residents and sending them to their rooms like disobedient children. Calypso couldn't even deliver the glass of water – she was sent to her apartment. So was Rafael, who had to abandon his garden work.

Liam and Lester were separated and ordered to stay. One was sent to the lounge, the other to the kitchen. Both silently radiated outrage. I was sure they would charge me double for this indignity.

That's when Detective Jordan DeMille arrived. DeMille was almost too pretty to be a cop. He was in his mid-thirties. His eyelashes were enviably long, and you could build condos on his cheekbones. He had a strong chin, stronger shoulders and long, muscular legs. Even his dark hair looked strong.

Most women's hearts beat faster if DeMille showed up on their doorstep.

Not mine. When I saw DeMille enter the Florodora courtyard, my heart stuttered and nearly stopped. He was the Peerless Point detective who'd heard me arguing with Sammie back in April. He'd heard me scream I would 'never, ever rent that apartment to you. I will rent it over my dead body. Or better yet, yours.'

And here was Sammie in my yard. Deader than disco.

A force as small as Peerless Point can't afford a full-time homicide detective, so DeMille investigated serious crimes.

He stared down into the hole that Liam and Lester had created. It was about four feet deep and the thin, tan soil was dry and crumbly. At the bottom was the pathetic pile of bones, skin rags and stained clothes.

'The victim wore mostly plastic and polyester,' DeMille said. 'That doesn't deteriorate as fast as natural fabrics.'

We could see the remains of a muddy red blouse, a pleather mini skirt, and red heels with rhinestone butterflies. The victim had long, dirty blonde hair. That was a description – the hair was muddy. Sammie's hair color was brassy, like her porn star profession.

Sammie had worn that outfit the last time I saw her. Except for the gold bikini top wrapped around the neck.

'Any idea who this is?' DeMille asked.

'No!' I sounded startled – and guilty.

'I don't know anyone who looks like that,' I added, truthfully. The remains were black and shriveled as a month-old banana skin.

DeMille was no dummy. 'That could be Sammie Lant,' he said.

'Really? Haven't seen her in months,' I said.

'Her agent reported her missing,' DeMille said, 'when she didn't show up for the premier of her movie, *Sex on the Beach*.'

'Porn movies have premieres?' I said.

'Her agent said it was an adult art film.'

'With no costume budget,' I said.

'I seem to remember you had a knock-down, drag-out fight with her.'

'I remember telling Sammie I wouldn't rent an apartment to her,' I said. 'Have you ID'd this person already, Detective? Do you know it's Sammie Lant? Or are you theorizing in advance of the facts?' That was a line from Sherlock Holmes I liked.

'The crime scene techs will be here shortly,' he said. 'Please wait in your apartment while I talk to the other witnesses.'

I was glad to leave the scene before DeMille asked more uncomfortable questions. He was a good cop. Once he reread the police report, he would consider our altercation a motive for murder. I'd have to be careful.

I could have taken the elevator, but I couldn't stand to be cooped up in that coffin-sized device. By the time I climbed the four flights to my apartment, I'd stopped shaking. My apartment was my refuge. I'd kept most of my grandmother's furniture – she had some delightful funky stuff, including a lamp with two frogs singing under glass flower shades, a stone gargoyle named Dolly, and offbeat collages by her favorite Florida artist, Dorothy Simpson Krause.

I also kept Grandma's offbeat collection of Florida souvenirs, including ceramic flamingo salt-and-pepper shakers, a needle-point pillow that said, 'Salt Margaritas, Not Sidewalks,' and weirdest of all, a manatee in a snow globe. Why that poor creature was trapped in a fake snowstorm I'll never know.

I kneeled on the comfortable white couch by the living-room window and carefully pushed aside the curtain. I saw the hole, with a ladder going into it. Crowded into the hole were two techs wearing white hooded suits, and their case of tools. The techs were moving carefully in the hole, but I couldn't hear them.

I eased up the window, hoping they couldn't hear it squeak.

Sound carries at the beach. The hot sticky air rushed in, and I heard the woman tech say, 'Glad this one is in the final stage of decomp, Art. There's almost no stink.'

Art said, 'I'm not gonna use it for aftershave, Em, but at least we can stand it. Florida has one of the fastest decomp rates in the country.'

Another reason to live here, I thought. Florida leads the nation in corruption.

'Hey,' Art said. 'The decedent has breast implants. They're numbered, so we can ID her if she doesn't have dental records. And look at this,' he continued. Next to the body was a gold beach bag. At least I think it was gold – it was badly stained by body fluids.

Art photographed the bag in place, then removed it and photographed it again.

'It's Gucci,' Art said, pointing to the designer logo.

Emily snorted. 'It's fake, Art. Like her tits. Something is spelled out in rhinestones on the bag. What's it say?'

Art peered at the bag and read, 'I Have Sand in My Happy Place.'

Emily snorted. 'Tacky.'

Art photographed the beach bag's interior, then fished out a pink wallet and opened it. 'Well, well,' he said. 'Looks like our dead woman is Sammie Lant, star of *Sex on the Beach*.'

Suddenly, the spring break scandal fell into place for me. Sammie had seduced that poor young football player on purpose. His undoing was publicity for her porn movie.

'There's a receipt in the wallet,' Art said. He photographed a strip of white paper and whistled. 'That woman could pound it down. She went to the Beach Bar and had six strawberry margaritas at fourteen dollars each, and a cheeseburger. Her lunch was a hundred thirty bucks with tip.'

'Is there a readable date on there?' Emily asked.

'Friday, April nineteenth. At 1:03 p.m. I'd better text DeMille. He'll want to know this.'

While Art contacted the detective, Emily pulled a tube of suntan lotion from the beach bag, photographed it, put it in a plastic bag, and wrote something on it. She called that process 'bagging and tagging.' A plastic hairbrush was next, followed by a black lipstick tube and a beach towel.

She also found the bottom half of a gold string bikini, and held it up.

Art frowned. 'What is that?'

'Butt floss,' Emily said.

Art looked puzzled.

'It's the bottom of a string bikini.' Emily's lip curled as she picked up the skimpy item to bag and tag it. 'Glad I'm wearing gloves.'

'You sure?' Art said. 'That's not enough material for a Band-Aid.'

I watched DeMille hurry over to the two techs, and peer down into the hole. 'You got something for me?'

'It looks like the victim is Sammie Lant, the porn star,' Art said. 'We found her wallet.'

'Good,' DeMille said. 'We'll have to confirm it with dental records to make it official.'

'If she doesn't have dental records, she has implants, so we can use those.' Emily's face – the part visible in her white hooded suit – was bright pink, and not from the sun. She had a crush on DeMille. Couldn't blame her. The man was quite the hunk in his dark suit pants and starched blue shirt, sleeves rolled to the elbow.

'We—' Art started to say, but Emily talked right over him.

'—found a receipt from the Beach Bar dated Friday, April nineteenth. Should I call the credit card company and find out if the card has been used since then?'

DeMille smiled at Emily, and she turned even redder. Some of her long blonde hair had escaped her hood, and she tucked it back inside. Even in the shapeless white suit, Emily had a knockout figure. Art was short, skinny and bald.

'Good idea, Emily,' DeMille said.

'I need you two to stop work right now. I'll have to get a search warrant ASAP. Emily, I'll be inside, working on the search warrant. Let me know what you find out when you call the credit card company.'

DeMille headed toward the Florodora. Once the detective was inside, Art taunted the tech with a nursery rhyme.

'DeMille and Emily sitting in a tree, K-I-S-S-I-N-G. First comes love, then comes marriage, Then comes baby in a baby carriage.'

Emily was fire-faced now. 'Shut up, Art,' she said.

'You like him,' Art said.

'Professionally,' she said. 'And you're jealous.'

'Why would I be jealous? Sure, his muscles have muscles, but I have a massive brain. You never seem to admire that.'

'I do,' Emily said. 'I like working with you. You're smart and . . . and . . . nice.'

'*Nice!*' Art staggered backward in pretend horror, and clutched his heart. 'Nice? You wound me. Sweet old grannies are nice. Kitten calendars are nice. Men should be more.'

'I have to make a call, Art.' Emily picked up the bagged credit card, climbed out of the hole, and sat on a deckchair in the shade. I heard her make the call, pretending to be Sammie.

Art began packing up their tools.

Judging by the bland music coming from her phone, Emily was on hold. Finally, she started talking, asking about the card. I caught parts of her conversation.

'So the card hasn't been used since last spring,' she said.

Silence. Then she said, 'I understand why you canceled it. That's all I needed to know.' Emily hung up, pulled her hood off, brushed her long hair, then brought out a mirror and checked her face. After another coat of lipstick, she stood up.

'Sammie's credit card hasn't been used since April nineteenth, Art. One more indicator that she's the dead woman. I'm going to tell DeMille.'

Emily practically skipped into the Florodora. 'This is good news,' she said.

For the detective, I thought. But not for me.

THREE

I watched Detective DeMille order yellow crime scene tape strung around the yard. Then he posted a uniform at the dig and another at the gate. A third uniform blocked off the sidewalk along Ocean Drive and a fourth was on the Beachwalk to keep sightseers away. Emily helped Art put a tent over the hole to hide the remains. Then the two techs hauled away their gear and left. Detective DeMille followed them.

I couldn't watch any more. I was certain that Sammie Lant was dead, and she'd been strangled at the Florodora.

I was heartsick someone had been murdered at my beloved home, and horrified that a resident might be a killer. I wanted to feel some sympathy for Sammie, but couldn't. I wasn't Mother Teresa.

I shut the window and tried to run downstairs to Willow. She was growing weed on her balcony, and that was illegal in Florida. Possession of more than twenty grams was a felony, and Willow could get up to five years in prison and a five-thousand-dollar fine. Last time I checked, she had a couple of pounds of dried buds and at least six plants on the balcony. The cops would lock her up and throw away the key.

I couldn't call her – the cops had taken away our cell phones when they sent us to our rooms. Willow didn't have a landline like I did. If I went out of my room to see her, the uniform on guard would send me back.

Willow would never survive prison. She was too otherworldly. As I worried about Willow, I paced my living room. The décor was a combination of my grandmother's quirky personality and my own touches.

The walls were white, and most were covered with bookcases stuffed with much-read favorites. Next to the white couch was a mahogany carved chair, which Grandma said once belonged to a beer baron. He must have consumed a lot of his own product, since the seat was pretty wide. The floor had a beachy woven seagrass carpet.

Finally, worn out by pointless pacing, I flopped on my couch, and stared at the silver-framed photo of my grandparents, taken the day they eloped in 1922. At twenty-one, Grandpa was a handsome devil, with dark center-parted hair and a wicked smile. Grandma carried a big bouquet of white lilies, and looked at her groom with adoring eyes. She was only sixteen, and she loved him passionately until the day he died. Which was only a year away.

Staring at the photo, I could almost feel my grandparents' comforting spirits. And then I remembered Grandma's secret staircase. It ran from a door on the beach side of the building up to my apartment. Maybe I could use it to warn Willow.

The staircase door ended in my bedroom closet. I opened the closet, frantically pulled out the clothes on hangers, and threw them on my bed. My shoeboxes followed. I slid aside a painting of a tall tree that was actually the door. Grabbing the flashlight in my bedside nightstand, I crept down the dusty staircase. Just past the third floor, I saw something pillowy on the steps. The flashlight revealed a Ziploc bag bulging with weed. Two more, the size of throw pillows, were next to it. A small box with bongs, pipes, rolling papers and other paraphernalia nestled by the pot bags. On the lower stairs were two rows of pot plants. As in weed, not potted plants.

Willow wasn't as otherworldly as I thought. She'd discovered Grandma's secret staircase. It was hard to keep secrets in this old building. I collapsed on the staircase for a moment, weak with relief.

Then I hurried up the hidden stairs to my bedroom and carefully shut the door. I needed something in front of that door to put off the searchers. I ran to my bathroom closet, and carried in the rattan storage shelves where I kept my stash of tampons, panty shields and other 'unmentionable' items. The shelves were tall enough to hide the door. I restocked them, and added a few more embarrassing items. The Peerless Point force were all men. If I knew them, they'd avoid rooting around in my personal hygiene products.

I rehung my clothes and piled my shoeboxes back in the closet.

While I waited for DeMille to return with the warrants, I wondered which one of my residents might have murdered

Sammie. Surely not Rafael. The maintenance man was a quiet immigrant from Colombia who kept to himself. Except wasn't that what neighbors told the media when they learned a killer had been living in their building?

I figured Willow was safe for now. I didn't think Lennox, the actor who lived next door to Willow, had much involvement with Sammie. He was stuck somewhere in 1595, rehearsing his role in *A Midsummer Night's Dream*. Sammie didn't exist in his Shakesperean universe. Lennox got more upset when someone said *Macbeth* instead of 'the Scottish play.' He made the offender go outside and turn around three times to undo the bad luck.

Mickey the artist lived on the ground floor, and loved funny signs. I hoped DeMille didn't remember that sourpuss who called the cops about Mickey's latest beach sign: 'Please to do not leave cigarette butts in the sand. The fish come out at night and smoke them.'

On the third floor was Billie the banana bandit, a movie buff who perpetually held his own personal filmfest. He'd turned his obsession into a successful writing career. Billie was researching his new book, *Seeing in the Dark*. This week it was the Rocky movies, and Billie was looking for the thirty-five goofs and plot holes that were supposedly in the Sly Stallone boxing movies. That's how he prepared for his work, by looking for the mistakes in the movies.

Yesterday, he proudly told us he spotted the famous elevated train in South Philly. 'Adrian – she's Rocky's future wife – and Rocky are talking,' Billie said, 'on a street in South Philadelphia, and there's a train in the background. Except there are no elevated trains in South Philly.'

'Does finding the mistakes ruin the movies for you, Billie?' I asked.

'No.' He smiled. 'They help me understand the technique.'

Next door to Billie lived Calypso, our housekeeper. I worried about her the most. Calypso was outspoken and loathed Sammie. Hot-tempered, she was strong enough to strangle the troublesome Sammie and toss her in the hole. I hoped Calypso would keep her mouth shut about her opinion of Sammie. Especially since the porn star had insulted Calypso the day Sammie was probably murdered.

My neighbor on the top floor, Dean the diver, was lucky to be out lobster fishing. I hoped he'd bring me some 'bugs' for dinner. Dean would probably miss today's drama, but he'd never paid much attention to Sammie.

That left me. Suspect Number One. The woman who said she'd rent to Sammie over her dead body. The mantel clock, Tuberoses, bonged twice. Grandma had named the clock for its funereal sound. Apparently spikes of fragrant tuberoses were used at funerals when she was young.

I jumped when I heard car doors slam in my drive. Detective DeMille was back with a fistful of warrants and a gang of six cops. They were going to search the Florodora. I tried to leave, but couldn't. I had to wait until DeMille arrived.

Finally, I heard the knock on my door. Judgment Day.

'Come in.'

Detective DeMille looked hot and frazzled. His blue shirt was wrinkled and sweat-stained.

'May I get you some water?' I asked.

He accepted a cold bottle, put it against his forehead to cool himself, then opened the bottle and took a long sip. He showed me the stack of warrants. 'I have permission to search the Florodora and all eight apartments,' he said.

'Help yourself.' I couldn't stop him. He handed all but two warrants to the uniform at the door, and sent him downstairs to give them to the gaggle of cops he brought along. Through my open door, I could hear groans and protests from my residents.

DeMille sat in the beer baron's carved wooden chair, and I sank into the couch.

'Thanks for the water,' he said. 'Before we search your apartment, what I really want from you, Ms McCarthy, are answers. It's not official yet, but it looks like the deceased is Sammie Lant.'

'Oh.' I tried to keep that sound as neutral as possible.

Now the detective rubbed the cold bottle along his right wrist. The man needed a full-body icepack. I stood up and lowered the air-conditioner temperature to 'wind off an iceberg' level. 'I've made it cooler.'

He nodded his thanks and asked, 'When was the last time you saw Ms Lant?'

'Sometime in April,' I said. 'She came here wanting to rent an apartment at the Florodora. I told her no.'

'You didn't tell her no,' he said. 'You had an altercation so loud someone called nine-one-one. I answered that call.'

'Yes,' I said.

'Why didn't you want Ms Lant to rent the apartment?'

'I didn't think she'd be a good fit, and neither did the other residents.'

He raised an eyebrow. 'They have a say in who rents the apartments here?'

'Yes, we're a small building, and it's more pleasant if we all get along.'

'Why didn't they like her?'

'You'll have to ask them.'

'Why didn't you like her?'

'Because she ruined a young man's athletic career with her sex on the beach stunt and didn't care. She seduced that poor young man and bragged about it.'

'So her death and burial here was a conspiracy.' It wasn't a question. It was a flat statement.

'A what?'

'A conspiracy. You were all in it, like in that Kenneth Branagh movie, *Murder on the Orient Express*.'

'No!' I was outraged. Was he trying to rile me with his stupid theory? Hoping I'd slip up and say something useful? I fought to control my anger, so I didn't blurt out something foolish. I didn't even mention the movie was based on a story by Agatha Christie.

'So who dug the hole?' he asked.

I must have stared at him, because he said, 'The hole Ms Lant was buried in. By the pool. Someone here would have seen the killer digging the hole in the courtyard.'

'We all saw who dug the hole, and it wasn't a killer,' I said. 'It was the plumbers, Lester and Liam Sykes. That pool has given us trouble for decades – back to when my grandma was still running the Florodora. The brothers have six kids between them, and I think the Florodora sent them all to college.'

I stopped, waiting for him to laugh.

He didn't. 'And?'

'Back in April, the plumbing was acting up again,' I said, 'so Liam and Lester removed the pavers in the courtyard and dug that hole. Again. The trouble always seems to be under the courtyard. At least according to them.'

'Exactly how long have you been having trouble with the pool plumbing?' DeMille asked.

I thought for a moment. 'Since the early Nineties. Other companies have looked at the problem, but they want to tear up the pool, and that would ruin the mosaic on the bottom. Liam and Lester say they can fix the pool without destroying it, and they can. For a while, anyway. But every six or eight months, the plumbing starts acting up again.'

'Let's go back to the last time you saw Ms Lant. What was she wearing?'

'Not sure.' I was sure, just like I knew when I'd last seen her, but I wanted to be careful. That encounter was burned in my mind. 'I think she wore a red blouse that was very low-cut, and a skirt. Not sure about her shoes.'

'What about her purse?'

I pretended to think for a moment. 'I don't think she had a purse. She had some kind of beach bag. Told me it was a nice day and she planned to go swimming.'

'And did she?'

'I don't know. I didn't keep track of her after she left.'

'Who do you think killed Ms Lant?'

'I have no idea.'

'Have you rented the apartment she wanted yet?'

'No.'

'How long have you known Ms Lant?'

'I don't really know her. I know *of* her.'

'And what's that?' he asked.

'Just what I read in the papers. She's a porn star and she caused a scandal by having sex on the beach with a college football star. She seduced him to further her career.'

'Do you know if she has any enemies?'

'No.'

'Do you know who wanted to kill her?'

'No.'

'Did you want to kill her?'

'No reason to.' I shrugged. 'You escorted her off the property. I wasn't required to rent to her.'

'Isn't she a minority?'

I laughed. 'Detective, pale busty blondes are not a protected minority. Not even in Florida. Neither are porn stars.'

'And you're sure you've had no contact with Sammie Lant since she left here last April.'

'Positive.'

DeMille stood up. 'I'm going to start with your office on the first floor. You can come with me to observe or stay up here.'

'I'll observe downstairs,' I said.

I couldn't stay alone in my apartment. I was too scared that a searcher would find the secret staircase stuffed with Willow's stash.

FOUR

'This is the best thing that's happened to me all day,' I said, dipping a bite of Caribbean lobster into the rum butter. The lobster was so fresh, it tasted of the sea.

'My pleasure,' Dean the diver said. My next-door neighbor looked like a beach bum. The ex-cop was tanned and toned, with sun-bleached blond hair. Dean wore cut-offs and a black Mortal Kombat T-shirt, which he insisted was a collectible.

After the Peerless Point police completed their search and left about seven o'clock, Dean knocked on my door with a bouquet: four fresh-caught lobsters. We broiled them in a dark rum butter sauce. I baked potatoes and made a salad.

We used the rest of the rum to make a pitcher of Dark and Stormy cocktails. Dark and Stormies only need four ingredients: Fever-Tree ginger beer, rum, ice, and lime slices. I liked the spicy alcohol taste. Besides, they were easy to whip up.

We sat down to dinner in my dining room, which faces the beach. The restless water was ink-black, dotted with the shimmering lights of cruise and cargo ships in the distance.

The dining room was as beachy as the view. I'd painted it light turquoise. The oval table was oak. On the wall was a wreath of seashells, which Calypso complained was a dust-catcher since the day my grandmother brought it home.

Dean set the table with bamboo mats and colorful linen napkins, while I plated the split lobsters and potatoes. When I sat down, Dean poured me a generous glass of the cocktail.

'Whoa. That's a bit much.' I held my hand over the top of my glass.

'You deserve it.'

'Yes, I do.' I moved my hand and Dean filled the glass to the brim.

'You had a heck of a day,' he said.

'I was terrified the cops would find Grandma's secret staircase and discover Willow's pot stash. They could have thrown her in prison.'

'But they didn't.' Dean tried to reassure me.

'No, but that doesn't mean I wasn't on pins and needles for five hours.'

I helped myself to the salad and passed the bowl to him.

'Did the police take anything during the search?' Dean refilled my glass. The last Dark and Stormy had disappeared.

'Some records from my office, including the letters I wrote Sammie Lant when I turned down her applications. Fortunately, the letters were polite – unlike my conversations with her.'

'Good. There's nothing on record that shows you were rude to Sammie.'

'Just the nine-one-one call, when Detective DeMille heard me yelling at her.' I crunched a bite of crisp green salad.

He shrugged. 'A good lawyer can debate that.'

'I hope it doesn't go that far.'

'Are you prepared for tomorrow?' he asked.

My mouth was full of rum-buttered lobster. I managed to raise a questioning eyebrow.

'The cops and techs will be back,' Dean said, 'bringing even more disruption.'

'They never really left,' I said. 'The yard's strung with crime scene tape. Uniforms are posted at the gate. The sidewalks on the streetside and beachside are closed. DeMille even has a guard by the tent he put over the remains.'

'Smart,' Dean said. 'Can't have Spot running off with a bone.'

I made a face. 'Do you mind? I'm trying to eat.'

'It's only going to get worse,' he said.

'How could it?' I stopped eating.

'What if they find more bodies?'

'What do you mean, more bodies?' I took a huge gulp of the Dark and Stormy.

'They've found one so far.'

'So far? Who do you think lives here: John Wayne Gacy? The Florodora residents aren't murdering people and burying them around the building.' I swallowed the last of my drink.

'Of course not.' Dean sounded soothing now. 'But the cops

have to do their job, and they'll look for more bodies. They'll bring in GPR.'

I didn't want to hear any more about bodies. 'What's GPR?' Dean loved to explain cop stuff. 'Ground penetrating radar. A machine that uses radar pulses to image the subsurface. It will tell them if there are other bodies buried in the yard.'

'OK.' I spoke slowly.

'It's way better than what they used to do. The cops would dig up your whole yard, front and back. GPR is nonintrusive.'

'That's good.' I didn't sound as enthusiastic as Dean did.

'Well, it beats the alternative. Now, how are you going to handle the media? They'll find out any time now, and go crazy when they learn a porn star was buried on your property.'

'Won't the cops keep the press away?'

'They'll keep them from entering your property, but that's all. The press can stand on the sidewalk side or the beach and photograph the Florodora and nobody can stop them. Expect a zillion TV trucks.'

'Can't wait. We'll have to pull down the window shades and close the curtains.'

'It's going to take more than that,' Dean said. 'None of us will be able to leave the building without being pursued by reporters.'

'I'll call a group meeting tomorrow morning and warn everyone.'

'Some of the residents are going to want publicity,' Dean said. 'Lennox might use it to plug his new play. What if Mickey wants to talk about her guerilla art?'

'That's two residents,' I said. 'Rafael rarely talks to outsiders. Calypso won't be shy about giving them a piece of her mind – that might be worth watching. Willow and Billie will be hiding. Willow knows she's had a narrow escape. Billie's still afraid he'll be arrested for boosting those hot dogs.'

'I doubt there's still an outstanding warrant for robbery with a deadly banana,' Dean said, and laughed.

'Well, it was loaded,' I said. 'Good thing he ate the evidence after the hold-up.' This struck me as hilarious, and I started giggling uncontrollably.

Finally, I pulled myself together and sat up straight. 'No, seriously,' I said. 'Could Billie be in trouble?' I took a big bite of buttery potato, hoping it would absorb the alcohol.

'Did the convenience store night clerk report the robbery?'

'No, and don't ask me why. There was no police report, either.'

'Was it that store on Dixie Highway? Near the car repair shop?'

'That's the one.'

'Billie's safe. The night clerk has a side gig selling weed. Last thing he'd want was cops crawling around that store. Why did Billie hold up the store?'

'Something about research for his book,' I said.

'When did Billlie commit this crime?' Dean asked.

'Three years ago,' I said. 'Before you moved in.'

'Oh, then Billie's in the clear. Even in a place as weird as Florida, a banana is not a deadly weapon. Were there any injuries?'

'There was extensive bruising,' I said. 'To the banana.' This time I stifled the giggles and took a long, sobering drink of water, followed by several bites of potato, salad, and more lobster.

'Back to your problem,' Dean said. 'Your phone will ring off the hook tomorrow. What are you going to say to the callers?'

'I have no idea.'

'You should have some kind of statement ready,' he said. 'Something like: We deeply regret the death of Ms Lant and extend our sympathy to her family and friends.'

'Not bad,' I said. 'Maybe add: We don't know why the porn star—'

Dean interrupted with a correction: '—adult entertainer—'

'That's good,' I said. 'We don't know why the adult entertainer was found on our property, but we are cooperating fully with the police.'

'You've got it,' he said.

I grabbed the grocery list pad off the kitchen counter and wrote down the statement, then sat back down to dinner. Dean had refilled my glass with more Dark and Stormy.

I had another butter-soaked bite of lobster. 'I love Caribbean lobsters,' I said. 'They taste so much better than Maine lobsters. Those are bland and flabby. At least to me.'

'Maine lobsters do have meat-filled claws,' he said. 'Caribbean lobsters are related to crawfish.'

'I used to go crawfishing with Grandma,' I said. 'Crawfish live in freshwater streams. We'd pack a lunch and go fishing.'

'Did you use a trap and a net?' he asked.

'Those are for sissies,' I said. 'We would tie a string around a hunk of raw bacon and dangle it near a rockpile in the water. The crawfish would nip out and grab the bacon. When it bit, I had to whip my string out of the water and throw it on the bank. Grandma would grab the crawfish behind the claws and drop it in a bucket of water.'

'That's not too far off from how I caught these lobsters,' Dean said. 'I go to my favorite lobster hole just past the pier, where there's this pile of old coral rocks, the perfect home for lobsters.'

I peeled the last morsel of lobster out of the shell.

'I take out my tickle stick.'

I'd had enough rum to be giggly again. 'Your what?'

'Tickle stick.' Dean tried to keep a straight face. 'Lobster hunters use them. A tickle stick is a lightweight aluminum rod. Here, I'll show you.' He used his knife as a stick and the long wicker bread basket as the lobster. 'When I see a lobster hiding in a hole, I slide the tickle stick behind the lobster.' He slid his knife alongside the basket. 'Then I lightly tap the lobster on its tail.' He tapped the basket. 'Your average lobster will walk slowly forward.' He moved the basket toward himself. 'Then I can use the tickle stick to sweep the lobster out of the hole.'

He swept the breadbasket close to his plate, nearly knocking over the pepper shaker. I caught it just in time.

'Once the lobster is out of its hole, I put my net behind it and trap the lobster between the ground and the net.' He dropped his napkin over the breadbasket. 'Boom! Dinner.'

I applauded.

Dean lowered his voice. 'But some lobsters are wily. Then I have to be wilier.' He raised his eyebrows and smiled at me. 'I use the lobster's natural instincts against it.' He took the napkin 'net' off the breadbasket and said, 'I tap the lobster on the forehead.' He tapped the front of the breadbasket. 'That will make the lobster shoot back into my net. It's trapped. And then it's dinner.'

Dean grinned at me. I laughed.

'When's the best time to hunt lobsters?' I asked.

'Well, they're most active at night. That's when they come out of hiding and crawl around on the bottom. But I don't like to go night-diving alone. Daytime is more sporting. I have to work hard to get the bugs out of their holes.'

'Why are they called bugs?' As soon as I asked that question, I knew I would be sorry.

'Lobsters and other bugs are part of the phylum Arthropoda. That includes all sorts of insects, and crustaceans like lobsters and crabs, and arachnids – those include spiders, scorpions, ticks, mites, and more.'

'Yum.' I was glad I'd finished my lobsters, which were looking buggier by the minute.

'Arthropoda all have hard exoskeletons.' He tapped the lobster's shell. 'You know what's really cool about lobsters?' he asked. 'Lobsters talk to one another when they pee in each other's faces.'

Inside every man was a fifteen-year-old boy, I thought, who enjoyed grossing out girls.

'Lovely,' I said.

'It's true,' Dean said. 'They have these nozzles under their eyes, and use peeing in each other's faces to communicate. They pee at each other during fights or courtship.'

'Amazing.' I took a last gulp of my drink, and began gathering up the plates and taking them to the kitchen. Dean followed with the breadbasket and nuzzled my neck.

'Can I spend the night?' he asked.

'As long as you don't engage in any lobster antics.'

He laughed and kissed me. I set the dishes on the counter and kissed him back. He picked me up and carried me off to my bedroom, teasing me with kisses all the way.

He was a skilled and inventive lover, and I enjoyed our romp in the sheets.

Afterward, Dean fell asleep, snoring lightly with his arm around me. The moon had risen, leaving a silver path across the sea. My grandmother had looked out that window at that same moon.

Dean and I didn't love each other, not really, but we enjoyed each other's company.

I wondered if I would ever love a man as passionately as my grandmother had loved her husband, Johnny Harriman.

FIVE

'**N**orah, wake up! Look at this.'
Dean stuck his phone in my face when I was sound asleep. I rolled over and growled like a hibernating bear. 'Huh? Wha? What time is it?' I blinked at Dean's cell phone screen, trying to focus. The bright light nearly blinded me.

'Five in the morning,' he said.

A rush of rage made me instantly alert. 'Dean, are you nuts? Why are you waking me at this obscene hour?'

'The first story about Sammie Lant is on the web, and it's a doozy. Here, look at it. It's a special report on Channel Eighteen.' Dean's tousled hair gave him a little boy look. I almost forgave him for waking me at this awful hour.

By this time, my eyes were able to focus. I saw a video of the Florodora front yard, shot from above. An announcer said, 'Two plumbers working to repair the plumbing at the historic Florodora Apartments found a body buried in an unmarked grave.'

The station had the decency to blur the gruesome sight of the victim. I could see the white-suited techs at work. Then the video switched to the white privacy tent erected over the grave and the yellow crime scene tape strung around the yard.

The announcer said, 'Peerless Point police obtained warrants and conducted a search at the property. Uniformed police carried bankers boxes out of the apartment building.'

'Who is taking these videos, Dean? Is the station using a helicopter? Or a drone?'

'You forget about your neighbors in the condos on either side of the Florodora,' he said. 'So-called "citizen journalists" are everywhere. Everybody has a cell phone video camera and they love to see their name on the TV screen. You know, "video courtesy Sally Sleuth."'

In this case, the video was 'courtesy of Dana Drumm of Peerless Point,' according to the announcer.

'Is that it?' I sat up in bed.

'Nope, it's just started,' Dean said. 'Check out this headline.'
It said: 'Sleazy Come, Sleazy Go. Body of Missing Porn Star Believed Buried at the Florodora.'

The photo featured a photo of Sammie from her latest adult epic, *Sex on the Beach*. Her teeny cropped shirt barely covered bazongas the size of basketballs, and they looked just as hard. She wore only a thin gold string and a gold postage stamp to cover her not-so-private parts.

The photo caption said: 'Sports lover takes dirt nap.'

'What publication is this?' I asked.

'The local online newspaper, *What's the Point?*'

'Oh, that rag,' I said. 'Nobody takes it seriously. Other papers won't print that trash.'

'Oh, they'll print this story,' Dean said. 'It's too juicy to resist.'

I hoped he was wrong, but I knew better. Even though it was still dark, I got out of bed. As soon as I stood, the hangover hit me. I'd pounded down too many Dark and Stormies last night, and my gut was roiling. I headed for the bathroom. A hot shower helped. Now I needed coffee – intravenously, if possible.

I started the coffee while Dean cleaned the kitchen. That was another thing I liked about him. Dean didn't believe in men's or women's work. If there was a job to do, he pitched in and did it.

When the coffee was ready and the dishwasher was humming, Dean and I sat at my dining table and drank the fragrant brew, simultaneously thumbing through the news feeds on our cell phones.

As Dean had predicted, none of the papers, not even the staid *South Florida Times*, could resist the porn star story. In fact, that paper had one of the more salacious headlines: 'The Naked and the Dead – Missing Porn Star Believed Buried at Historic Apartment House.'

The *Peerless Gazette* shrieked: 'Down and Dirty. Is missing porn star six feet under?'

'I never liked Sammie,' I said, 'but she deserves a little respect.'

'Wait till the press finds out Sammie was murdered.' Dean took a long drink of coffee, then added, 'At least there's some good news. Read the first couple paragraphs of the *Peerless Gazette* story.'

I did. It said:

> The body of missing adult entertainment actress Sammie Lant may have been buried by the pool at the historic Florodora Apartments. Sources close to the police say that the remains, found yesterday by two plumbers digging in the yard, could be that of Ms Lant, age 30. Ms Lant was reported missing by her agent April 19 when she failed to show for the premier of her new adult entertainment film, *Sex on the Beach*. She has not been seen since.
>
> Detective Jordan DeMille, crimes against persons detective with the Peerless Point police, said, 'We can neither confirm nor deny the identity of the deceased until the medical examiner makes a determination.'

'OK, I read it, but I don't see why that's good news.'

'Because the body hasn't been officially identified as Sammie's,' Dean said. 'When the media contacts you today, just fob them off on Detective DeMille. At least until the ID is official.'

He looked up at the kitchen clock. 'It's six,' he said. 'We should let everyone here know the news.'

'Let's start with Calypso. She's an early riser. I'll go down and check.'

I hurried down the steps, and knocked on her door. Calypso answered, dressed for the day's work in a bright green pantsuit.

'Can you come upstairs, please?' I asked. 'We need to discuss some developments in the Sammie Lant case.'

Calypso joined us for coffee, while we told her what was happening.

'Huh! I'm not gonna lie. If anyone asks me, I'll tell them the truth.' Calypso stuck out her chin. 'That *jungaless*! She only got those dirty movies because of her big *bubbies*. You won't see me doing no weeping and wailing.'

When Calypso was upset, she'd lapse into Bahamian dialect. I'd been around her long enough to know that a 'jungaless' was a loudmouth, a person with no manners. 'Bubbies' were breasts.

'I agree,' Dean said. 'But please don't spout off your true feelings, especially to the cops. This crime will generate tons of publicity, which means the police are under pressure to make an arrest in a hurry. Let's not give them a quick, easy – and wrong – arrest. That's why we wanted to talk to you.'

Calypso crossed her arms. 'Well, you'd better talk to everyone here then, because there isn't a person in this building who has a good word to say about that woman. Not even Rafael, and you know how he keeps to himself.'

'Good idea,' I said. 'Let's gather everyone and warn them. Right now.'

'We can,' Dean said, 'but they won't be happy.'

'Invite them here for breakfast,' Calypso said. 'I'll make my French toast. Do you have heavy cream, Norah?'

'No.'

'Should have known,' she said. 'Skinny little flat-assed thing like you isn't going to have any real food.'

'Hey!' I didn't know whether to be angry or flattered by her description. 'I don't have heavy cream, but I have all the other ingredients: butter, vanilla, eggs, sugar, syrup, and cinnamon.'

'What about bread?' That was a three-word challenge.

'Whole wheat,' I said.

'Hah! Can't make good French toast with that stuff. I have cream along with brioche bread in my freezer. Day old. The best kind for French toast. Breakfast will be ready in half an hour. Norah, start making coffee. Dean, you get to wake everyone up.'

Dean gulped the last of his coffee to fortify himself before rousting the Florodora residents. Fortunately, he had a powerful incentive to get them out of bed. The dead would wake for Calypso's French toast.

About forty minutes later, all the residents were assembled in my living room, most looking sleepy and surly. Especially the habitual late risers, like Willow and Lennox. Rafael, an early riser like Calypso, was happy to start his day with French toast.

As the residents walked through my door, the rich cinnamon smell of Calypso's special breakfast soon had them smiling.

I'd filled the thirty-cup coffee urn, and made sure everyone had a mug of the steaming brew. The dining room had been turned into a buffet. My guests filled their plates and found a seat in the living room. As soon as everyone had wolfed down a round of French toast slathered in butter and warm syrup, I was ready to begin.

'It looks like the body found by the pool will turn out to be the missing porn star, Sammie Lant,' I said.

The banana bandit spoke up first. 'Good riddance,' Billie said. 'That means she can't ever rent here.'

'I'd already turned her down three times,' I said. 'She was never going to rent here. But once the police say the dead woman is Sammie, we'll be inundated with reporters. Please be careful what you say. I don't think any of us liked the woman, but the police are going to be looking for a quick arrest. Let's not give them an excuse by saying something careless to a reporter.'

'Can't we keep the press off the property?' Mickey asked. The artist wore what looked like a silk caftan, with her dark hair in a green silk turban.

'Yes, but if we want to leave here, reporters have the right to hang around outside the grounds on the streetside and the beach-side. They could chase us down with microphones.'

'I'm not going anywhere,' Willow said, and shrugged. 'Won't bother me.' Our hippie resident looked ethereal in a gauzy white gown.

'I'll be watching movies all day,' Billie said. He crossed his arms over his plaid bathrobe. 'Still finishing my Sly Stone retrospective.'

Lennox looked positively theatrical in a purple silk dressing gown and white ascot. 'I have rehearsal at noon,' he said, 'but I'll use this as a chance to educate the masses on south Florida's cultural opportunities, including *A Midsummer Night's Dream*.'

'That should keep the press away,' Billie said under his breath. I shot him a glare.

Rafael restored everyone's good humor by saying, 'I'll use my usual excuse. I'll look confused and say, "No spik Engleesh." Always works.'

It did, too. 'Rafael,' I said. 'Eventually you're going to get caught. You speak excellent English. You were a judge in Colombia.' As soon as the words passed my lips I wished I could take them back.

The sudden sadness in Rafael's eyes was a terrible rebuke. Rafael fled Medellin in 1986, after Pablo Escobar killed the judge's wife and baby son. Grandma hired him, and he'd worked at the Florodora ever since. His ambition died with his family.

Late at night, I'd often see Rafael sitting on the flat roof of his garage apartment staring at the ocean, as if he could see all the way to his troubled country.

Rafael never discussed his family's murders. He hid his heartbreak with superficial jokes and his 'no-spik-Engleesh' routine. I mentally kicked myself for inflicting more pain.

'I asked you all here this morning,' I said, 'because I don't want anyone to get ambushed and blurt out something – like what we really thought of Sammie.'

'Not much,' Mickey said.

'Right now, we don't have to worry,' I said. 'The body hasn't been officially identified. Just tell everyone to check with Detective DeMille. He can take the heat.'

'What happens when they know for sure who it is?' Billie asked.

'When the reporters come sniffing around, I'll shoo them away like chickens,' said Calypso, bringing another platter of French toast to the table. 'Come on, everyone. Eat this while it's hot.'

The group didn't need encouragement. They rose as one and headed to the table for refills.

'You may want to take coffee and French toast down to the uniforms on duty,' Dean said to me. 'Never hurts to do a cop a kindness.'

'There's four of them,' I said.

'I'll help,' Mickey said.

It was almost seven o'clock when we clattered down the stairs with the food. The warm salt air smelled fresh and clean, and the sky was a delicate pink.

I delivered breakfast on a tray to the closest uniform, whose name was Ted Jameson. He was sitting in a deckchair by the hole. His face brightened when he saw me. 'Thank you!' he said and smiled.

We got similar reactions from Steve, Nick and Cal, the other uniforms.

When we returned, Dean looked out the beachside window in the dining room and said, 'It's started. I see two TV trucks on the beach.'

I peeked out the front room and saw the street was a traffic jam of TV trucks, bristling with antennas and satellite dishes.

Dean joined me. 'Brace yourself,' he said. 'They'll be ringing the doorbell any minute now.'

SIX

The doorbell rang on cue.

'I'll get it. Bye, everybody!' I waved at the roomful of residents, stuffing their faces with French toast. I heard a few goodbye grunts as I skimmed down the stairs, practicing my lines to evade the TV interviews: 'Please contact Detective DeMille. I have no information.'

I threw open the front door and said, 'Please contact—' then put on the brakes. Officer Ted Jameson was on my doorstep, holding a stack of trays piled with empty coffee cups and syrup-sticky plates.

'Steve, Nick, Cal and I wanted to thank you for the breakfast, Ms McCarthy,' he said. 'You were so thoughtful. That was the best French toast we've ever had.'

'You're welcome,' I said. 'All of you. Calypso made the French toast. She's an amazing cook.'

'Also' – Ted pointed toward the gates – 'the TV stations want to come in to interview you and the residents.'

'No, please,' I said.

'That's what I thought, ma'am. Sorry I can't do anything about those buzzards hanging out on their balconies.'

Sure enough, I saw at least ten people at the Croak Us standing on their condo balconies, some wearing flimsy pajamas. I started to raise my hand to flip them the bird, but Ted shoved the trays into my hands before I could complete the gesture.

'You don't want to do that,' he said. 'The stations will just blur your finger and go out of their way to talk trash about you.'

'You're right. Thank you. I'd better go upstairs.'

'One more thing,' Ted said. 'Detective DeMille should be here shortly, along with the techs and the GPR operator.'

'Thanks. Would you like more coffee or a bottle of water?'

'No, we're good,' he said.

Back upstairs, everyone had left my apartment except for Dean and Calypso, who were cleaning up. I went into the kitchen to help, but Calypso threw me out. 'This is a two-butt kitchen,' she said. 'It isn't big enough for three people. Go tidy up the living room.'

I collected the sticky paper napkins, put the chairs back in place and fluffed the couch pillows, all while watching out the front window.

Ten minutes later, Detective DeMille arrived, along with the CSI techs, Art and Emily, both wearing white suits, and four more uniforms. The night watch cops were relieved of duty. The new uniforms pushed back the media horde and kept them off the Florodora grounds.

The two techs disappeared under the white tent, complaining about the heat.

Bringing up the rear of this law enforcement parade was a man in khakis, an orange safety vest and a yellow hardhat. He was rolling a machine that looked like a lawn mower with a digital screen between the handles.

He rolled the machine back and forth in my front yard, as if he was mowing the grass, all while watching the screen.

'Dean,' I said, 'is this man using GPR? Ground penetrating radar?'

Dean came out of the kitchen, wiping his hands on his pants. He looked out the window. 'That's it,' he said. 'Look at the TV photographers trampling one another to get video of the GPR tech.'

I glanced up at the tall condos flanking the Florodora. At the Croak Us 'citizen journalists' leaned over their balconies. 'That old guy in the striped pajamas is going to fall over the railing,' I said.

'Better hope he doesn't,' Dean said. 'It will just delay this investigation.'

The GPR machine didn't seem to make any noise, but I eased open my front window, hoping to hear something interesting.

'Look at that.' Dean pointed to a fifty-something man with a thin face and iron gray hair, wearing a white lab coat. 'I think that's the county medical examiner.'

Judging by the excited buzz from the TV reporters, the man was someone important.

'Does an ME have to pronounce the victim dead?' I asked.

'Not in Florida,' Dean said. 'I'm guessing the ME is here to make sure the techs have all the victim's bones. That way, if the techs find anything else, they'll know they have another body.'

'Please, Dean, don't even say that. Besides, they can't get the GPR machine in that hole. The machine's too big.'

'There are smaller versions,' he said.

'You're no comfort at all.'

Calypso had left, and I heard her vacuuming the hallway.

Tired of pacing, I sat on my couch. Dean and I stared silently at the tent. I was too frightened to say anything. My heart was beating fast and the French toast breakfast roiled.

Dean seemed to understand how I felt. He held my hand. Meanwhile, the GPR operator went back and forth across my front yard. When he finished, he rolled the machine around to the backyard, facing the beach.

A black van arrived, and two men in dark uniforms climbed out and pulled out a stretcher.

'Wow, look at the news photographers and TV camera guys pushing and shoving,' Dean said.

'Ooh! The TV cameraman in the khaki vest elbowed the newspaper reporter in the nose,' I said. 'The reporter's nose is bleeding. Look! He slugged the cameraman. Three cameramen are videoing the press fight.

'Hah! Look at that,' I continued. 'The woman camera operator with the ponytail snuck past them all and she's the only one videoing the stretcher going inside the gate. The police are trying to stop the fight.'

'Sorry to break up the color commentary,' Dean said, 'but you're rooting for someone who is videoing the Florodora.'

'Oh, right.'

It had been almost twenty-four hours since the remains had been found, and there was still no official confirmation. Judging by the clothes, I was sure the body would be Sammie's.

By this time, the men in dark uniforms had emerged from the white tent with a body bag on the stretcher. The black body bag was nearly flat except for a few pathetic lumps. The mortal remains of Sammie Lant.

The GPR operator rolled his machine out the gates and into a truck parked next to the sidewalk. He returned with a red machine with black wheels, about the size of a toaster. It looked like a child's toy. Now DeMille and the two techs were out of the tent. The GPR operator carried the small, wheeled machine inside the tent.

'Finally, some air,' Art said. He sat in a deckchair in the shade.

Emily stayed next to DeMille. She pulled back her hood, took off her gloves, and ran her fingers through her long, sweaty blonde hair. I couldn't hear what she said to DeMille, but she giggled and smiled a lot. Art scowled.

The Florodora's front door opened and out stepped Lennox.

'Oh, no,' I said. 'Lennox is walking to rehearsal. He'll be sure to tell the media they are missing south Florida's cultural opportunities.'

'Is that so bad?' Dean asked.

'Depends on how he does it,' I said.

Lennox was dressed in his flamboyant best: white ruffled shirt, tight black bell bottoms and a fitted maroon frock coat, circa 1968. His longish gray hair was swept back. He looked good in his outré outfit.

As he reached the gate, a microphone was thrust in his face and a hard-faced, hair-sprayed brunette TV reporter asked, 'What can you tell us about the victim buried by the pool?'

'Nothing,' Lennox said. 'Nothing at all.'

He was using his theater voice, and I could hear every word.

'Why bother with such ephemera when you can see the immortal Bard's comedy, *A Midsummer Night's Dream*?' he asked. 'The Peerless Point Players present numerous cultural opportunities all year round.'

The reporter retreated and signaled the cameraman to back away. I sighed with relief. Then a brash young TV reporter pushed his way through the crowd, a cruel smile on his face.

He stepped forward to interview Lennox. 'Excuse me, sir,' he said. 'What part do you have in this play?'

Lennox stood up straight and threw back his shoulders. 'I am Bottom,' he said majestically.

'I'm not surprised,' the reporter said. 'You look like one in that get-up.'

'Excuse me?' Lennox asked.

'Dean, I have to go out there and save Lennox.' I turned to run for the door but Dean grabbed me.

'You can't, Norah. If you go out there, you'll only make this more of a spectacle.' He held me tightly, but I couldn't tell if it was for comfort or restraint. Either way, I had to listen to the interview.

'Can you tell us what a Bottom does?' the reporter asked, his voice sly.

'I play Piramus in the play within a play, *Piramus and Thisbe*. It's a precursor to *Romeo and Juliet*. As Bottom, I'm enchanted and have an ass's head.'

'So let me get this straight,' said the reporter, barely concealing his laughter. 'You're an ass on top and a Bottom on the bottom.'

'Something like that. You can see *A Midsummer Night's Dream* throughout the month of December at the Peerless Playhouse.'

'Can't wait,' said the reporter. Lennox missed the sarcasm and beamed.

'Viewers, I have just interviewed the most prominent Bottom in Peerless Point,' the reporter said. I longed to slap that grin off his smug face.

Lennox ignored the snickers and walked toward the playhouse.

I was glad for the distraction when the GPR operator crawled out of the tent, red-faced and sweating, holding the toylike red machine. 'Detective DeMille?' he said. 'Looks like there's another one down there.'

'Another body?' My voice was trembling. I turned to Dean. 'What am I going to do?'

'Nothing.' He held me tightly in his arms. This time, it felt like comfort.

'Norah, you had nothing to do with this body. You don't even know if it's a murder victim. The person probably died before you were born. It could be a burial by an early settler. A shipwrecked sailor who washed ashore. Or a Native American who died before the Europeans arrived.

'Now you have to do the hard part,' Dean said.

'What's that?' I asked.

'Wait and see.'

SEVEN

Detective DeMille ended the CSI techs' break. 'GPR says there's more down there,' he said. 'Start digging.'

'How far?' asked a sweaty, surly Art.

'Down to China if you have to,' DeMille said. 'I want to make sure we get all the bodies out of there.'

All the bodies? The detective's words chilled me, even on a steamy September afternoon. Was there a mass grave at the Florodora? Grandma built it in the Twenties, and we're right on the coast. Was someone running booze during Prohibition? Was the Florodora the site of a secret St Valentine's Day massacre?

Emily gave DeMille a dazzling smile (which he missed), then pulled up her hood, pushed her hair back inside, put on her gloves, and went into the tent. Art joined her, grumbling.

I needed something to occupy my mind. I tried reading a mystery, but abandoned it after one chapter. It wasn't the writer's fault. I couldn't concentrate. Instead, I went downstairs to the first-floor office to work on accounts. I had backup in the Cloud for the information the cops took during the search, and it was time to pay bills. My desk was by the front window. Once again I carefully opened the window and angled the wooden blinds so I could see and hear what was happening.

After Art complained about the heat, DeMille let them roll up the side of the tent closest to my window for some air. The other sides had to stay down to block the view.

For almost an hour I listened to Art gripe and the steady *chunk, chunk* of the shovels as they dug in the thin, sandy soil. Then Emily shouted, 'Stop! Stop! I see something. Something gold. Right there by the tip of your shovel.'

There was a scratching, scrabbling sound and then Emily shouted in triumph, 'Aha!'

'What is it?' Art asked.

'Let me show DeMille,' she said, running up the ladder and calling the detective's name.

Art followed her, whining, 'You could at least let me see it first.'
I backed away from the window and watched from the side.
'Look at this, Detective DeMille,' Emily said, elbowing Art
out of the way.

The detective examined the item with gloved hands. 'Looks
like a man's gold ID bracelet with diamonds.'

'It's engraved,' Emily said. 'What's it say?'

'Just three initials,' DeMille said. 'M.E.C.'

Those initials made me uneasy, though I wasn't sure why.

'Maybe someone dropped it,' Art said, hopefully.

'The GPR says there's someone down there,' DeMille said.
'Keep digging.'

Once again, Art groaned. Now the dig proceeded slowly, inch
by inch, as I worked through the stack of bills and two bottles
of water.

An hour later, I heard excited cries from Emily and Art. 'We've
got something!' Art shouted.

'Bones,' Emily said. 'Bones with clothes.'

Time for me to go on an errand of mercy, I thought.

Upstairs in my kitchen, I filled two big, insulated pitchers –
one with lemonade and the other with ice water – then loaded a
platter with chocolate-chip cookies and added paper cups. This
time I took the Florodora's creaky elevator. I braced myself when
it landed with a thud, and nothing fell off the tray.

'Hi, everyone,' I said. 'It's hot out here, so I thought you could
use a cool drink and a snack.' I set the cookies and drinks on a
table in the courtyard.

Emily and Art didn't wait for permission. They hurried over
to the refreshments.

DeMille helped himself to a cookie and a cup of water and
regarded me with suspicious eyes. 'May I show you something,
Ms McCarthy?'

'Sure.'

He held up a plastic evidence bag containing the diamond-
studded ID bracelet. 'Any idea who this might belong to?'

I studied the bracelet, my uneasiness growing, while the
diamonds sparkled in the sun. Why were the initials M.E.C.
familiar? I pushed down my fears, frowned and said almost the
same thing as Art. 'Someone who dropped it?'

I tried to look innocent as I edged toward the hole, until I got a look at the victim.

I bit my lip so I wouldn't gasp at the horrible sight. The remains were mostly bones, with some clothes. The dead person seemed to be about five-feet-ten inches tall, but that was hard to tell. I couldn't make out the hair color.

Parts of the clothes remained. It looked like the dead person wore a leather biker jacket. Designer, I thought. It didn't have the colors and other insignia of a real biker's jacket. The lines were too stylish. I saw badly stained Dolce and Gabbana jeans, and iconic high-top kicks, the '91 Nike Air Classic BW. Was that color Persian violet? It was difficult to tell. The clothing was stained by sandy dirt and body fluids.

The dig was divided by string into a grid, so each section could be sifted through a screen for evidence.

'Party's over, people,' DeMille said, startling me. I edged away from the hole. 'Art and Emily, back to work. Ms McCarthy, thank you for the refreshments. Please stay in the building and away from the dig site. I'll return the tray and pitchers.'

I returned to my office to wrestle with the bills. I was patting myself on the back for navigating Florida Power & Light's tricky 'pay by phone' system when I heard Art shout, 'I found a wallet.'

He ignored Emily's cry of 'Let me see!' and raced up the ladder, Emily trailing behind.

Art handed the wallet to DeMille, who examined it with gloved hands. 'Looks like it's alligator,' the detective said. 'Let's see what's inside this gator.' He carefully opened it. 'A driver's license. It belongs to a Maximillian Evan Clifford.'

The bottom dropped out of my stomach. Max Clifford killed my parents. In 1988. I was only four years old at the time. I wasn't familiar with his full name, but my confusion had been brief. There could be no doubt who DeMille was talking about.

My vision went gray, and I couldn't hear anyone talking. I was hit by a flood of memories. I remembered the doorbell ringing late one night, and then Grandma screaming. It was a terrible sound. I was staying in her apartment. I started to run downstairs to Grandma, but Uncle Lennox grabbed me and took me back upstairs.

'What's wrong?' I asked.

'It's OK, sweetheart,' Lennox said. 'Calypso is with your grandmother. Would you like some warm milk and a cookie?'

Lennox carefully warmed the milk in a pan and poured it into my favorite cup, which had a starfish on it.

'Drink it down,' he said.

I did and ate a cookie. Then my eyes started closing. Lennox carried me to my bedroom at Grandma's and tucked me in, then stayed with me until I fell asleep.

I slept restlessly that night, occasionally awakened by weeping and whispering. In the morning, when I padded out to the kitchen, Calypso was fixing breakfast.

'Your grandma isn't feeling well.' She handed me a glass of orange juice. 'I'm making you pancakes.'

'Yay! With chocolate chips?'

'Of course, darling.'

Lennox pushed his pancakes around on his plate, uneaten, but I polished mine off and asked for more.

After I devoured the pancakes, I asked, 'When are Mommy and Daddy coming home?'

'Uh . . .' Calypso said, and started sniffling. She wiped her eyes with her apron.

Lennox cleared his throat and said, 'Why don't you ask Grandma when she wakes up?'

Later that day, I learned that Mom and Dad weren't coming home. Ever.

'They're in heaven with God,' Grandma said.

'Why?'

'Because God wanted two beautiful angels,' Grandma said. She didn't talk for a long time after that.

I knew my parents were beautiful. My mother, Dot, was a model, and my daddy, Joey, could have been. He was a talented wood carver. They looked like movie stars when they went out at night, Mother in her sequin-spangled clothes, Daddy wearing the bright colors and offbeat patterns of high-Eighties fashion.

I don't remember much during their double funeral, which was closed casket, except asking, 'Are Mommy and Daddy in those boxes?'

'Yes, dear,' Grandma said. She was dressed completely in black.

'Can I see them?' I asked.

'No,' she said. 'They're with God now.'

'Who's going to take care of me?'

'I am,' Grandma said.

'But what if God wants you?'

'He doesn't,' she said. 'I'm too ornery.'

And she did take care of me. At age eighty-three, she took on the job of raising me, and the other Florodora residents became my honorary uncles and aunts. Aunts Tillie and Lacey, former Florodora Girls, let me play with their pretty things. Uncle Lennox was my favorite. Calypso was my nanny, and Rafael would talk to me about my parents. Though he never mentioned the murder of his family, it seemed to give him a special understanding of sorrow.

As I grew older, I understood my dazzling parents weren't the most responsible couple. They loved parties and champagne. They had a special medicine, a whitish powder for their noses that Mommy said I must never touch. When they wanted to go out, they would send me upstairs to Grandma's apartment. My mother had me at age forty-four, and I must have seriously interrupted their party life.

I also understood that even if my parents had lived, Grandma would have probably taken care of me. And put them both in rehab. After the funeral, Grandma put my parents' things in storage. Eventually, Calypso moved into their apartment on the third floor. I moved upstairs with Grandma, where I've lived ever since.

Max Clifford was drunk when he killed my parents. He blew through a red light in his sporty '88 Mercedes SL and smashed into their tiny Alpha Romeo. Thanks to Max, Mom and Dad were buried in closed caskets.

Max had had several DUI arrests, but his wealthy family always managed to get him out of the charges. This time, it must have cost the Cliffords a bundle, but Max got a paltry two years in prison for making me an orphan.

The mists were starting to clear, and I could hear people talking again. I took a deep breath and heard Art, the CSI tech, ask DeMille, 'Is Max Clifford's family the same people who own half of Peerless Point?'

'Yes, that's them. If I remember right, he got out of jail some-time in '91 or '92. Then he disappeared. His parents said he was a missing person. Judging by the designer sneaks, looks like Max died sometime in the early Nineties, right after he got out of prison.'

'If that's Max in the hole, I'd say he died of a broken neck,' Emily said. 'Do you think he got drunk, fell in and then died?'

'Don't know,' DeMille said. 'But burying his body is definitely suspicious.'

EIGHT

By late afternoon, black clouds were scudding across the sky. The wind had picked up and the ocean turned rough and restless.

Art, the CSI tech, climbed out of the hole and stretched. 'Ah. The weather's changing. It's getting cooler. It feels so good.'

Emily followed him. She shivered. 'I wish I'd brought a sweater.'

'Time to pack it in,' Detective DeMille told the techs. 'Your work will be easier for a few days. It's going to be cold. Real cold. There's an iguana warning.'

Florida's downright weird, but iguana warnings are one of the state's strangest customs. Even the National Weather Service will issue iguana alerts.

The green spiky lizards are native to the rainforests of Central and South America. Here in Florida iguanas are an invasive species. The destructive critters eat flowers and burrow into seawalls, causing major damage. Iguanas also transmit salmonella to pets and cause erosion near lakes and canals. They're prolific pests who lay up to seventy eggs a year.

When temperatures drop below forty-five degrees, the cold-blooded iguanas fall out of trees. Iguanas can weigh some thirty pounds and grow more than five feet long, which is a small dinosaur in my opinion.

The paralyzed iguanas look dead, but they'll warm up and come back to life, as one poor guy found out the hard way. He gathered a bunch of 'dead' iguanas in trash bags and tossed them in his van. On the way to the dump, the iguanas revived and clawed their way out of the bags. His van was crawling with the critters.

Nobody questioned why it would be so cold in September – thanks to global warming we're used to offbeat weather. But we never tire of falling iguanas.

After the techs left and DeMille posted four more uniforms for overnight guard duty, he began interviewing the Florodora residents again, this time about Max Clifford.

He started with me in my office. I tried to distract him by saying, 'I hear tomorrow it's supposed to rain lizards.'

'That's the forecast. Cloudy with a chance of iguanas.' DeMille leaned against the wall by my desk. 'I'm glad I'm on this case. I hate working iguana days,' he said. 'The phone never stops ringing. We get the callers who are upset because a thirty-pound iguana dented their car hood. That's not a police matter. Go call the insurance company.'

'Does insurance cover frozen lizard damage?' I asked.

'So far as I know,' he said. 'Besides the car owners, we get the nitwits who want to know how to save the little frozen bastards. They get upset when I tell them, "Don't revive them. Let them die. They don't belong here." They think I'm cruel.

'Do you know the old woman who lives in that turquoise house on Beach Road?' he asked.

I shook my head no.

'She knits them sweaters. Sweaters for lizards! Bright pink sweaters. She was interviewed on TV, showing off photos of the lizards in their little sweaters. We're out there freezing our asses off and she's worried about keeping freakin' lizards warm.'

'Would you like something to drink?' I asked.

'No,' he said. 'We've found some ID in the wallet that probably belonged to the decedent. Do you know a Maximillian Evan Clifford?'

My heart was pounding with fear. I forced myself to stare at my desk so my lying eyes wouldn't betray me.

'No.' That was the truth. Sort of. I never met the man who killed my parents.

I tried to stave off more detailed questions by asking, 'Do you know when he died?'

'Best guess is the early Nineties,' he said.

'Oh,' I said. 'I was born in 1984. I would have only been six or seven years old then.'

Also true. But the name of the man who killed my parents was burned into my brain.

'Is this Maximillian Clifford the person buried in the hole?' I asked.

'The ME will have to confirm it with dental records, but we

think so.' DeMille handed me his card. 'You know how to reach me if you think of anything else.'

Then he asked, 'Are all the other residents at home?'

'Everyone but Lennox,' I said. 'He's at rehearsal.'

Detective DeMille began knocking on apartment doors, rousting the residents and questioning them. Two hours later he knocked on my apartment door. I could tell by the slump of his shoulders he was tired and discouraged.

'One more thing,' he said.

Hm. The *Columbo* trick. I had to answer this question carefully.

He pulled out an evidence bag with a rhinestone butterfly pin, badly stained by something brown.

'Do you recognize this?' he asked.

I studied it. 'I think Sammie was wearing this. She had rhinestone butterflies on her shoes and a big butterfly pin on her blouse.'

'It wasn't on the victim's blouse when the pathologist found it,' DeMille said. 'Someone shoved this butterfly pin down her throat. After she was dead. The pathologist found it during the autopsy. I wanted to confirm Ms Lant was wearing it the day she died.'

'She was.' I wanted to throw up. The room spun and I sat in a nearby chair. 'That's horrible.'

'Yes, it is,' DeMille said. 'And I don't want to see or read about this pin in the media. We're holding back this information in case any nutcases confess to killing Sammie Lant to get attention.'

'I won't say a word.'

'Good.' He glared at me. 'Because I'll know where it came from.'

'That mean the body was Sammie Lant?' I asked.

'Yes, it's official,' he said.

Once I was sure DeMille was gone, I took some time to recover from the sight of the rhinestone pin that had been crammed down Sammie's throat. When I didn't feel so shaky, I contacted all the residents for a meeting in the lounge. I opened wine and set out cold water bottles on the credenza.

The lounge was furnished by Grandma in Twenties' high style – a sort of Hollywood Spanish. The walls were white and the furniture was dark walnut. Overhead was a wrought-iron chandelier. I expected Gloria Swanson to swan about the room. The residents drifted in one by one. Calypso was first. She poured herself a stiff drink at the credenza and plopped down on the big three-cushion couch. Willow helped herself to a bottle of water and settled in one of the thronelike walnut chairs, encrusted with carved knobs and curlicues. She stared dreamily at the art nouveau print of a woman kissing the moon.

Billie the banana bandit entered, poured himself some wine and collapsed on the couch. Mickey the artistic vandal was next, clad in a funky orange-striped caftan. She poured herself a hefty glass of wine and chose one of the walnut thrones.

Hot on her heels was Rafael. The maintenance man looked gleeful. 'Tomorrow it will rain iguanas,' he said. 'And I will kill them. They're not feasting on my flowers any more.'

'How do you kill them?' Mickey asked.

'Cryogenically,' I said.

Mickey looked puzzled. Rafael said, 'I throw the lizards in the old freezer in the garage, and when they are frozen solid, I put them in the trash. They don't come back from that.'

'It's humane,' I said. 'They go to sleep and never wake up.'

'A lot kinder than what those beasts do to my garden,' Rafael said.

Dean the diver was the last to arrive. He brought his own drink, a bottle of Heineken, and settled in another throne. I took the last tall chair, and thanked everyone for coming.

'First, I wanted to let you know that the body the plumbers found belonged to Sammie Lant.'

'Good,' Calypso said. Everyone else was silent, but they didn't seem too broken up by this news.

'I wanted to warn you because we're going to have even more media at our gates,' I said, 'so be prepared.'

Calypso started to get up, but I said, 'Please, there's more. I want to know what you told the detective about Max Clifford.'

'Nothing.' Willow shrugged. 'I didn't live here in the Nineties.'

'Me, either,' Mickey and Billie said at the same time.

'I moved in here two years ago,' Dean said.

'And I was a little girl at the time,' I said. 'That leaves Rafael, Calypso and Lennox, and he's at rehearsal right now.'

'I told the detective I no spik Engleesh,' Rafael said.

I rolled my eyes. 'Your English is better than his. What are you going to do when DeMille finds out?'

'I'll worry about that when it happens,' Rafael said.

'Calypso?' I asked.

'I said I never heard of Max Clifford,' she said.

'But you know who he is,' I said.

Calypso set her face in a stubborn mask and crossed her arms over her generous chest. 'That detective doesn't know what I know and he can't prove it,' she said, 'unless he can read my mind. And I don't think he can.'

Dean weighed in with his opinion, and I listened carefully. He was an ex-police officer.

'This Max Clifford is the drunk driver who killed your parents, right?' Dean asked me.

'That's the man, and I hope he's frying in hell,' I said.

'OK, let's think about what information would be available to the detective from the early Nineties,' Dean said. 'The era of this crime is mostly pre-cell phone, so texting is probably out.'

'I don't text,' Calypso said. 'And I don't email. If I want to talk to someone I pick up the phone.'

'That's good,' Dean said. 'Detective DeMille can't find anything to contradict what you told him.'

Dean took a long drink of his beer and then asked, 'When this Clifford went missing, was he paroled or on probation?'

'No, his family lawyer made sure he didn't have probation,' I said. 'Another perk of having rich parents.'

'Was the DUI driver supposed to make any restitution payments to your family, Norah?'

'One payment, which Grandma put in trust for my college fund,' I said.

'Did this Max guy have a credit card?'

'I think so,' I said.

'Then the time he stopped charging on it will help the police create a date of death,' Dean said.

'Here's another question. What happened to Max Clifford's car?'

'It was totaled,' I said. 'Along with my parents' car.'

'Were any other repairs done in the area of the current dig, where the bodies were found?'

'No, just the hole dug by the plumbers,' I said. 'The Sykes brothers.'

'The same ones?' Dean asked.

'No, the current brothers were in high school. Their father, Lemuel, was working back then.'

'Did Lemuel have a beef with Max?'

'No,' I said.

'Lem was a drunk,' Calypso said, 'but he was harmless.'

'Did anyone else dig up the yard by the pool?' Dean asked.

'No,' Calypso said, then stood up and helped herself to more wine.

'Does Max Clifford have a family?' Dean asked.

'Oh, yeah, Alberta and Reginald Clifford,' I said. 'As in *The* Cliffords, the local bigwigs who own miles of waterfront property in Peerless Point.' I couldn't keep the bitterness out of my voice.

Rafael jumped in and said, 'Those are the same Cliffords who have been pressuring the city to condemn the Florodora. They want to get their slimy hands on this building and tear it down to build more ugly condos.' He finished off the last of his water.

'Thanks to Rafael's ingenious repairs, we've managed to hold them off,' I said.

'Let's not forget the Cliffords are major contributors to a long list of politicians, including the mayor, the state reps and the US senate campaigns,' Mickey added.

'Ouch,' Dean said. 'These people are going to put massive pressure on Detective DeMille.'

'And they'll get lots of help from the media,' Mickey said. 'The press will go crazy when they find out the dead man is Max Clifford.'

'More pressure on DeMille,' Dean said. 'He's going to wish he could crawl in that hole – and pull the dirt over him.' He leaned forward and looked at all of us, one by one. 'Please, everyone, be careful what you say. Very careful. Don't give DeMille an excuse to make a quick and easy arrest.

'There's something else to consider,' Dean said. 'We have two bodies. So, do we have one killer or two?'

I drank down my wine in one gulp.

NINE

Calypso lingered after most of the meeting goers had left the lounge. She poured herself another glass of wine.

'I might have someone to rent that empty apartment,' Calypso said.

'That's good. Who is it?'

'A young woman. Nettie Parker, one of my church lady friends, says she'd be a good fit. Nettie knows her well. She was almost Nettie's daughter-in-law. Katie Penrod.'

'Katie, the woman who was engaged to Chet, the football player in the sex on the beach scandal? I thought she dumped him after he got arrested.'

'No, Katie broke up with him before all that happened,' Calypso said. 'She still likes Chet, but realized they're better as just good friends.'

'Right,' I said.

'Don't sound so judgmental,' Calypso said. 'Nettie understands why Katie called off the wedding, but she loves that girl like a daughter. Katie still goes to our church.'

'Huh,' I said. I was madly scrambling for an excuse to get out of this. Calypso could read my face. I was a bad poker player.

'Don't look at me like that,' she said. 'I know you think church people are hypocrites, and some of them are. But Katie is a good person. Even though she broke up with Chet, she still volunteers five days a week at our Hope Blooms shop. That's the plant shop that raises money for needy children.'

I didn't say anything. Calypso asked, 'Will you at least talk to Katie? As a favor to me?'

Now I was embarrassed. 'You don't have to beg me, Calypso. Of course, I'll talk to Katie. I won't make any promises, but I'll talk to her.'

'That's all I ask.' Calypso was all smiles. 'I know you'll like her. I cleaned the apartment, and it's ready to show. Katie can be here in an hour. Is that OK?'

'This evening?' I'd been ambushed.

'Yes,' Calypso said.

'OK, send her up to my apartment, please.'

Much as I liked Calypso, I was wary of church ladies. Priscilla, a former tenant who'd rented that same apartment, had been a disaster, judging the other residents and meddling in my grandmother's business. She was my grandmother's one failure at picking tenants. I didn't want another renter like Priscilla. But Calypso was also a church lady, and she was smart, generous, open-hearted, and open-minded. I needed to be more openminded, too.

Back in my apartment, I was booting up my laptop when Mickey knocked on my door.

'I overheard Calypso talking about a renter for the apartment next to mine,' she said. 'Who is it?'

'Calypso wants me to rent the empty apartment to Katie Penrod.'

'The ex-fiancée of the sex on the beach guy?' Mickey asked.

'That's her. Katie goes to Calypso's church.'

'I'm going to have to live next to a church lady?'

I saw panic in Mickey's eyes.

'Only if I approve her,' I said. 'She'll be here in an hour. Meanwhile, I'm trying to find out what I can about her online. I found her wedding website.'

'Katie and Chet broke up,' Mickey said.

'Websites last longer than love,' I said. I opened weddingbliss. com and went to the Peerless Point section.

I scrolled down until I saw a soft-focus photo of Chet and an ethereal blonde in a wispy pink chiffon dress, walking hand-inhand on the beach at sunset. The evening sky was smeared pink, purple and coral.

Chet looked formidable in his university football uniform, which was black with pink piping and a hot pink helmet.

'What's with the pink helmet?' I asked.

'Some teams are adopting them for breast cancer awareness,' Mickey said. 'The pink helmets raise money for the cause. The teams say real men aren't afraid to wear pink. They are warriors for change.'

'Chet sure makes his fiancée look tiny,' I said. 'I bet she weighs

ninety pounds. She's barefoot and Chet's wearing football cleats,
Look at his shoeprints in the sand.'

'Hope he didn't step on her foot,' Mickey said.

After we quit laughing, I started reading the website out loud.

I looked at the flossy type across the top of the page: 'Katie
and Chet. The story of our love.'

It was a short story:

> When I first saw Chet Parker, I knew he was the man for
> me. He was so strong and handsome. Everyone said he
> would be an NFL star, and when the pro scouts showed up
> at Chet's games, I knew he had a brilliant future. I can't
> wait to change my name from Katie Penrod to Katie Parker.
> Our goal? To live happily ever after.

'That isn't the story of Katie and Chet's love,' I said. 'That's
Katie's story. Chet doesn't get a say.'

I skimmed through the website pages.

'The wedding colors were shades of pink, from pastel to
flamingo,' I said. 'The wedding and reception were supposed to
be at The Breakers Palm Beach.'

Mickey whistled. 'I can't even afford to say that hotel's name,
much less stay there. Katie's family must have some bucks. Wait!
Is Katie Penrod the daughter of the family that owns Penrod's
Peerless Luxury Cars?'

Mickey pulled out her phone and typed in some names. 'Yep,
that's her. She even starred in one of her family's TV commer-
cials. Here she is in the driver's seat of a Rolls.'

I studied the commercial.

The dainty blonde looked overwhelmed by the massive car.
She gave a stiff smile and spoke in a flat voice, 'Get Peerless
luxury in a new Rolls. You deserve the best at a Peerless price.'

'Hm,' I said. 'Born with a silver hood ornament in her hand.'

'Not only does Daddy have plenty of dough,' Mickey said,
'Mommy also has money. She's a hotshot trial lawyer, Patricia
Penrod.'

'Oh, boy,' I said.

'Can I sit in on this interview?' Mickey asked.

'Sure. You can be head of our tenant association.'

I made coffee and put out a plate of cookies. We didn't have long to wait. Calypso knocked on the door and said, 'Katie Penrod is here.'

I opened the door. Katie did not make a good first impression – not to Mickey and me, anyway. The small blonde was so pale, she seemed made of porcelain. Her long hair was icy white, and her pink-flowered dress looked like a Lilly Pulitzer, designed for ladies' lunches in Palm Beach.

I could almost read Mickey's thoughts: way too conventional to live here.

'Thank you for seeing me on short notice,' Katie said. 'I really love this place.'

I introduced Mickey and myself and asked her to sit down. Katie took a seat on the couch, next to me. Mickey was settled into the beer baron's chair. I poured Katie a cup of black coffee and she took a cookie.

'I have just a few questions for you, Katie,' I said. 'Are you employed?'

'I do volunteer work at Hope Blooms, the Peerless Point African Methodist Church's plant shop, five mornings a week, from nine to noon.'

'Isn't that an odd choice for a church?' Mickey asked.

'Because I'm white?' Katie said. 'Not really. I was engaged to a man who went to that church.' She looked at the floor. 'We called off the wedding, but I'm still fond of him and his family. Our church welcomes everyone. You should come to our Sunday service. Calypso sings in the choir and the music is heavenly.'

OK, she'd sidestepped her engagement to Chet slightly, but her answer was good.

'Are you dating anyone now?' I asked.

'No,' she said. 'I need to get my head straight. I thought I was madly in love with Chet, but once we were engaged, I realized he was a friend, not a lover. I called off the engagement. Chet was sweet, kind, hot and smart, but the spark wasn't there, you know.'

'Yes.' I knew all too well. Those were my feelings for Dean.

'How did Chet take the break-up?'

'He took it well. The engagement proved we weren't right for each other. Chet's still my best friend, and we want to keep it that way.'

'So his fling with Sammie Lant didn't upset you?'

'Of course it did,' she said. 'How would you feel if your best friend was in a major scandal? Chet was humiliated. He'd embarrassed himself and his family. He lost his scholarship and his reputation.'

'Did you ever meet Sammie?'

Katie looked angry. 'No, and I didn't want to,' she said. 'The woman's disgusting.'

'How did Sammie get her hooks in Chet?' Mickey asked.

'Chet's not sophisticated when it comes to women,' Katie said.

'That's a surprise,' Mickey said.

Katie smiled. 'I know. It seems hard to believe because you've seen his photos. Chet is an incredible hunk, but he has no idea how attractive he is. Most football heroes have big egos, but not Chet. It's one of the many things that makes me so fond of him.'

Katie paused and studied her coffee. 'Chet is so innocent, I think I was his first . . . uh, his first . . . Chet was easy prey for someone like Sammie.'

Mickey asked, 'How did Chet feel when the Sammie story hit the media?'

'He was devastated,' Katie said. 'Even though our romance was over, he came to me for comfort. He cried. Real tears. It broke my heart to see that big, kind-hearted man so lost and miserable.'

'Why would Chet have sex with Sammie on a public beach?' Mickey asked. 'Is he some kind of exhibitionist?'

'Chet? No way,' Katie said. 'Sammie got him drunk. Chet doesn't drink much, especially when he's in training. He was running on the beach and stopped for a burger at the Beach Bar, and Sammie spotted him. She was drinking strawberry margaritas, and she asked if he wanted one. The drink had little paper umbrellas and lots of fruit, and Chet didn't take it seriously.'

'A couple of those sweet drinks can clobber you,' I said. I was speaking from personal experience.

'Exactly. That's what happened to Chet.'

Katie looked uneasy and I changed the subject. 'Do you work anywhere else besides the flower shop?'

'Most evenings, I take acting classes in Miami,' Katie said. 'I canceled tonight because this interview is important.'

Points for the acting classes, I thought.

'I saw your TV ad for Penrod's Peerless Luxury Cars,' Mickey said.

Katie's white skin blushed strawberry red. 'I wasn't very good in that,' she said. 'I only got the job because my daddy owns the dealership. But I want to improve. That's why I'm taking acting classes.'

Two points for Katie, I thought. She has a realistic view of her first effort and she admitted her father gave her the job. I was starting to warm to her.

'Do you own a weapon?' I asked.

'I own a gun, a small one.'

'I don't allow firearms at the Florodora,' I said.

'No problem,' she said. 'I keep it behind the counter at the plant shop. For protection. The shop's in an iffy area.'

'What's your favorite alcoholic drink?' Mickey asked.

'Beer,' she said. 'I like a cold beer. When I can find them, I like Samuel Adams Noble Pils and Russian River's Pliny the Elder.'

'Glass or bottle?' Mickey asked.

'Bottle, usually.'

Mickey gave me a wink. Definitely the right answers.

Now for the important one. 'Have you ever been arrested?' I asked.

'Uh, yes.' She bit into her cookie to buy time, and chewed carefully. Finally, she said, 'There was a drunk college student on the beach, Bryce Carson. He was juggling a live fish, a red snapper. Bryce was showing off to his girlfriend and she was laughing. What he was doing was cruel.

'I was outraged. I told him, "Quit playing with that fish. You're torturing it. Put it back in the water."

'"Make me," he said, and laughed at me. He kept throwing the fish around. I saw the poor thing gasping for air. His girlfriend was giggling. She said, "Chill. It's just a fish." They both laughed.

'I was so mad, I picked up my beach chair and hit him in the face. I kept hitting him until he dropped the fish back in the water. The police showed up and arrested me for felony assault and battery. At least I saw that poor fish swim away. It was still alive. Bryce needed seventeen stitches in his head.

'I called my mother from jail. She's Pattie Penrod, the trial lawyer.'

'I've heard she's good,' I said.

'Mom saved my bacon. I was lucky to have her. Also, the judge was an animal lover. The charges were reduced from felony assault to a misdemeanor. I had to pay Bryce's medical bills, including a plastic surgeon, and do six months' community service. That's how I started volunteering at Hope Blooms. I liked working there so I kept it up.

'Not included in the judge's punishment was the lecture I got from Mom. She billed me for the time she spent on my case, and she charges eight hundred an hour. Mom made me pay it out of my money.'

She looked at me, and said, 'My grandmother left me some money. I'm using it for my acting lessons. That's also how I'll pay the rent.'

'How long have you lived at your current residence?' I asked. 'Do you have references?'

Katie laughed. 'I'm living with my parents, so twenty-two years. My mom will tell you I don't clean my room enough. I don't have pets. It's time I leave the family nest. I really like this building and I'd love to live on the beach. Can I rent here? Pretty please?'

'Let me discuss this with the head of the tenants association,' I said.

Mickey and I walked to my guest bedroom and I shut the door.

'What do you think?' I said.

'I like her,' Mickey said. 'I didn't at first, but she sort of grows on you.'

'What about her break-up with Chet?'

'She seems fairly mature,' Mickey said. 'It also sounds like we won't have to worry about her ex-boyfriend coming here and causing a scene: she and Chet seem OK.'

'That fish story is crazy enough to make her a real Florida Woman,' I said. 'And Calypso says she's good.'

'Then she's in,' Mickey said. 'Let's give her the good news.'

TEN

Katie moved in the next morning. Mickey and I tried to help, but the burly movers said they could handle it. Most of her furniture looked new, and most of it was pink with black accents. The men in gray coveralls hauled in a bed with a pink leather headboard, three pink lamps, a pink couch and two black-and-pink side chairs.

'Where did she get this stuff?' Mickey said. 'Barbie's Dream House?'

'Sh,' I said. 'I'm happy to have a decent renter.'

'At least Katie's money is green,' Mickey said.

'That reminds me,' I said. 'We'd better prepare her. Once Max Clifford is officially identified, the media will be all over this place like ants on a candy bar.'

I was glad Katie took the news in stride.

That afternoon, Mickey knocked on my apartment door and said, 'I'm walking over to Frannie's for coconut ice cream.' Frannie ran a closet-sized snack shop on Ocean Drive, north of the bus stop. Frannie's specialty was homemade coconut ice cream in a coconut shell. 'Can I bring you some?'

'Of course,' I said. 'But how will you get past the media?'

'Watch,' Mickey said.

She was carrying a yellow tote bag with a picture of a rubber duck on it. Mickey reached in and pulled out a cape with a rubber duck print. Underneath each yellow bath toy was the word 'duck' in an elaborate curly script. On closer examination each 'D' was actually an 'F.' Same with the tote.

Mickey tied the cape on and added a 'duck' turban.

'The turban will take care of those buzzards hanging off the balconies of the Croak Us,' she said. 'No way they will get this outfit on TV. I'm holding this tote in front of my face, which will take care of anyone who tries to stick a microphone in my face.'

'But what about Frannie?' She was an older woman, and very proper.

'I'll take the cape and turban off before I get to her store,' Mickey said.

'Bring back two dozen and we'll give them to the residents.' I reached for my purse but Mickey waved my hand away.

'My treat,' she said, and left with mischief in her eyes.

I watched her progress after she left the Florodora. As predicted, the press surged forward when they saw Mickey. She held up the tote, and the reporters backed away like vampires facing garlic.

Mickey returned an hour later, and the Florodora had an ice cream party.

Two days later, when the dead man was officially identified as Max Clifford, the news exploded like a bomb. It hit the front page of all the south Florida papers. It played endlessly on TV newscasts. Ravenous reporters camped out on the edge of my property, demanding I make a statement.

I spent the day dodging phone calls from the media. I was under siege.

From what I could figure out, Max Clifford disappeared Friday, November fifteenth, 1991, a month after his release from prison. He talked to his mother at two thirty in the afternoon and said he wouldn't be home for supper. His last credit card charge was the same day. He bought a six-pack of beer and a bag of chips. After November fifteenth, no one heard from Max again.

Dean stopped by late that afternoon with a couple of sirloin steaks he'd had in his freezer. We made a salad, broiled the steaks, baked some potatoes and settled in front of the TV with a glass of Merlot to watch the six o'clock news.

We turned on Channel Eighteen, where a reporter, a bald veteran with a heavily powdered forehead, was interviewing Alberta Clifford, Max's mother, in her living room. Her white hair was sprayed into spun-sugar curls and she wore dead black. Her sweet old lady look was spoiled by her blood-red mouth and long red talons.

Alberta was ensconced in a flowered wingback chair. The reporter sat across from her, nodding his head sympathetically as she wept through her story.

'My son, my only son, was buried at that derelict apartment.'

'Derelict!' I said. 'The Florodora has never been derelict. It's historic.'

'Shh!' Dean said.

Alberta paused to dab her eyes with a lace-edged handkerchief and continued, 'My sweet boy has been missing for more than thirty years. And all along, that sleazy, senile showgirl, Eleanor Harriman, killed him. Yes, killed him. And buried him on her property. My boy's been there all these years. Alone.'

'Sleazy, senile showgirl!' I was shouting now. I jumped up, abandoning my dinner. 'She just called my grandmother a murderer.'

'Hey,' Dean said. 'Where are you going?'

'To set the record straight.' I pounded down the stairs.

Dean followed me, shouting, 'Norah, this is a bad idea.'

'The truth is never a bad idea.' I paused long enough to run my fingers through my hair and add a slash of lipstick, and I was out the door and marching toward the reporters. My blood was boiling. How dare she!

I stood at the fence and said, 'My name is Norah McCarthy. I'm the owner of the historic Florodora Apartments, which I inherited from my grandmother, Eleanor Harriman. I'd like to make a statement to answer Alberta Clifford's allegations.'

The reporters crowded closer. The bald reporter who'd interviewed Alberta stepped forward and shoved his microphone in my face.

'You're the one who let Alberta Clifford call my grandmother a sleazy, senile showgirl,' I told him.

'Uh,' he said.

'Mrs Clifford was wrong. My grandmother was not senile. She was a showgirl, and that's a fact. She was a Florodora Girl, a superstar. That's a second fact.'

Out of the corner of my eye, I could see Dean rushing toward me.

'Here's a third fact. Max Clifford was a drunk. He'd been arrested twice for drunken driving, and each time his blood alcohol content was above the legal limit. He should have had his license revoked for six months to a year, but his parents' lawyers got him off.'

Dean was getting closer. I had seconds to state my case.

'Just three months after Max's second DUI arrest, his car plowed into my parents' car. Max was drunk again, and this time he killed both my parents. Once again Max's rich parents got him a lawyer, and Max went to prison for two years. Two years! He served only a year for killing my father and another year for my mother. That's all. Two young and beautiful people were destroyed by his drunken behavior.

'Never mind that when he killed my parents, Max committed a second-degree felony. By rights, he should have served up to fifteen years in prison. Instead, he was back out in two years. The Cliffords used their money to buy their son a shorter sentence.

'So Max left me an orphan, and my grandmother, at age eighty-three, took over the job of raising a four-year-old. Me.' Tears welled in my eyes and my voice grew wobbly. 'I cried for my parents every night.'

I felt Dean behind me. He gripped my arm in some kind of police hold that hurt like hell. 'My grandmother, Eleanor Harriman would never kill anyone. Ever.'

'Come along,' he whispered in my ear. I'm sure on television, he looked like he was comforting me.

The reporters erupted into questions. 'Ms McCarthy, do you know how Mr Clifford came to be buried in your yard?'

'Do you know who killed him?'

'His parents killed him,' I said. 'If Max had served the full fifteen years – or even the minimum of four years – he'd still be alive today. He's a victim of their privilege.'

I started to say more, but Dean pinched something in my arm that made me gasp.

'As you can see, Ms McCarthy has been traumatized by the unwarranted accusations against her family,' Dean said. 'Her innocent family. There will be no more comment. Please respect her privacy.'

He appeared to help me into the building, though he really frog-marched me to the Florodora.

Once inside, when the door was shut, he said, 'What the hell were you doing?'

'Defending Grandma's good name. And my parents' memory.'

Dean put his arm around me and guided me upstairs. 'They're dead, Norah. They can't be hurt any more.'

'But I can,' I said.

'Come upstairs. Let's talk about this,' he said.

We went back to my apartment and sat on the white couch. Dean turned off the TV, and took my plate into the kitchen, where he nuked my steak and potato to warm them up.

He brought back the plate and said, 'Finish your dinner. I'll make some coffee.'

Dean returned a while later with two mugs of fragrant coffee. I wrapped my hands around the mug, feeling its comforting warmth.

Dean's voice was soft. 'You know I'm an ex-cop. Lying to a detective is criminally stupid. You're going to need DeMille's help. The Cliffords are a big deal in south Florida, and they can make trouble for you.'

I nodded my head in agreement and took a small sip of coffee.

'Now you're seen on TV barreling toward the cameras, demanding an interview so you can spout all sorts of information about Max Clifford. Detailed information. How are you going to explain that to DeMille?'

'Easy,' I said. 'DeMille called him Maximillian Evan Clifford. I didn't make the connection instantly. I'll say that I didn't realize who he was until I googled Max Clifford's name. His arrests are on the record.'

'I hope DeMille believes that,' Dean said.

We sipped our coffee in silence, while Dean played with one of my curls. Finally I said, 'I'm afraid the killer lives at the Florodora, Dean. One of our residents put both those bodies in that hole.

'At least I know it wasn't Katie. She's just moved in. She wasn't alive in the Eighties. But I'm worried about our long-time residents. No one else could have known the yard was torn up by the pool back then.'

Dean laughed. 'You're kidding, right? Anyone passing here can see what's going on,' he said. 'We have a bus stop in front of the building, and the fence isn't that difficult to climb over.'

'It's covered with bougainvillea, which has thorns.'

'The beachside fence doesn't. It's only about three-feet high. A child could get over it.'

'What if one of our residents invited Max in, killed him, and pushed his body into the open hole?'

'I doubt that,' Dean said. 'The only residents from that time still living here are Rafael, Calypso, and Lennox. I can't see any of them burying a body in secret.'

'If the killer didn't live here, could they carry a body over the fence? A man's body? How would they get Max to the fence?'

'Every day, we see dozens of people pulling folding beach wagons,' Dean said. 'No one goes to the beach with just a chair and a towel these days. They practically camp on the sand. Beachgoers fill their portable wagons with beer, soda, snacks, towels, umbrellas, even shade tents. It would be easy to put a body in a wagon, cover it with towels, and haul it to the low beachside wall.

'All they have to do is drag the body over, then the wagon, put the body back in and roll it to the hole.'

'It's possible.' I wasn't convinced and wanted to change the subject. 'I want to make this mess go away. I can start by finding out who killed Sammie. That could lead me to Max.'

'Why?' Dean asked.

'Because I think the two murders are connected,' I said.

'I'm not convinced they are,' Dean said. 'You should leave murder investigations to the professionals.'

'Amateurs have advantages,' I said. 'They're friendlier than the police. They don't frighten people the way the cops do, so witnesses are more likely to talk to them. They can search without warrants and don't have to follow the rules of evidence.'

'You can bungle an investigation if you don't follow the rules,' Dean said. 'You can get yourself killed. Remember, whoever killed Sammie has already killed once. Maybe twice. You aren't trained to defend yourself.'

Dean's 'I'm a pro and I know more than you do' was beginning to annoy me. I tried not to snap at him as he outlined what else I didn't know.

'The cops know if Sammie has a rap sheet, and who her known associates are. They can get her records. What do you know about her?'

'She's a porn star,' I said. Big deal, I thought. Everyone knew that.

'What else?' Dean asked.

'She has fake boobs and cheap clothes.'

Dean rolled his eyes. 'You're quite the crack investigator. What else can you tell me about the dead woman?'

'OK, I don't know anything about her,' I said. 'I don't know where she lived. Or where she worked. Or how she supported herself when she wasn't making porn films. Unless it was on her back.' I sounded snippy, but it could be true.

'If it's true she was a working girl, then this investigation is even more dangerous,' Dean said. 'What if she has a pimp? He won't hesitate to kill you if you start poking around in his business. And there will be a long list of suspects. Maybe a john killed Sammie and dumped her in your yard.'

'How am I going to find that out?'

'You don't have to.' Dean put his mug on the coffee table and faced me. He was speaking earnestly, almost pleading with me. 'Norah, if you insist on getting involved, then you should focus on giving DeMille more information so he doesn't take the easy way and arrest you. But you have to be careful.'

'I can do that.'

'Good. Try to find out if Sammie had any rivals who wanted her dead. How much money did she have? Where did she keep it? And why did she decide to ruin that young man's career?'

'I guess he's a suspect, too,' I said.

'Yes, but so are you. And you have a police report to confirm you hated Sammie. The prosecution will be waving that in front of a jury.'

The events of the last few days were finally sinking in.

'You're frightening me,' I said.

'Yes,' Dean said. 'You need to take this seriously. You're a prime suspect in Sammie's murder and your motive is on paper. In a police report. You could lose everything, including the Florodora.'

'At least I'm too young to have killed Max Clifford,' I said.

'We'll deal with that problem later,' he said.

'First thing tomorrow,' I said, 'I'll start investigating Sammie.'

ELEVEN

I was up the next morning at sunrise, and slipped out the Florodora's back door before the media watch began. The press had gone wild after Max Clifford's identity was confirmed. 'Slain Scion of Prominent Peerless Family Buried at Historic Apartment House,' screamed one headline. 'Double Death on the Beach,' said another.

The worst one said, 'Peerless Mother Mourns Lost Son. Showgirl's Granddaughter Blames Victim's Family for His Death.'

That was technically accurate, but it made me the bad guy. I wondered what the fallout would be.

After a sleepless night, I needed a calming walk along the water, and the soothing sounds of the ocean. This morning, the sunrise sky was a raucous burst of hot pink reflected in the silver ocean. The beach was nearly empty. Peace.

Too bad it was forty-five degrees and I was freezing. In the north, that temperature would be a spring day. In fact, that's how we can tell the tourists down here in Florida: they wear shorts and sandals on cold days. Some even go shirtless.

Floridians are weather wimps. I wore my warmest jacket, then piled on a knit scarf and gloves. Together with my jeans and sweater, these were more clothes than I wore in a week.

And I was still cold.

I stopped at Egg-Zack-Lee-Rite, the beachside breakfast spot owned by Zack Lee, and bought two black coffees.

I was on a mission to meet my favorite Beachwalk cop, Ben Abbott.

I saw him just past the lifeguard station, watching the volunteers collect the turtle eggs laid overnight on the beach. During sea turtle nesting season, volunteers monitored the nests to keep the eggs safe.

Ben had short, unruly gray hair, leathery tanned skin, and a generous paunch my grandmother called an 'alderman.' His khaki uniform looked starched and his shoes were polished into mirrors. Ben's eyes were kind but sharp. He didn't miss much on his beat.

He thanked me for the coffee and then asked, 'What do you need, Norah?'

Ben was hard to fool. He was sixty-something, and had been a friend of Grandma's. I sort of inherited him.

'You arrested Sammie Lant and Chet Parker during spring break, right?' I took a long drink of coffee and felt its welcome warmth.

'Chet. That poor kid.' Ben shook his head. 'I had to arrest them both. They were going at it on the beach. In broad daylight. I felt sorry for Chet. Thanks to Sammie, Chet lost everything, including his college scholarship. His fiancée broke up with him. But Chet had one bit of luck.'

'What's that?' I sipped more hot coffee, but it didn't stop my shivers.

'He had a felony arrest for beating up another player on his team,' Ben said. 'Sent the guy to the ER. Chet's arrest never made the papers during the Sammie scandal.'

'Is Chet dangerous?'

'Who knows?' Ben shrugged. 'He went along quietly with me. That scumbag Sammie did a number on him. He was really out of it. I suspected Chet was drugged, but the tox screen didn't show anything.'

'And what did Sammie get for her shameless stunt? More publicity for her so-called adult film. Didn't do her any good, though, did it? She's dead.' Ben looked positively gleeful.

'Did Sammie have any rivals?'

'Yeah, lots of women in Florida make pornos. But one was really mad at her. Countess Cora Crawlie.'

'Like the Countess Crawley in *Downton Abbey*?'

'Sort of. You'll see this countess crawling aboard just about anyone in her flicks, but the only thing she's counting is her money. Her movies are hardcore.

'Anyway, the countess was outraged when Sammie had a sports-themed skin flick coming out at the same time as the countess's movie. Sammie's raunchy stunt on the beach sucked up all the publicity, and Countess Crawlie's sports flick, *Big Balls and Forward Passes*, flopped.'

'So the countess's career was ruined?' I sipped more coffee. I was turning into an icicle.

'Let's just say Sammie deflated the countess's bank account significantly. But I wouldn't count out the countess. She's signed on with Sammie's old agent, Vixen Tamer.'

'That's his name?' Another gulp of coffee. It was lukewarm.

'It's not the one his mother gave him, but I'm pretty sure Mama wouldn't want to know how Vix makes his money.'

'Do you watch those movies?' I tried not to sound judgy.

'Don't need to,' Ben said. 'I see enough porn on the beach, and it's all free. What really excites me these days are fully dressed women.' He grinned at me.

Oops, time to change the subject. 'Do you know where Sammie lived?'

Ben pointed north. 'Up that way, about two blocks. Sammie had a room at the Blue Mermaid on Surf Road and Palm. The landlady is Edna Goodrich, a retired good-time girl who saved enough to buy an old motel and rent the rooms by the month.

'You going there?' Ben asked.

'Yes.'

'Be careful, Norah. Edna's clientele isn't the finest. Do you have my phone number?'

I shook my head no, and Ben punched his number into my cell phone.

'You're cold, aren't you?' he said. 'Your teeth are chattering.'

'I'm all bundled up.'

'You're wearing sandals. Next time try shoes and socks,' he said. 'You'll be warmer.'

Right. No wonder I was cold. I didn't even know how to dress.

I saluted him with my almost empty coffee cup and headed toward Sammie's apartment. Surf Road ran parallel to the beach, but was more like an alley. A block from the ocean, the Surf Road view mostly featured condo garages and reeking dumpsters. The brisk walk there warmed me up a bit.

The Blue Mermaid was a U-shaped art deco building with faded blue paint. The courtyard had a concrete fountain with an injured mermaid. Her tail was broken and her nose chipped. The basin was overflowing with sun-bleached seashells, beer cans and pint liquor bottles.

The first door said 'mange' in stick-on gold letters. It could have been a statement about the door's peeling paint, but I guessed this was the manager's apartment. Judging by the blaring TV coming from the apartment, Edna was awake.

I knocked on the door and heard a cigarette-ravaged voice shout, 'Just a freakin' minute.'

The door opened and the sight of Edna seared my eyes. She was a flabby eighty in a bikini, holding a dish towel. There was more material in the dish towel than on Edna.

'Whad' ya want?' I could see traces of her former good looks in her wrinkled face. Her eyes sparkled with humor. Her hair was dyed a brassy blonde. In one hand was a lit filter-tip cigarette.

'Ms Goodrich? I'd like to ask you about Sammie Lant.'

'She's dead,' Edna said, 'and she owes me two months' back rent. Come in, will ya? You look like you're freezing your ass off.'

'I am.' I was grateful to duck into the warm kitchen, even if it did reek of stale cigarette smoke. The room was just big enough for a Formica table for two and a battered fridge that whined like a giant wasp. The table's centerpiece was a turkey platter holding a mountain of ash and old cigarette butts.

'You interrupted me when I was smoking breakfast,' she said, and tapped her cigarette's ash on to the platter. 'Take a seat.'

I did and she sat opposite me. I tried not to stare at the gray pile of ashes, which threatened to slide on to the table.

The good humor was gone from Edna's eyes. 'Now why should I talk to you about Sammie?' she said. 'If you're police, I got nothing to say to you.'

'I'm not,' I said. 'I run the Florodora down the road. I'm an apartment manager, just like you. Sammie was found dead in a hole on my property and I don't want the cops blaming me, or any of my residents.'

Edna took a long, thoughtful draw on her cigarette and said, 'I saw something about that on TV. I liked how you ran out and defended your grandmother when Mrs Lah-Dee-Dah Clifford ran her down. You got spunk going up against the Cliffords.

'You can call me Edna. So what can I tell you about Sammie?'

'Did she have any boyfriends?' I asked.

'Lots. They were noisy, too. Kept us all awake.' Edna blew out a long stream of smoke.

'Does she have any family?' I asked.

'A father somewhere up north. Heard he was a Baptist preacher. You know what they say about preacher's daughters: wild as March hares. I let him know his daughter died. So did the police. He ignored us. I don't think he wants to claim her body.' More smoke.

For the first time, I felt a pang of pity for Sammie.

'I'm sorry,' I said.

Edna shrugged. 'So much for Christian forgiveness.'

'Why didn't you report Sammie missing?' I asked.

'I was glad to see her gone,' the landlady said. 'We all were.'

'Could I look through Sammie's belongings?' I asked.

'The police took everything in her room, and made a big mess. Plus, I overheard one of those bastards in blue call me an old bag with saggy tits. In my own building. That's just rude.'

'It is,' I said.

'When I found two boxes of Sammie's things in my storage room, I didn't bother to call them. You can take them. No one's going to claim them. You'll be doing me a favor. I need the space. I'll be right back.'

Edna disappeared down a short hall. I glanced at the kitchen clock. 8:03. I had to get back home. The press siege of the Florodora would start any minute.

Edna returned with two beat-up cardboard boxes. On top of them was a floppy straw hat. I thanked Edna and headed toward the Florodora. Surf Road dead-ended at my property. Three TV trucks were camped at the beachside of the Florodora. Rafael was working in the side lot, throwing cold-stunned lizards into a wheelbarrow. He wore thick gloves and a heavy shirt. Iguana spines cut like razors.

Rafael waved me over to the side fence and held up a five-feet-long iguana, its back bristling with serious spikes.

'I've found Godzilla,' he said. 'It's exhausted after destroying Japan.'

I laughed and said, 'Rafael, are there any TV trucks out front?'

'At least ten of them. Your interview yesterday really stirred things up. There's three more on the beachside.'

'It wasn't my brightest move. I need to get in the back way. Can you create a diversion on the beachside?'

'No problem,' he said. 'I have lizards. No Florida reporter can resist them. Give me five minutes.' He tossed two more bright green lizards in his wheelbarrow and trundled toward the backyard.

A well-groomed redheaded reporter spotted Rafael and waved him over to the fence. 'Sir! Oh, sir! Do you live at the Florodora?' Rafael parked the wheelbarrow at the farthest end of the backyard and smiled. The reporter sprinted over, her high heels clicking on the Beachwalk, her green wool coat dress rippling in the breeze.

'No spik Engleesh,' Rafael said, launching into his clueless immigrant routine. He picked up Godzilla. The lizard was so big, Rafael needed both hands. Holding Godzilla in his arms like a baby, he said, 'Es una iguana enorme.' My Spanish was pretty limited, but I thought that meant, 'It's a huge iguana.'

I wondered what the Spanish-speaking audience would think of Rafael's performance. A large iguana is a stand-in for a man's large you-know-what.

'Uh, yes.' The reporter turned as green as her dress.

Rafael was definitely enjoying this. All three TV cameras were focused on Rafael, the giant lizard, and the reporter.

'Es super lindo,' Rafael said. (He's super cute.)

He smooched the cold-stunned lizard on its scaly head and said, 'Me encanta besar a mi niñito.' (I love kissing my little baby.)

He held the enormous lizard under its front legs and presented it to the reporter. 'Ahora, bésalo tú.' (Now, you kiss him.)

The lizard twitched one leg. The reporter screamed and dropped her mic. I stuck the straw hat on my head, grabbed the boxes, and scurried in the back way, laughing so hard my sides hurt. I leaned against the wall in the back hall, trying to catch my breath.

'Open up! Police! Right now!' a man demanded at the front door.

Uh, oh. I knew that voice. Detective DeMille. He sounded furious.

TWELVE

My laughter died when I heard DeMille's outraged shouts. The Florodora seemed to shake from his furious pounding. What if he tried to batter down the front door? Or shoot out the lock?

Calypso shut off her vacuum and ran down the stairs, while I stashed Sammie's boxes in the back closet, then tore off the straw hat, coat, scarf and gloves and threw them in, too. I ran toward the front door, skidded to a stop, and peeked around the corner.

Calypso was calmly opening the door. Her voice soothing as a sea breeze, she greeted the man with a smile. 'Detective DeMille. Why all this shouting? And at eight thirty in the morning. No need for that. Come in. Let me make you some hot coffee.'

I could see DeMille on the doorstep, his face stroke-red, his hair standing almost straight up.

'I don't want coffee,' he said. 'I want to see Ms McCarthy. Now.'

I took a deep breath, then stepped into the entry. 'I'm here. What can I do for you?'

DeMille was so sizzling mad, he could hardly spit out the words. 'What you can do . . . what you can do . . . is tell the truth!'

I tried to look innocent. 'I did. Why don't we discuss your concerns upstairs in my apartment?'

I wasn't about to get in that cramped elevator with an angry DeMille. It might explode. Also, I hoped the four-story climb would tire him out and calm him down.

He followed me up the stairs. Once in my apartment, he said, 'Mind if I look around?'

'Help yourself.' I was glad I'd stashed Sammie's boxes in the downstairs closet.

'Should I make us some coffee?' I asked.

He spit out one word. 'Yes.'

While I busied myself in the kitchen, DeMille checked out

my apartment as if I'd hidden an assassin in it. He looked in my bedroom, bathroom, closets, and dining room. He even shook the living-room curtains, but no one was behind them. Finally, he sat down on my living-room couch, facing the door.

The impromptu search seemed to have drained away some anger. Maybe he was trying to intimidate me, but I hadn't done anything wrong. Well, not too much.

I brought in two mugs of hot coffee and a plate of sugar cookies, then sat in the beer baron's carved chair.

He gulped the hot coffee, and resentfully crunched a cookie before he started talking. He picked up a second cookie, and pointed it at me.

'You lied,' he said. 'I asked you if you knew a Max Clifford and you said no.'

'No, you asked me if I knew a *Maximillian Evan* Clifford. I didn't recognize his full name.'

'You sure knew enough to go on TV last night and talk about him. Dates and details. Where did you get that information about him?'

'I googled it. That's when I remembered who Max Clifford was. The man who killed my parents.'

'And instead of telling me, you went on TV.'

'I had to. I was responding to Alberta Clifford's statement, calling my grandmother a sleazy, senile showgirl, and a killer.'

'Don't you have any respect for a mother who just found out where her lost child had been? She's never had a funeral for Max.'

'What about me?' I said. 'What about a child who lost both parents? Parents who were killed by a drunken driver? Max should have been locked up. He was so drunk, he smashed into my parents' car and turned them into hamburger. They had to be buried in closed caskets. I never saw them again.'

'But I did get two funerals.' I glared at the detective. 'Then I turned on the TV news and heard Alberta blackening my grand-mother's name. The woman who raised me. At age eighty-three, she took on a confused and rebellious child.

'And no, I didn't remember who Maximillian Evan Clifford was. Not right away. So lock me up.'

I threw up my hands.

DeMille's fury seemed to have vanished. Now his voice was soothing. 'Calm down,' he said. 'I'm not going to arrest you. This time. But I want you to give me the names of everyone who lived in the Florodora when your grandmother was alive.'

I was wary of his sudden mood switch. I said, 'That would be Calypso and Lennox.' I felt like I was betraying them.

'Are they home?'

'You just saw Calypso,' I said. 'I think Lennox is here, too. His rehearsal usually starts at noon. Rafael the maintenance man lived here, too, if you want to wait for an interpreter who speaks Spanish.'

'Never mind Rafael,' he said. 'Calypso and Lennox will do for now.'

Fifteen minutes later, a sleepy (and possibly hungover) Lennox stumbled into my apartment, and plopped down next to Calypso on the sofa. I served more coffee to everyone. Lennox grabbed the mug gratefully.

'Calypso,' DeMille asked, 'where were you November fifteenth, 1991?'

'I have no idea,' Calypso said.

'You didn't have anything to do with the death of Max Clifford?'

'Hell, no,' she said.

'What about you, Lennox? Did you kill Max Clifford?'

'Of course not,' Lennox said.

Calypso stared at the detective resentfully. Lennox looked a little more alert. I wondered why DeMille even asked them. Did he expect Calypso or Lennox to confess if they had killed Max Clifford?

DeMille suddenly shifted his line of questioning. 'Do you know what Google Earth is?' he asked. 'Calypso?'

'Something to do with the internet, and I don't bother with it.' Calypso sounded defiant.

'What about you, Lennox?'

He shrugged and looked apologetic. 'Sorry, old man. Like Calypso, I know it has something to do with the internet, but I don't know anything about it. Computers aren't my thing.'

'Norah?'

'Uh, it's some kind of a computer program, and it shows the

earth in three dimensions. Doesn't Google use mostly satellite imagery?'

I didn't sound confident at all.

'Not bad, Norah.' DeMille metaphorically patted me on the head, then lapsed into full teaching mode.

He began his lecture. 'Google Earth has a so-called "historical view." I can go to Google Earth Pro on a computer, select a location, and pull down "view." Then I slide the bar back in time to see different views from different years from various satellites on the same site.

'Anyway, I went all the way back to 1991 and got a historical view of the Florodora. In mid-October of '91, it showed disturbed earth near the pool. I didn't see anyone tossing a body into the disturbed earth, but I'm still looking.'

He paused and glared at each of us. I took a long sip of coffee to break his gaze.

DeMille continued. 'The disturbed earth near the pool' (I guess that was cop talk for hole), 'was date-stamped November fifteenth. The view also showed the cars in the parking lot.'

I recognized the Sykes brothers' black plumbing truck, though I didn't see them digging the hole. I didn't remember anything about that plumbing project, either. The Florodora had too many over the years.

'I also saw a 1987 white Cadillac,' DeMille said.

'That belonged to my grandmother,' I said.

DeMille didn't look pleased with the interruption. 'I already knew that, Norah. I also saw Rafael's pickup truck. I didn't see a car for Lennox or Calypso.'

'We don't drive,' Calypso said, proud of that sentence. 'We walk, take the bus, or someone drives us.'

'Economical and better for the environment,' Lennox said, sounding righteous.

DeMille nodded, and then hit us with a nasty surprise. 'I did see one other car, an '89 Yugo.'

Oh, no. I felt like I'd been sucker-punched. I glanced at Calypso, and then Lennox. We all looked stunned.

DeMille gave us a nasty smile. 'So which Florodora resident owned a Yugo, one of the worst cars ever made? And don't tell me you don't remember, because no one ever forgets a Yugo.

Besides, I could make out the license plate. This is a test, people. Are you lying or are you telling the truth?'

The silence was deafening. Finally, Lennox said, 'It definitely didn't belong to Max Clifford. He liked fast cars. The Yugo was a bucket of bolts that crapped out if you went over forty.'

'Quit stalling,' DeMille's voice was hard.

Calypso and Lennox stayed still and silent as Easter Island statues.

Finally, I said, 'The car belonged to Priscilla Pennington.' I gulped and added, 'At least, I think that's what Grandma said. She thought Priscilla would be a good tenant, but she didn't work out. Grandma called her a wet blanket and a killjoy. Priscilla lived in apartment 101. On the first floor. She moved out in November, 1991.'

'Why was that?' DeMille said.

'I don't remember.' I did, but I didn't want to give him any ammunition against Lennox and Calypso.

'One reason Priscilla moved out was because she disapproved of us,' Calypso said. 'Every one of us, except Norah, who was just a little bit of a thing. I had me a boyfriend, a big, handsome island man, and Priscilla saw him leaving my room late one night. Took it upon herself to lecture me about sin and the sanctity of marriage. I told her to shove her opinions where the sun don't shine.'

Calypso grew more defiant as she talked. 'Personally, I think she was jealous. She was skeleton skinny, with no bubbies and matchstick legs. She looked down her nose at everyone and everything. That's why she was alone. Not because of her looks. She had a bad attitude.'

Silence descended like a curtain, until Lennox finally spoke up. 'I was another reason Priscilla left the Florodora,' he said. 'She was snooping around in the halls one night and saw a man leave my room. A young man, the star of the Scottish play.'

'You mean *Macbeth*?' DeMille said.

The blood drained from Lennox's face. 'You can't say that word. It's bad luck. You have to go outside and turn around three times to undo it. If you don't I won't say another word.' He folded his arms and set his jaw at a stubborn angle.

'I just said it,' DeMille said, 'and I'll say it again . . . *Ma—*'

I stopped him mid-word. 'No, Detective, please. You can't name the Scottish play. It's a time-honored theater tradition.'

'It's superstition,' he said. 'And I don't believe in it.'

'You should,' I said. Lennox had schooled me in *Macbeth* folklore since I was a little girl. I launched into what he'd taught me.

'Supposedly, the play has been cursed since the days of Shakespeare, because he used real incantations for his witches scene. That ticked off a coven, and they put a curse on the play. At the first performance, the actor playing Lady Macbeth died suddenly, so Shakespeare had to take the part.'

DeMille interrupted. 'Wait, Shakespeare played a woman?'

'Yes,' I said. 'Women weren't allowed to go on the stage back then.'

Lennox nodded his approval at my explanation.

'There were more problems. Sometimes real daggers were used instead of props, so King Duncan really was killed. Ever since, actors in the Scottish play have died, fallen off the stage, or been seriously injured. Even saying the name out loud could bankrupt the theater. *Macbeth* was bad luck if it was said inside a theater, but Lennox didn't like it said at all.

'If you want to hear the rest of what Lennox has to say, will you please go outside and spin around three times to undo the curse?'

'That's ridiculous,' DeMille said. 'I'm not going up and down those steps because of some loony idea.' He glared at Lennox. Lennox glared right back.

I needed a compromise. 'Lennox, could Detective DeMille undo the curse if he stepped outside my apartment and turned around three times in the hall?'

Lennox gave a magisterial nod.

'Come on, Detective,' I said. 'It's not a big deal.'

'I could throw his ass in jail until he talks,' DeMille said. 'I'll charge him with obstruction of justice.'

'You could, but this is a lot quicker,' I said.

This could easily turn into a childish power struggle. I tried to remember what Dean told me that cops really hated, and fished out my final argument. 'Plus, there's no paperwork this way.'

It worked. DeMille grumbled about how this was pathetic, stupid and idiotic all the way out to the hall, where I watched him turn around three times.

'It's OK, Lennox,' I said.

A grumpy DeMille plopped back down on the couch, crunched another cookie, gulped some coffee and said, 'OK. Talk.'

'Once Priscilla discovered I was a sodomite – her word, not mine – she refused to talk to me. Eleanor, your grandmother, told me this story. This happened right before Max Clifford disappeared, when he was released from prison in October of '91.'

My mouth dropped open. I'd never heard this story before.

'Eleanor said Max Clifford came to the Florodora one night after he got out of prison. It was late, almost midnight, and Priscilla was sitting out by the pool. Max rang the doorbell, but no one answered.'

No one ever answered the doorbell that late, I thought.

'Priscilla called out to Max,' Lennox said, 'and he introduced himself. He said he'd found God in prison and he wanted to apologize, but Eleanor refused to talk to him.'

'Of course she did,' I said. 'You can't apologize for what he did.'

'Well, he was spouting Bible verses right and left, telling Priscilla, "If we confess our sins, God is faithful and just. He will forgive us our sins and cleanse us from all unrighteousness." Max claimed to be cleansed of his sins and wanted to tell your grandmother.

'Priscilla stayed with him, and they prayed up a storm by the pool. Then at one in the morning, she and Max rang the doorbell at the Florodora and confronted your grandmother. Priscilla said Max was washed in the blood of the Lord and God had forgiven him.

'Your grandmother was outraged. She told Max, "Get the hell out of my house before I run down your sorry ass."

'Then your grandma said, "Priscilla, that goes for you, too. I want you out by tomorrow morning. Got it?"

'Priscilla said, "I don't want to live in such a godless place." That woman was gone the next day.'

'And good riddance.' Calypso looked triumphant.

THIRTEEN

Detective DeMille didn't bother finishing his coffee. 'I'll check this information when I talk to Ms Pennington,' he said. 'She's moved to Wellington.'

'Wellington is one of the ten most boring places in south Florida,' I said. 'It's perfect for her.'

'She won't have a good word to say about us,' Calypso said.

'That's why I'm going to talk to her.' He stalked out, slamming my door. The three of us – Lennox, Calypso and I – looked at one another and shrugged.

Lennox gave me a quick goodbye kiss on the cheek and said, 'I have rehearsal, dear.'

'I'm gonna finish vacuuming,' Calypso said.

I heard the detective's car start and checked to make sure he was really gone. It was pouring rain. I hurried downstairs to get my stash in the back closet.

I stuck Sammie's straw hat on my head and squeezed into the elevator with both her boxes. As the elevator thumped and thudded up to my floor, I wished I'd wrestled those boxes up the stairs. When the elevator landed with a final clonk, I hauled the boxes into my living room and set them on the coffee table.

Two battered cardboard boxes were a pathetic summary of Sammie's life. The contents were even sadder. The first box held a satiny silver dress with the tags still on it. It was cheap and shiny. Was that the dress Sammie planned to wear to her porn movie premier? Or somewhere else? Why was it in storage?

Under the dress were sparkly high-heeled sandals.

Next was a color photo of a smiling blonde girl and a dark-haired boy, shyly holding hands in front of the Burnlocks Baptist Church in Burnlocks, Missouri, a tiny town north of St. Louis. The church marquee said, 'Pastor Samuel Lant,' and reminded viewers: 'Pride is like summer. Always followed by a fall.'

The girl's hair was in long, golden ringlets. Her blue dress, with its long sleeves and high collar, was suitable for an Amish wife. The boy's black suit looked uncomfortable. Were those his church clothes?

On the back of the photo was 'Sammie and Jimmy, Graduation Day, May 12, 2002' in purple ink, with a heart dotting each letter 'i.'

The photo delivered several shocks. First, the guileless blonde in the frumpy dress was Sammie, the future adult entertainer. I would have voted her least likely to be a mattress actress. Second, she was about forty-one when she was murdered. A bit long in the tooth for a porn star. No wonder she pulled that desperate stunt with Chet, the football player.

And jeez Louise, Sammie's father was Samuel Lant. She was named for her preacher father, and used that name as a porn star. Bet Daddy Dearest was madder than hell.

Underneath the photo of Sammie and her high school sweetheart was a framed ad for Sammie's movie, *Sex on the Beach*. Same Sammie, but her breasts, bottom, and lips looked like they'd been inflated by a bicycle pump, and she had yards of bleached blonde hair. She was stretched out on the sand under a hunky football player. The backfield was definitely in motion.

At the bottom of the box was a wrinkled program for a convention in Las Vegas for the AVN Awards, 'recognizing achievement in American pornographic films.' Also known as the Oscars of porn.

Some of the categories, such as Best Film, Best Director, Feature, and Best Director, Foreign, could have been at the traditional Oscars. Others, such as Best MILF Release and Most Outrageous Sex Scene, could not.

Sammie had been nominated for Best Ingenue in the movie, *Teacher's Pet, Extra Credit*. She didn't win, but she did get a laminated certificate.

The second box was mostly clothes, club clothes made of pleather, polyester, and other unnatural fabrics. I spotted a heap of colorful shoe strings, which turned out to be string bikinis. Accent on string.

At the very bottom was a business card with a busty woman on the front with a winking fox's head. The back said, 'Vixen Tamer, repping the hottest stars in adult entertainment.' The address was in downtown Peerless Point and the phone number was 786-555-RACK.

Tasteful. Vix was next on my list. I bet he was fat, bald and smoked cigars.

I felt sorry for Sammie. Her life had come to a shabby end.

I checked her straw hat last. The hat's crown was lined with polka-dot fabric. On the inside. Odd. Odder still, the lining was lumpy.

I carefully peeled it back and saw how Sammie had seduced Chet Parker, the college football hunk. In the lining was a small, crushed white box with blue letters: 'Rohypnol. Flunitrazepam, 1 mg.'

Inside the box were bubble packs of olive green tablets. Roofies. Four of the twenty slots were empty.

Ben the cop was right. Chet had been drugged. Cynical Sammie wanted publicity for her new movie, so she roofied the un-suspecting college student and ruined his life. She'd date-raped Chet.

My sympathy for Sammie vanished.

It was time to see Vixen Tamer, the agent for the hottest porn stars.

South Florida had a major role in modern porn. The 1972 movie *Deep Throat,* starring Linda Lovelace, was filmed in a North Miami motel that later became a college dorm. Linda said that she was forced to make the film by her abusive husband. The movie became a top grosser (in more ways than one), and was partly backed by mob money. The dirty movie helped the mob launder money.

Deep Throat launched what was known as 'porno chic,' when so-called nice people not only watched it, they told everyone, sometimes on national TV. *Deep Throat* was banned in the UK for ten years, and also in parts of the US. That only made it more attractive. Then Watergate came along, and the source who helped topple a president was called Deep Throat. The movie became a legend.

The Florida adult film industry jogged along for more than fifty years, secure in its landmark legacy, until Covid-19 made the state a porn film hotspot. In March 2020, when Covid was on the rise, the country shut down. Restaurants, businesses and schools closed. Hospitals were overwhelmed. People were told stay home, and when they did go out they had to wear masks or risk fines.

Florida Governor Ron DeSantis saved the day in the Sunshine State. In May 2020, DeSantis removed many of the worst restrictions and declared, 'The state of Florida is probably the most open big state in the country.'

The adult entertainment industry greeted this news with open arms, as well as other body parts, and the newly free state became a haven for adult entertainment films, second only to Los Angeles.

And Vixen Tamer rose out of the swamp to exploit the sun-tanned flesh of south Florida.

Since I was going to a sketchy part of town, I let Calypso know. Actually, I shouted the information while she was vacuuming the downstairs office. I wasn't sure she heard me.

The cops were no longer guarding the burial site by the pool and today's pouring rain had chased off the perpetual press watch. I hopped in Wicked Red, my '68 Mustang convertible. Driving Red always made me feel better, and he was wicked. It was love at first sight: Red has a black body with red pinstripes, a red convertible top and red leather seats.

I'd road-tested him on a deserted highway and got Red up to 120 miles an hour with no shimmy or shake.

My good mood quickly evaporated when I reached Vix Tamer's office.

As expected, his office building looked dodgy: a concrete cube with scabrous gray paint. I parked in front, waded through the potholed parking lot, and opened a glass door that had more fingerprints than an FBI lab.

The office was dusty, dominated by a dark wood desk that had to be at least six feet wide, piled with papers. A brass name plaque said, 'Vixen Tamer, Agent.'

Behind it was a man who looked like an aging frat boy, with brassy blond hair and a pink polo shirt. On the wall was a poster promoting *Big Balls and Forward Passes*, featuring Countess Crawlie, a busty brunette holding two footballs to cover her chest. The rest of her body was covered with frilly bits of a French maid costume. *Downton Abbey* must have been on hard times if it couldn't afford full uniforms.

Vix Tamer held up a single finger and then pointed to his cell phone.

I sat in a leather club chair in front of his desk and eaves-dropped. 'Yeah, yeah, she'll be there at eight tomorrow morning for the shoot. You're going to use the gym for the orgy scene. Of course, that's OK. Yeah, she can screw on an exercise bike. Better her than me.'

Blech! I'd never get that image out of my mind. I studied the intricate carvings on his giant desk.

Vix laughed, hung up the phone and said, 'I see you've noticed my desk. It's the Resolute desk, the same one that's in the Oval Office. Queen Victoria gave it to the president in 1880.'

He stopped, and said, 'Well, not the same desk. Mine's a copy. Cost me nine thousand dollars. About what my daddy made in a year.' He slapped the desk top and an avalanche of paper landed by my feet.

I gathered the errant papers, which looked like contracts, and handed them to Vix.

'How can I help you, honey? If you're looking for a job, you're cute but a little old.' He gave me an appraising look and said, 'Jugs could be bigger, but that can be fixed. Well, maybe I could use a MILF.'

I didn't know whether to laugh or stomp out of there. Finally, I said, 'I'm not looking for a job. I'm Norah McCarthy. I own the Florodora Apartments by the beach, and one of your clients turned up at my place. Dead.'

He raised a questioning eyebrow.

'Sammie Lant,' I said. 'She was buried on my property.'

'Oh, yeah, yeah. Sammie. Poor girl.' Not a trace of regret. He could have been talking about roadkill.

'When was the last time you saw her?'

'Two days before the premier of her movie. I had the press and everything for the premiere in Miami, and then she didn't show up on the night. I was frantic. I kept calling her, but she ghosted me.'

'She sure did,' I said. 'She was dead.'

'I didn't know that.' He sounded defensive.

'What happens now? To her movie.'

'Nothing.' He shrugged. 'She's dead. No heirs to bother me. Her residuals are my retirement plan.'

He leaned back in his chair and said, 'Truth to tell, Sammie was getting a little long in the tooth. Overexposed, if you know what I mean. She was pushing thirty-five.'

More like forty-five, I thought. I leaned back so I wasn't too close to the conniving creep. 'I see that you signed Countess Crawlie.'

Now he was enthusiastic. He gave me a big smile. 'Oh, yeah, the countess is a hot talent. And that rack is real.'

'I'm sure,' I said.

'So am I.' He leered at me. 'I road-test all my stars.'

Yuck. I scooted my chair back and asked, 'Weren't the countess and Sammie rivals?'

'Nothing serious. Just friendly stuff.'

'So you and the countess didn't have any reason to kill Sammie?'

'Of course not,' he said. 'Now, you want a job or not?'

'No. Not just no, but hell no. You're a nasty little sleaze. I bet you're short, too. And I'm not talking about your height. That's why you have to road-test your stars.'

He stood up so quickly another pile of papers slid off the desk, and landed on my shoes. I kicked them away.

'Get out!' he screamed. 'I've seen warts bigger than your jugs . . .'

I left, and shrugged off his insults. Sticks and stones.

FOURTEEN

I was happy to escape Vix Tamer's office, even if I did run out into a hard rain. Wicked Red wasn't perfect. He had a leak in the convertible roof that dripped down my back. There are only three days a year when I can drive a convertible in Florida. The rest are too hot or too wet. The steady drip, drip reminded me this was not one of those days.

It was only twelve thirty, and I wasn't ready to go back to the Florodora. Ben the cop told me that Chet Parker, the college football star whose career Sammie had ruined, had transferred to Hallandale Beach College, where the young man was studying computer science.

Hallandale College was known for three things: its Olympic-level beach volleyball team; its excellence in intermural beer drinking (periodically beating even the top-seeded University of Florida); and its prestigious computer science program.

The green campus grounds were nearly deserted. I parked in a palm-fringed visitor lot and ran through the warm drizzle to the student cafeteria, where I found a friendly group eating lunch near the door.

'Do you know where I can find Chet Parker?' I asked a young woman in Hallandale College sweats.

She looked puzzled by my question, and then said, 'Oh, you mean Big Chet? He's the dude in the green shirt, using his laptop.' She pointed to a table in the far corner.

Chet was sitting alone, pounding his laptop and drinking a Coke. A basket of French fries and a pile of paper napkins sat next to him. The former football player wasn't just big, he seemed built on a different scale. He was about 230 well-muscled pounds. His beard was trimmed and his brown hair was short.

Chet had massive shoulders, mahogany skin, and a sweet face. Could he really send another man to the emergency room? He didn't look like a dangerous felon.

'Chet Parker?' I asked.

He frowned at me. 'I'm Chet Parker. Why are you asking?'

I told him that Sammie had been buried in my backyard. I didn't mention I was trying to figure out if Chet killed her.

'Beat it,' Chet said.

'What? I'm not a reporter.'

'I don't care. Get out of here. I don't want to talk about that woman. Ever again. And I don't have to. So get out before I wring your neck.'

He stood up, glowering at me. I backed away and knocked over a chair. The cafeteria went stone-cold quiet.

I left in a hurry.

Back in the parking lot, I searched for photos of Chet's mother online. She'd been interviewed by Channel Eighteen. She seemed like a spirited woman, but I doubted she weighed more than a hundred pounds. And she used a wheelchair.

I called Chet's coach at his school. The switchboard operator said, 'Coach Sullivan is out of town.'

'Do you know when he'll be back?'

'Don't know,' said the bored voice.

Two interviews. One useless and one a possible death threat. Enough sleuthing for the day. Except maybe my encounter with Vix wasn't useless. Could Vix have killed Sammie? He certainly showed no regret – or even interest – in her death. He complained she was getting old. He said Sammie had 'no heirs to bother me. Her residuals are part of my retirement plan.'

Was he bragging or telling the truth?

As soon as Sammie was out of the way, he signed up the countess, a younger, fresher talent. I didn't believe Sammie and the countess were friendly rivals. Not for a minute. I also didn't believe Lennox or Calypso could have killed Sammie. She was a brief annoyance, but she didn't affect their lives.

I drove back to the Florodora, leaving huge rooster tails of water in my wake on flooded Ocean Drive.

By the time I got home, the rain had stopped and the sun was out. I could smell the salt on the ocean breeze. I hoped it would blow away the cobwebs from my encounter with the boorish Vix Tamer and the threatening Chet Parker. Watching innocent people laugh and play in the waves lightened my mood.

Ben, my favorite beach cop, ran after me, calling my name.

'What's wrong, Ben? You look out of breath.'

He shrugged. 'I'm fine. Just had to deal with a teenage shoplifter. The T-shirt store called me. They caught the kid trying to walk out with the shirt stuffed in his cargo shorts. I rounded up the boy's mother at the motel next door. She told us that her darling boy would never steal a shirt that said, "Freelance Gynecologist – No Appointment Needed." The store agreed not to press charges if she paid for the shirt plus a hundred-dollar "restocking" fee.' He laughed.

'And you were OK with that?' I asked.

'Less paperwork for me. Besides, that kid's going to get an earful all the way home to Ohio.'

We laughed. Ben looked around and made sure no one was near us, then lowered his voice. 'My sources are telling me you should be careful of the Clifford family.'

'I don't expect them to nominate me Peerless Person of the Year.'

'It's worse than that. They want a piece of your hide after you insulted Alberta Clifford on TV.'

'She deserved it,' I said.

'I'm not arguing with you,' Ben said. 'That family blames your grandma for killing their son.'

'Blames her? Ben, Alberta came right out on TV and said Grandma killed Max.'

'I know. I saw the interview,' Ben said. 'Rumor around City Hall is that the Cliffords are using pressure to send city inspectors to your building and condemn it.'

'Thanks, Ben. I'll let Rafael know.'

'Be careful,' he said. 'The Cliffords' knives are sharpened. You know they'd love to get their mitts on the Florodora land.'

At home, I delivered the news to Rafael. 'We've beat them before,' he said. 'We can do it again.'

Our conversation was cut short by a call from Liam Sykes. The police had cleared the plumbers to continue working. 'We'll start tomorrow,' he said. 'Shouldn't take too long. You'll have your pool back in a day or two.'

That was good news for the Florodora. The pool was our gathering place. As I climbed the stairs to my apartment, I felt a glow of satisfaction. Life was improving. Soon the Florodora would be back to normal.

Willow, our resident hippie, knocked on my door about three that afternoon, balancing a tray with a plate of chocolate muffins and two mugs of tea. Her long blonde hair formed a golden halo, and her eyes were bright with suppressed glee.

'I have to tell you something,' Willow said. 'Do you have time for tea?'

'Yes,' I said. 'Especially when you bring it.'

I crossed my fingers that Willow didn't serve one of her healthy teas, like stinging nettle leaf, milk thistle, or dandelion. Chamomile was OK, but tasted like fancy dishwater.

Willow set the tea tray on the coffee table, and we settled in for a chat on the sofa.

'What's up?' I asked, as I reached for a muffin. It was still warm. Then I sipped the tea. 'Not bad,' I said.

'It's Dragon Well green tea,' she said.

'So what happened?'

'I was meditating on the beach this morning, when this man approached me. He was wearing a Hawaiian shirt and a banana sack.'

'Ick.' A banana sack was a skimpy Speedo.

'He asked me for a date,' she said. 'When I said no thanks, he wanted to know where he could meet girls. "Friendly girls." Those were his words, not mine.'

I took another bite of muffin. It was like eating melted chocolate.

Willow kept talking. 'I asked him if he was from Texas. I could tell he was by his accent. *Austin. I'm here on business*, he told me. Then I asked what kind of women did he want to meet? *Young ones*, he said. *No offense, but younger than you.* Twenties, teens? I asked him. *Younger*, he said. *Preteen, if possible.*'

'I want to throw up,' I said. I gulped my cooling tea.

'I know,' Willow said. 'But I wanted to take him out of circulation. So I asked him, do you want "untouched" preteens? Can you pay for the privilege?

'He was so excited he was almost drooling. *Money's no object*, he said. I lowered my voice and told him that the best-kept secret in Peerless Point is a place called the Police Station. That it looks just like a 1920s' cop shop. The bouncers and the madam are dressed in realistic police uniforms, and dummy police cars are parked around the station. I told him to bring seven thousand dollars in cash. Cash only, got it? He said yes. I told him to go to the person at the front desk, they'll be wearing a police uniform, and tell them you want a "preteen girl, untouched." Remember that. Ask for a "preteen girl, untouched." You may have to ask several times. Then use the password: "Detective DeMille sent me." Got that?

'*Detective DeMille sent me*, he repeated. I said, if you drink, bring your own booze. They don't serve alcohol. Better hurry. The untouched ones don't last. He ran off to the cop shop, and that's the last I heard from him.'

I was laughing so hard, I snorted tea out of my nose. 'Willow, you're brilliant.'

I toasted her with my tea. 'You're a true Florida Woman. I'm proud to know you.'

'Well, we don't know if it worked yet,' she said. 'But I expect it will be on TV or in the papers in a day or so.'

'Why do you think he asked you?'

'I was about the only person on the beach at that hour. And I'm kind of hippie-looking, so I guess he thought I was safe.'

'That will show him,' I said.

'Please don't say anything to anyone,' she said. 'Not even Dean. I don't want this to get back to DeMille.'

'Deal,' I said. We spent the next hour talking and drinking tea before Willow went back to her apartment.

Dean stopped by my apartment about seven thirty that night with a six-pack. I was happy to see the blond hunk. I ordered pizza and we drank beer and ate greasy slabs of pepperoni pizza in my living room.

'You seem kind of subdued,' he said, popping the top on another beer.

'I am.' I left out Chet Parker, because I didn't want to hear 'I told you so.' I did tell him about my morning with Vix Tamer.

'He offered me a job in a porn movie, Dean. He said I could work as a MILF, but I'd need implants.'

Dean laughed so hard beer spurted out his nose.

'What's so funny?' I asked.

'That man's an idiot,' he said. 'You don't need any changes. You're perfect the way you are.'

'You're not bad yourself,' I said, toasting him with my beer. He was way handsomer than the football player on the Countess Crawlie's porn poster. If anything, he gotten better looking since he'd moved in here. Dean was leaner, tanned and more muscular since he'd been fishing almost daily.

'I think I hit a nerve with that sleaze, Vix,' I said.

'Maybe.' Dean shrugged. 'Maybe he hates women who stand up to him. Especially ones he can't test-drive.'

I swatted him, and he made a grab for the last piece of pizza.

Dean didn't ask to stay with me that night. I wasn't in the mood. Vix left me feeling out of sorts, and Dean seemed to sense that. He was good at reading my moods.

He knew me well. We were compatible in so many ways. Too bad the spark was missing.

FIFTEEN

The Bobcat's growl tore through the still morning air, waking me at the ungodly hour of seven.

I padded over to the front window and saw the source of the noise. The Sykes brothers were back at work, using the small excavator to attack the hole and fix the pool's faulty plumbing. I'd already sent their crop of kids to college. I hoped none of their children were going after post-graduate degrees, or I'd be paying for those, too.

Suddenly, the machine's growls ceased, followed by muscular curses and hearty cheers. Liam, the taller, older brother, dropped a ladder into the hole, and scrambled down. He emerged shouting, 'I got the blasted thing!'

Liam held a mud-encrusted hunk of metal overhead like the Heisman Trophy.

'About time.' His brother Lester climbed out of the Bobcat, wiped his forehead with a red bandana, and stuck it in the back pocket of his overalls.

The two brothers poked and prodded the mud-coated metal, then celebrated their success with a fifteen-minute coffee break under a palm tree.

Coffee was a good idea, I decided, and fortified myself with a pot of hot, black coffee. It was eighty-two degrees already this morning, another scorcher in south Florida, where the four seasons were hot, hotter, hottest and hurricane. I could hear some of the residents of the Florodora stirring – hacking coughs, shower noises, and Calypso singing 'Believe for It' as she cleaned.

When the doorbell rang at eight o'clock, I ran downstairs to greet a rotund man in a hardhat, neon safety vest and gray coveralls. He had a wispy mouse-colored mustache and weedy patches of hair clinging to his sweaty scalp. In fact, with his round body, gray coveralls and twitchy nose, he looked like a cartoon mouse. But there was nothing funny about this man.

He brandished a gold badge and a clipboard filled with forms.

'Elwin Sandford, Peerless Point city code enforcement,' he said. 'My colleagues and I are here to inspect your property.' Behind him was a gaggle of inspectors, all men, all dressed the same.

Oh, boy, I thought. Ben had warned me this would happen, but I hoped it wouldn't be so soon.

'On what grounds?' I asked.

'We've received complaints regarding the safety of this dwelling.'

'From whom?' Mrs Neibauer, my English teacher, would be so proud of that 'whom.'

'The complaints were made anonymously,' Elwin said. 'I'm not required to reveal who made them.'

'Let me guess: it's someone in the Clifford family.'

'I can neither confirm nor deny that.'

His oily smile confirmed it. I wanted to slap that smug look off his fat face.

Dean rushed down the stairs to the front door, sounding out of breath. 'Phone call for you, Norah.'

I hesitated, wanting to needle the crooked inspector more, but Dean grabbed my arm and dragged me inside and up the stairs.

When we reached the second floor, I asked, 'What phone call?'

'Mine. Calling you to return to sanity,' he said. 'Teasing government drones won't do you any good. It will make this bad situation worse.'

Dean was right. Hot anger had burned through my common sense.

'Go wake up Willow and make sure her pot plants are hidden,' Dean said, 'before she gets arrested. I'll check that Mickey doesn't have any pranks in progress that the inspectors can see in her apartment.'

'Billie, Katie, and Lennox should be OK,' I said. 'Rafael and Calypso will be fine.'

I encountered Calypso, in a bright yellow sundress, coming down the hall with her cleaning caddy.

'The city inspectors just arrived and they're hot to take the Florodora apart,' I said. 'Can you create a diversion on the stairs to delay the inspectors from coming up to Willow's apartment right away?'

Calypso grinned, showing her white teeth. 'I certainly can. I'll take my own sweet time scrubbing these stairs. On my hands and knees.'

She plunked herself down on the stairs, grabbed a spray bottle, and began working on each step.

'That looks hard on your knees, Calypso. Can I get you a rug or a cushion?'

'No, I'm fine.'

'I owe you,' I said.

'You certainly do. Now, go. It's our job to save your grandma's building.'

I pounded on Willow's door. She must have been sound asleep, because she didn't answer. I heard an inspector arguing with Mickey on the first floor. There was no time to waste.

I used to my master key to Willow's apartment, a portal to 1968. The place reeked of weed. Willow, in a long tie-dyed shirt, was stretched out on her couch, deep in doobie dreams.

'Willow, wake up!' I shook her shoulders. She groaned and rolled over.

After several tries, I finally woke her.

'Wha's wrong?' She brushed her long blonde hair out of her face.

'The city inspectors are here. We have to hide your bohemian broccoli.'

'Oh, gawd, what do I do?'

'Open the windows and turn on the fan. Light some incense. I'll stash your plants in the secret staircase.'

I headed to her balcony and picked up a large, leafy plant. Willow called, 'Careful! That's my Jelly Rancher. It's a hybrid made from a cross between Very Cherry and Notorious THC.'

'Maybe you'd better carry it,' I said.

She rushed in to rescue the prized plant and said, 'Take those two, Wedding Cake and Gorilla Glue.'

'Why's it called Gorilla Glue?'

'Because it's so strong it glues you to the couch.'

In the hall, I pressed the edge of the gold frame on a giant painting of *September Morn*, which showed a nude young woman standing in a pool of water, gilded by the sun. It was a scandalous artwork when Grandma built the place.

In fact, the Miami police made a respectable bookstore take the painting out of its window. A Miami paper regretted the removal of this artwork because 'the great majority of men and almost all boys under twenty cannot see art as art when it is dressed up in undress.'

I suspected that's why crafty Grandma used the pervy painting to cover this door to her secret stairway. No one would want to be caught contemplating the nude vision, so they passed by, eyes averted.

The hidden door creaked open. At the top landing, out of sight, I set down the two pots of pot. Willow carried her precious Jelly Rancher up to safety.

'Jelly Rancher. Is that what you smoked last night?' I asked.

'No, I had another classic,' she said. 'Northern Lights. It's good for chilling.'

We carried up three more plants. Back in Willow's apartment, I rearranged the other plants on her balcony, mostly short, leafy palms and philodendron, to fill in the spaces left by her pot farm.

'What's next?' she asked.

'Hide your stash,' I said. 'In the staircase.'

Willow came out of her bedroom with a bulging Ziploc bag and ran out to the hall. Next, she carried a box filled with bongs, a hookah and other paraphernalia, and then made sure the secret door was shut.

Meanwhile, I spotted an overflowing painted clay ashtray on the coffee table and flushed the contents down the toilet. Twice. And washed the ashtray. Next, I straightened the Indian cotton spread on her couch, fluffed the throw pillows, and moved *The I Ching* and *The Way of Zen* to the end table.

Willow had slipped into jeans and sandals and brushed her hair. We surveyed our work.

The overhead fan was whirring, and the ocean breeze did its best to air out the apartment. I gave the apartment a final scan and a deep inhale.

'What do you think?' Willow asked.

'I can still detect a hint of weed,' I said.

'Time to break out the big guns.' Willow returned with a red bottle called Mule Head Brand Stinkinator Extreme Odor Eliminator and sprayed that around. Next, she lit cinnamon incense.

'Have a seat on the couch,' she said. 'I'll make tea.'

I heard Willow clanking around in the kitchen, and the teakettle shriek. Soon she brought out the teapot, mugs, a jar of honey, and a plate of blueberry muffins on a tray.

'Help yourself,' she said. 'Everything is organic. I know you like the tea, Dragon Well green.'

I did. The green tea was delicate and the muffins were fresh. As we ate and sipped tea, I told Willow the Clifford family was after the Florodora. 'They called the city inspector on us. Alberta Clifford wants revenge because she thinks my grandmother killed her son.'

'Do you?' Willow asked.

'Do I what?' I helped myself to a second muffin.

'Do you think your grandmother killed him? Max murdered her only child and left you an orphan.'

'No, of course not,' I said quickly. Too quickly. Grandma was in her eighties when Max Clifford got out of jail. Was she strong enough to kill a grown man, throw him in a hole and cover him with several feet of dirt? I didn't think so. I quickly shut down those thoughts.

'I don't think Grandma would go after revenge.'

'Your grandmother was wise. You know what Gandhi said about revenge? "An eye for an eye will only make the whole world blind."'

'Exactly,' I said.

Willow turned the conversation to safer subjects. 'I met Katie, the new resident,' she said. 'She stopped by and introduced herself. She's a good addition to the Florodora. You chose well.'

'I'm glad she's working out,' I said.

We talked about the beach, the heat, and the latest Florida craziness.

'Did you hear about the Catholic priest who bit a woman?' Willow asked.

'You're making that up,' I said.

'Hah! You know better than that,' Willow said. 'Not in this state.'

She opened her phone and showed me the story. The headline said, 'Florida Priest Bites Woman Who Grabbed Holy Communion Wafers.'

The priest said he bit the woman's hand, but only to avoid an act of desecration. The woman didn't seem familiar with communion and tried to grab a handful of communion wafers, which she called 'cookies.' The priest was holding the ciborium, when she reached in and grabbed a handful of wafers. He bit her to protect the wafers from this sacrilege.

'That's nuts,' I said. 'Even for Florida.'

We were interrupted by a knock on the door. Willow answered. It was Elwin, the mouselike city inspector. Actually, he looked like a giant rat, at least to me.

His clipboard was thick with triplicate forms, filled out in black ink. I looked at it with dread.

'I'm going to have to ask you ladies to step out, please,' he said.

I passed Elwin with my hands clasped together, to keep from punching the man.

SIXTEEN

D ownstairs, I paced back and forth in my office, anxious and angry, while the city inspectors invaded the Florodora. I counted five of them. Willow stayed with me until her apartment was cleared. 'It will be OK, Norah.' She patted my arm.

I didn't share her optimism.

Calypso delivered periodic reports to the office, along with pitchers of lemonade and cookies.

'Those fools didn't find the entrance to the secret staircase,' she said, her voice almost a whisper. 'They were in and out of Willow's apartment with no comment.'

Two bits of good news. Willow and I sighed with relief.

'I'd like to go upstairs and meditate,' she said.

'Go. Chill.'

I wasn't alone for long. I heard angry voices coming from Billie's apartment. He stomped down the stairs and found me in my office.

'What the heck is going on here?' Billie said. 'I've been thrown out of my own apartment by a bunch of government goldbricks.'

His face was bright red and his brown hair was plastered to his scalp.

'Billie, I'm sorry,' I said. 'The city is after us. The Cliffords complained that the Florodora is unsafe and sicced the city inspectors on us.'

'Oh.' Billie's anger vanished. 'I'm sorry I yelled at you, Norah. What can I do to help?'

'Nothing. We'll have to wait them out. Want some lemonade or a cookie?'

Billie drank two glasses and polished off half a dozen cookies. 'Will you sit down, please, Norah?' he asked. 'Your pacing is making me nervous.'

I thought Billie was more annoyed than nervous, but I sat. He was barefoot, wearing baggy jeans and a red Bruce Willis T-shirt

that read, 'I survived the Nakatomi Plaza Christmas party 1988.'
Nakatomi Plaza. The setting for *Die Hard.*

'Let me guess,' I said. 'You're also doing a *Die Hard* retro-spective for your new book.'

'Yep. Did you see the first *Die Hard* movie?'

'It's been a while, but I liked it.'

'Me, too. But there are supposed to be more than a hundred mistakes in the first movie alone, and I'm trying to find them all.'

'Like what?' I asked.

'Remember when the terrorists shot the rocket at the RV?'

Vaguely, I thought. I nodded yes.

'Well, they break the same window in the building. Twice.'

'I didn't notice that,' I said.

'I had to watch the movie three times to find it.' Billie sounded proud of his observation. 'Here's another error. The power was cut in the building, but the lights on a Christmas tree stay on for the whole movie.'

Billie regaled me with his findings for forty-five minutes, until Calypso announced his apartment was now inspector-free. Billie pocketed another cookie and left to continue his day with Bruce and his blunders.

'Sit down, Calypso,' I said. 'You must be exhausted.'

She poured herself a glass of lemonade, plopped in the chair by the window and drank it quickly. Before the ice melted in her glass, she jumped up. 'I don't have time to sit. I have to go back upstairs. The city slackers pulled down the stairs to the attic and climbed up into it.'

'Good. I hope they roast,' I said. 'It must be two hundred degrees in that attic.'

'Your place and Dean's apartment are clear if you want to go back up.'

'No, thanks,' I said. 'I need to stay far away from those people.'

'Be careful if you go outside. It's infested with media buzzards. They got all excited when they found out the city inspectors were here.'

'Gee, I wonder who tipped them off to that story?'

Calypso laughed and went upstairs. I resumed pacing.

I could hear the Sykes brothers working outside: pounding,

clanking, and occasionally cursing. 'Damn, it's hotter than the hinges of hell out here,' Liam said.

Should I bring the plumbers something cold to drink? Governor Ron DeSantis had signed a baffling bill, blocking communities from enacting ordinances providing heat and water breaks for outdoor workers. No mandatory shade, water, or rest breaks were allowed. Never mind that anywhere from ten to twenty-eight people died from heatstroke each year in Florida.

Not on my property. I looked out the window and saw the reporters at the edge of my land, sweating off their TV make-up. They'd be clamoring with questions as soon as I stepped outside.

I squared my shoulders. They weren't going to stop me from doing something decent. I'd ignore them.

I went in the kitchen behind the office, made lemonade in a plastic pitcher, collected plastic glasses and a package of cookies. Both brothers were working in the hole.

I kept myself focused on the tray with the lemonade and ignored the shouts from the media: 'Hey, Norah, what do you think of the city inspectors at your apartment? Who do you think called them? What will the inspectors find? Can they shut down the Florodora?'

I set the tray on a shady table by the pool and said, 'Liam and Lester, come out for a break. It's too hot.'

Both brothers climbed out of the hole. They were drenched in sweat.

'How's the work going?' I asked.

'Not bad,' Lester said, wiping his forehead. 'We should have this repaired today. Tomorrow we'll fill in the hole and put the pavers back. You should have your pool and courtyard in about two days.'

'Thanks, fellas.'

'Thank you,' they said.

Head high, ears deaf to the hurled media questions, I left the pitcher and returned to the Florodora, grateful for the air-conditioning. Too tired to pace any more, I sat at my computer and stared at the monthly bills, unable to work.

Elwin clomped down the steps, leading his parade of stooges, and stuck his head in my office door. 'We need to check the garage and parking area, and then I'll have my report.'

He gazed longingly at the frosty pitcher of lemonade on my desk. I ignored him, and hoped he'd die of thirst.

Forty-five minutes later, a sweating Elwin was back, grinning like it was Christmas morning. He presented me with a sheaf of papers. 'These are the citations. Please let me know if you need an explanation.'

I read through them, biting the inside of my cheek to avoid any reaction.

The electrical box needed to be updated. I'd expected that.

The smoke alarm in Billie's apartment had been disabled. That was a five-hundred-dollar fine. My guess was the alarm started beeping when the battery was low and Billie tore it off the wall. I'd have a talk with him about that.

The gutters and downspouts needed to be replaced.

The beachside entrance to the building was not ADA compliant. It needed a ramp and hand rails. I was a fan of the Americans with Disabilities Act, figuring at one time or another we all had a sprained ankle or broken leg and needed those accommodations. It wasn't enough to have my heart in the right place – I had to have a ramp and rails, too.

The elevator was cited for 'unusual noises, malfunctioning doors and erratic movements and stops.' Couldn't argue with that. I just hoped the parts were available for that antique.

And finally, there was a leak and 'substantial' mold in the attic, thanks to the barrel-tile roof. Red clay barrel tiles were long-lasting, but the Florodora's were more than a hundred years old. It was a constant battle to care for the aging roof. The rounded tiles are popular in Florida, and expensive to repair.

I prayed there was no structural damage underneath those old tiles.

The repair bills were now in the high five figures – that was my guess.

On to the garage and parking area. The garage was cited for rotted window sills and doors, lead paint, mold and roof issues. We parked on the sandy grass in front of the garage. Now the 'unimproved parking area' had to be paved with asphalt or concrete.

The requirements were spelled out in nearly incomprehensible bureaucratese. Spaces must be 'stenciled in reflective yellow or white paint and be nine-feet wide and eighteen-feet long, with one marked handicapped parking space per every twenty-five spaces.'

Out of the corner of my eye, I caught Elwin swaying slightly by the door, grinning like the evil clown Pennywise. Elwin was enjoying this.

I bit down harder on the inside of my cheek, and dug my fingernails into my hand. I'd be damned if I'd give him the satisfaction of seeing me angry.

I kept reading the requirements. The parking lot also had to be landscaped. 'One tree shall be planted for each eight square feet of landscaped area,' the citation said. 'Additionally, you are required to have ten square feet of landscaped area per parking space to plant trees and shrubs. Hedge or shrub materials shall be a minimum of eighteen inches in height at time of planting.'

I was so angry I thought my head would explode. Deep breaths, I thought. There's only one more section to read.

Lighting was also required. The parking lot 'shall be provided with a maintained minimum of one foot candle of light from dusk until dawn.' I had no idea what a foot candle was, but I was pretty sure it would burn a lot of money.

I smiled at Elwin. 'So, that's it? Anything else?'

He looked disappointed, but managed to ask, 'Any questions?'

'It's perfectly clear.' I smiled my brightest, hoping it matched one foot candle.

'The work has a thirty-day deadline.' Elwin gave me his most slap-worthy smile.

I forced myself to stay calm and keep my voice flat. 'Thirty days.'

'Of course, if you need more time, you can always appeal.' Another smirking smile.

'Who's the judge?'

'Catherine Clifford.' He said that with a flourish.

'Alberta's cousin?' I asked.

'No,' he said. 'Her sister.'

SEVENTEEN

Finally, Elwin and his band of boneheads left. But not before the city inspector delivered one more jab. He stood outside the gates and announced to the press throng, 'The violations for this multiple-family dwelling will be inputted in an hour.'

Inputted? What kind of word was that?

'After the report has been officially filed,' he said, 'these violations will be part of the public record and you can see them.'

'How many violations are there?' a sweat-soaked reporter asked.

'I can't say until they've been inputted,' he said.

'One? Two? Fifty?' another reporter asked.

'More than one,' he said. 'Definitely.' Giving his Pennywise smile, the evil clown and his crew climbed in the city van and left.

Seven TV reporters did stand-up intros for their reports using the Florodora as background. Within half an hour, the press pack was gone. I knew we'd be the lead story on the local news tonight.

The Sykes brothers left soon after, and the Florodora was quiet at last.

I closed the door to the office and reread the paperwork. I'd been too upset to study it the first time through. There were 117 violations, and I had only thirty days to fix them. A month! My stomach twisted and I felt sick. How was I going to get through this?

If only Grandma were here. I missed her every day. I thought about how I grew up in this big, rambling building, surrounded by loving, indulgent adults. Including Uncle Lennox and Aunt Lacey, another former Florodora Girl. Aunt Lacey wore Arpège perfume and let me play with the black and gold bottles. Uncle Lennox recited Shakespeare and would re-enact the fight scenes. My favorite was from *Henry V:* 'Once more unto the breach, dear friends, once more.' Aunt Tillie let me play dress-up in her old gowns, as long as I stayed off the stairs.

Aunts Lacey and Tillie were long gone. Mom and Dad were killed by Max Clifford. Thanks to him, I didn't have a family. Now I was going to lose my home.

I was close to tears when suddenly, I was overwhelmed with rage. I did have a family. Everyone who lived in the Florodora was my family. Time to stop the 'poor little orphan me' routine and call the residents for a meeting. I needed my family's help.

As soon as I made that decision, I felt better. Energized, I started getting the lounge ready. I opened some wine and set out snacks on the buffet. Maybe it was my mood, but the lounge's dark, carved furniture seemed gloomy. I opened the curtains, and sunlight flooded in. That helped.

I found Calypso and we rounded up the residents.

Willow arrived first, and helped herself to a glass of wine and potato chips. Billie loaded his plate with enough cheese, crackers and cashews to make a meal. Dean showed up with a twelve-pack of cold beer, took some chips and sat on a couch. Katie helped herself to a cold beer and Mickey poured herself a generous glass of red. So did Calypso.

Rafael was the last to arrive. The maintenance man took a cold beer and a big handful of chips. I filled my wineglass nearly to the brim. Dean raised an eyebrow, but I ignored him. I needed that wine.

The worried group was perched on the lounge's chairs and couches. Except for nods or quick hellos, no one talked. Once everyone was settled, Mickey said, 'Lennox is at rehearsal. I promised to give him the details.'

'Before we get to the serious stuff,' I said, 'let me introduce our newest resident, Katie Penrod. Katie is an aspiring actress who starred in at least one major TV ad campaign. Stand up and take a bow, Katie.'

Katie turned scarlet, but she stood and said, 'Hi, everyone. I've already met all of you and I'm happy to be at the historic Florodora.'

She sat down to whistles, claps and cheers.

When they died down, Dean got straight to the point. 'How bad is it, Norah? What did the city inspectors find? Can we save the Florodora?'

'It's bad,' I said. 'The Florodora will need work that's going to cost at least five figures – maybe six.'

'Can you afford that?' Billie asked.

'I can, but it's going to hurt. We've been cited for more than a hundred violations, some small, and some massive.'

Billie whistled.

'What kind of violations?' Mickey asked.

'One small violation is because a resident removed a smoke detector. That's a five-hundred-dollar fine.'

Billie looked sheepish. 'I'll pay the fine,' he said. 'I did that. It started beeping at two in the morning, and I couldn't sleep.'

'Thank you.' I was relieved he'd owned up.

I gulped some wine and said, 'Here are a few of the big repairs: we have mold in the attic, a leaking roof, and an outdated electrical box. We need new gutters and downspouts, and an ADA compliant ramp for the back entrance. The garage has lead paint, needs new windows and doors, and more. Also, the parking area has to be paved, landscaped and professionally lit.'

I held up the pack of citations. 'Here they are, if anyone wants to take a look.'

Rafael rummaged through the pages, looking grim. He shook his head, then handed the papers to Dean, who studied them closely.

'How soon does this work have to be finished?' Willow asked.

'In thirty days.'

'Thirty days!' Willow sounded shocked.

'Impossible,' Rafael said. 'Can't you appeal the decision?'

'Won't do any good. The judge is Max Clifford's aunt.'

A group groan.

'The city really clipped you,' Dean said.

'What are we going to do?' Billie asked. 'It's hard to find people who do carpentry and home repairs in Florida.'

'I know that.' I sounded sharper than I wanted. 'Any suggestions? I'm desperate.'

After a long, uneasy silence, Calypso spoke. 'I'd like to have a family reunion. I haven't seen my cousins in the Bahamas in five whole years.'

Huh? I stared at Calypso as if she had sunstroke.

'That's fine, Calypso, but why this sudden urge to see your family?' I asked.

'Because my cousins are first-rate carpenters and handymen. My great-great-uncle Nelson worked for a shipbuilder in the Abacos.'

'What are the Abacos?' Willow looked puzzled.

'Islands in the northern Bahamas, about two hundred miles east of here,' Calypso said. 'A lot of the white people left the US after the Revolutionary War and moved to the Abacos. The white Bahamians turned to shipbuilding, sailmaking and seafaring repairs. They hire us – the black Bahamians. Years ago, my Uncle Nelson worked at a shipbuilder's, and he trained his sons and grandsons to be carpenters.

'If I invite my family to Florida for a reunion, they could work for you.'

'Do they have the skills to make these repairs?' I felt a small stirring of hope.

'Are you kidding?' she said. 'They've been busy rebuilding and repairing houses in the islands since the last hurricane. They're used to making do.'

I heard the pride in Calypso's voice. 'My family can fix your roof, install new gutters, paint, install a new electrical box, remove mold, add an ADA ramp and more. They'll be able to fix nearly every one of those violations.'

Calypso's words gushed out, then suddenly stopped. It took a moment for me to register her offer, and then it hit me. Salvation! I felt the knot in my gut loosening. I could breathe again. I could keep my home. Hope surged through me.

'That's wonderful,' I said. 'I'll take care of their expenses and airfare, and pay them twenty-five dollars an hour. If they finish on time, each one will get a bonus. When do you think they'll be free?'

Calypso laughed. 'For those rates, they'll drop everything and come as soon as they can. That's more than they can make in the islands.'

The residents cheered and toasted one another. Except for Dean. 'Hold on,' he said. 'I hate to stomp all over everyone's good mood, but we need visas to import foreign workers.'

'That's why I'm calling this a family reunion,' Calypso said. 'If my family comes for a visit and want to help, that's their business.'

'I'll pay cash.' I gulped more wine.

'OK, if that's how you want to play it.' Dean shrugged. 'Just so you know it's a risk.'

'It is,' I said. 'But losing the Florodora is a bigger risk. There's no way we'd find enough Florida repair crews and get them to finish the work in time.'

'I think it would be better if we hired someone local for the elevator repair and electrical work,' Dean said. 'Just in case. They'll know how to pull the right permits.'

'Good idea. But I don't want anyone *too* local,' I said. 'We can't have the electricians talking to the city inspectors. Maybe we can hire a company out of Miami or Fort Lauderdale.'

'That's smart,' Dean said. 'What about the other permits?'

'Peerless has people who will stand in line for you at City Hall,' Rafael said. 'They're known as line standers. You give the line stander the list of work you want done and they stand in the lines at City Hall. If you give them a "tip."'

Dean interrupted. 'Is that a bribe?'

'Unofficially, yes,' Rafael said. 'If you give the line stander a tip, it speeds up the permit process. Depending on the size of the tip.'

'Sounds like a terrific job for the useless relatives of City Hall politicians,' Dean said.

'Beats standing in line.' Rafael shrugged.

'Back to the repairs,' Dean said. 'Rafael and I can do a lot of the outside work.'

'I'll help, too,' Billie said.

'Don't you have a book deadline?' I asked.

'Not until April. I have plenty of time.'

'Thank you, Billie.' I glanced at Dean. He raised an eyebrow. He knew the movie-loving couch potato probably wouldn't be much help.

'Can the three of you handle the gutters, the paving and the ramp?' I looked at my wineglass. It was empty.

While I refilled it, Calypso said, 'My youngest cousin, Oswald, can work with Rafael, Billie and Dean for the outside repairs. He's twenty and a strong young man. He looks and sounds the most American. Oswald works at a hotel and puts on a Bahamian accent for the tourists, but he'll blend in here.'

'Even better,' I said. 'Where should I put up your family?'

'Use my apartment,' Mickey said. 'I have three bedrooms and a sleeper sofa. If I can move in with someone, Calypso's family can bunk at my place.'

'Thanks, Mickey,' I said. 'You can stay at my apartment, if you want. How many cousins and second cousins do you have, Calypso?' I asked.

'Sixteen, but only four or five men will be the right age to work.'

'What about their wives and girlfriends?' I asked.

'They'll stay home with the kids.'

'Will they be happy about that?'

'They will if I ask them what they want from the States and make sure the men send it home. I'll also tell the women exactly how much money the men made.' She gave me a satisfied smile. Everyone laughed.

'I'll cook for them, too,' Calypso said.

'I'll help with the cleaning,' Mickey said.

'Me, too,' Willow and Katie added.

I felt lighter and happier. My family had come through and lifted this burden. Rafael and Dean sat together and began planning the materials they'd need and the equipment they'd have to rent. Billie took notes on his phone.

Calypso retired to her apartment to call her family. Katie stayed behind to help clean up. When the room was empty, Katie said, 'Norah, I have some money. I'll be happy to give it to you for repairs.' She turned as pink as her blouse.

'Thank you, Katie, but you don't have to do that. I can manage.'

'OK,' she said. 'But I'm here if you need me.'

'I appreciate your offer. Do you have time to talk for a minute?'

Katie nodded, and helped herself to another cold beer. I refilled my wineglass, and we sat on the sofa.

'How are you settling in?' I asked.

'I'm finally moved in and I've met the residents. It's fun being surrounded by so many creative people. Plus, I get to walk on the beach every day.'

'You know you can have your friends here,' I said. 'The pool will be fixed and that's a lovely place to hang out. Feel free to come in the lounge any time, too.'

'Yes, thank you. I'm guessing you want to know why Chet hasn't come around to see my new place.'

That was exactly what I wanted. 'It's none of my business, but yes.'

'Chet needs some space,' she said. 'He's not been himself since the Sammie thing.' Katie took a long drink of her beer.

'How so?'

'He's been so angry and guilty. He blames himself for what happened.'

Katie looked sad. I didn't know if she knew that Sammie had roofied Chet, but decided not to mention it, or the possibility that he'd been raped. I didn't want to make her feel any worse, and besides, I couldn't claim to know the truth of what happened on the beach. Only Chet knew that. Maybe he had confided in Katie. I felt a flash of guilt. I'd made off with the evidence that might have proved Chet was assaulted. The roofies were stashed in my closet.

'Is Chet getting counseling?' I asked.

'Counseling isn't the answer to everything,' she said. 'Chet spent a lot of time talking to me, and when I couldn't help him, he started talking to our pastor. He's turned to God for help.'

'Well, that's good,' I said.

'It's also good that Sammie's dead,' she said. 'He'll never have to worry about running into that woman again.'

Katie took a big gulp of her beer, then tipped back her bottle, and drank the last. For a small woman, Katie could hold her liquor. 'Nice talking to you,' she said.

Upstairs, I flipped on the TV and my worries kicked up a notch. I didn't know how the local press would spin the story about the Florodora's citations.

On Channel Eighteen, I saw a new reporter, Michele Meyer, a tall, slender woman with straight brown hair. I had no idea how she could wear a dark suit in this heat, but she did.

The reporter said, 'Another development at the historic Florodora Apartments.'

We've been upgraded to historic, I thought.

'Recently, two bodies were discovered on the grounds near the pool by plumbers digging up the yard,' the reporter said. 'Police identified one as porn star Sammie Lant, who disappeared shortly before the premier of her adult film. The other body was Maximillian Clifford, son of the prominent Clifford family. Max Clifford has been missing since 1991. Police sources say both persons were murdered. So far, they seem to have no suspects or leads on the two cases.

'Today, Peerless Point city inspectors cited the Florodora for one-hundred-seventeen code violations, ranging from mold to an unpaved parking lot.'

The reporter paused dramatically and then said, 'Will this latest development prove fatal for the century-old building?

'I'm Michele Meyer, for Channel Eighteen news.'

Not a bad report. I'd expected worse.

I heard someone hammering on my door and Dean shouting, 'Norah! Norah! Come quick!'

My heart was pounding as I flung open the door, and saw a worried Dean.

'What is it?' I said. 'Who's hurt? Calypso? Lennox?'

'It's not a person,' he said.

'Well, that's good.' I was slightly relieved.

'It's your car,' he said. 'I know how much you love that Mustang. Someone tore up your car.'

EIGHTEEN

'Red! Red!' I called my car's name as I flew down the stairs two at a time, Dean trailing behind me. Katie heard the commotion and followed us. I burst outside, and whipped around the side of the building.

To behold my ruined beauty.

'Red!' I cried, as if my desecrated car could hear me. His ragtop was ripped to ribbons. His red leather bucket seats were slashed. Carved in his black door was: 'Die, bitch!' Cut into the trunk was: 'Mind your own business.'

'No,' I said. 'Oh, no.' Tears of fury stung my eyes.

Dean wrapped me in his arms. 'It's OK,' he said.

'It's not!' I said. 'Red is ruined.'

'No, he's not,' Dean said. 'He's insured. He can be repaired. Peerless Point Auto Restoration is famous for antique car restorations. I know the owner. Carl will take care of Red.'

'Are you sure?' My voice trembled.

'The man is an artist,' Katie said. 'My father uses Carl.'

'Then let's call him.'

'After we file a report with the police first.' Dean called the police department and we waited in the shadow of the garage, the heat beating us like a hammer.

Rafael joined us, saw my car, and said something in Spanish that sounded like a swear word. Then he added, 'Norah, I am so sorry.' I finally calmed down enough to see that Red was parked next to Rafael's battered truck.

'Naturally, they didn't touch my wreck,' Rafael said.

I saw Dean stealing glances at his restored '76 Jeep. 'Go,' I said. 'Make sure your baby is safe.'

He ran over and examined every inch, making sure the vinyl windows, black fabric top and doors were unharmed, as well as the original paint job. 'It's fine,' he said. 'They didn't get it.'

I could hear his relief. Dean was proud to own what he called a 'real Jeep, before they turned into SUVs.' (Jeep drivers could be as snobbish as Bentley owners.)

Parked on the other side of Rafael's truck was Mickey's powder blue VW Bug. I ran over and checked it. All was well, right down to the sign in the back window: 'Adults on board. We want to live, too.'

'Looks like all the other cars were unharmed,' I said.

'Then this was a personal attack,' Dean said. 'Someone is threatening you.'

I heard the police sirens, and was glad the parking area was out of sight of the press. Another flock of vultures had gathered outside the gates, hungry for scraps of news.

Officer Ted Jameson pushed through the throng of reporters. Dean escorted the uniform. I smiled when I saw his friendly face. Ted was the officer who'd devoured Calypso's French toast when he was on guard duty here.

'I'm sorry you're having trouble, Norah,' Ted said. 'What's wrong?'

We'd reached the parking lot. 'Someone attacked my car.'

Ted stopped and studied the damage, then shook his head. 'What a shame,' he said. 'That's a sweet ride.'

I nodded my head, afraid to speak. I could feel the anger boiling up in me again. Dean squeezed my hand. Katie hovered in the background, looking worried.

'I'm calling Detective DeMille,' Ted said. 'This vandalism might be related to the other crimes.'

DeMille arrived a short time later. The reporters hurled pointed questions at him, but DeMille ignored them, parting the crowd as if they weren't there.

Dean brought the detective back to the parking lot. 'You're handling vandalism now?' I asked DeMille.

'For now I'm handling anything to do with the Florodora,' he said. 'It's a trouble spot.'

DeMille stopped in his tracks when he saw Red, and shook his head at the damage. 'Somebody was really mad at you,' he said. 'I'm calling CSI to print the car and take pictures. Ted will write up the report for your insurance.'

'You're really taking this seriously,' I said.

'It is serious,' he said. 'You've got a death threat cut into your car.'

'They didn't come after me,' I said.

'Yet.' DeMille's single word had a terrible finality that hung in the evening silence.

'Do you remember a divorce lawyer named Paxton Scottoline?' he asked.

'No.'

'Probably before your time,' DeMille said. 'Ask old Ben the Beachwalk cop about him. Paxton was a real go-for-the-throat lawyer,' he said, 'famous for wringing every last nickel out of his clients' spouses. In 1987, Paxton was shot and killed in his office in downtown Peerless. Shot him right in the . . . uh, posterior . . . as he was running out of his office. A week before he was killed, Paxton's car tires were slashed in his law office lot. Nobody paid much attention. Ben answered the call, took fingerprints, made a report and that was it. The lawyer didn't have a lot of fans on the force.

'The day Paxton was shot, the killer was too dumb, or too crazy, to wear gloves. He left his prints on the door to the lawyer's office. Ben compared the fingerprints on Paxton's car to the ones left by the killer. They were the same. Ben caught the killer.

'The killer was Milo Flynn, not a name you'd forget. Milo had good reason to be angry. He got itchy after thirty years of marriage and wanted to divorce his wife and abandon his three kids for a twenty-something girlfriend. Paxton stripped Milo of his vacation home, go-fast boat and money market accounts. Paxton even found Milo's off-shore banking account. Once Milo was broke, his much younger girlfriend took off. Milo blamed the lawyer instead of his own wandering eye.

'That's why I take vandalism seriously,' he said. 'You need to be careful, Norah.'

'I'll keep an eye on her,' Dean said.

'We all will,' Calypso said. Next to her were Rafael, Billie, Katie, and Mickey.

I smiled at them. 'Speaking of eyes,' I said. 'What about that condo?' I pointed at the Croak Us, the tall building south of us. 'Did any of their surveillance cameras pick up the vandalism?'

'Ted will check the buildings on either side,' DeMille said. 'When is the last time you drove your car?'

'Yesterday afternoon. I got home about three.' I didn't mention that I'd talked to a very angry Vix Tamer, the porn star agent. And DeMille didn't ask.

'I saw the car after the city inspectors left at three thirty this afternoon, and it was unharmed,' Dean said.

'So the vandal could have hit any time between three thirty and – what time is it?' DeMille looked at his watch. 'Seven o'clock. It's almost dark. Someone vandalized your car in broad daylight. Pretty bold, don't you think?' The detective looked at me, to make sure I got the point.

'Yes,' I said.

'Any idea who did this?'

'Someone connected with the Clifford family,' I said.

'There are lots of Cliffords,' the detective said, 'including a flock of them in city government. Has one in particular threatened you?'

'No. Alberta Clifford insulted my grandmother on TV the other night. But you know that.'

'Yes,' DeMille said, 'your outburst.'

'Response. I responded to Alberta's ugly lies about my grand-mother, who isn't around to defend herself.'

'I'd say you and Alberta were even when it came to insults.' Was that a slight smile on his face?

'But wouldn't my response give Alberta a reason to go after me?'

'What's your proof?' DeMille said.

'I don't have any,' I said.

'That's what I thought,' DeMille said. 'Did you have any visitors today?'

'We had the city inspectors. The building was cited for one-hundred-seventeen code violations.'

'Was that Elwin and his gang?' he asked.

'Yes.'

'I don't think he needs to destroy your car. He's done enough damage.' Again, that irritating ghost of a smile.

DeMille turned to the flock of Florodora residents. 'Did any of you hear or see anything unusual?'

He got a collective no.

'I discovered the damaged car when I went out to the garage,' Dean said. 'The threats look like they were carved in the paint with a pocket knife.'

'That's my guess,' DeMille said.

The CSI team arrived, two women who looked annoyed. The tall brunette was Quinn. The pint-sized redhead was Zoe. DeMille gave the CSI team instructions.

Quinn examined the damage to my car up close and said, 'Whoever did this deserves the death penalty.'

'I couldn't agree more,' I said.

DeMille glared at me. 'You need to cool it, Norah. This isn't a joke. Some nut could cut you up next.'

He turned to the knot of Florodora residents and said, 'Look after her, will you? I don't want to come back here for a third body.'

'I'll try not to inconvenience you,' I said.

DeMille ignored me. 'I'm leaving now, but Ted will be back with your report, Norah.'

Dark purple clouds signaled night was on the way, but it was still a steamy eighty-five degrees. The ocean breeze was a wind off a blast furnace.

Quinn was photographing the damage to my car while slapping at her neck and cursing the mosquitos. 'You'd think Noah could have left these needle-nosed pests off the Ark,' she said.

'Let's go inside before the bugs eat us alive,' Dean said. 'I think Calypso has some news.'

The residents reassembled in the lounge, while I brought out more wine. Everyone except Dean and Rafael, who were still working on the beer, poured themselves a glass.

Calypso stood in front of the group, looking like a tropical flower in her yellow sundress. 'Good news.' Her smile stretched across her face.

'We can use some,' Billie said.

'Four of my cousins can come to the reunion,' she said. 'Oswald, he's the young man I told you about, can help with the outdoor work. Eric, he's my oldest cousin and a master carpenter. Godfrey, he works with Eric. They have a business, carpentry and roofing. Also mold removal. And finally, Ian. You want Ian for the paintwork. He's fast and good. Norah, they accept your offer of payment.'

'And the bonus if they finish on time,' I added.

'Oh, they know about that. I suspect they've already spent it in their heads. I can't wait to see them all again.' Bubbling with energy, Calypso looked ten years younger.

We all cheered and toasted Calypso with our drinks.

'Norah, we need to make their travel plans,' she said, 'and buy the food. There's no time to waste.'

I stood up. 'Let's go.' The other residents scattered to their apartments.

I was following them when a knock on the front door stopped me in my tracks. A hot, tired Officer Ted Jameson was on the doorstep.

'I'm afraid I have bad news,' he said.

NINETEEN

Ted was dripping sweat on the concrete steps. 'Come in and get cool,' I said. 'Can I get you water or a beer?'

'I'd love a cold beer,' the uniform said. 'I'm off-duty after I talk to you.'

He followed me to the lounge. Dean had left two beers behind. I gave one to Ted and said, 'Help yourself to some snacks.'

He piled a plate with cashews, cheese and chips, popped the top on his beer, then sat in a big, thronelike chair. 'Now I feel like a king,' he said.

When Ted was settled and looked cooler, I asked, 'So what's the bad news?'

'I checked with both condos. No video on your car vandal was caught by either condo's surveillance cameras.'

That was bad news. 'What about the Croak Us residents who have been hanging off their balconies, taking videos of the Florodora?'

Ted seemed uneasy. 'There are more than four hundred people in that building. We don't have the manpower to track down everyone. I'm sorry, Norah. I really wanted to help.'

'It's OK,' I said. 'I can go there first thing tomorrow.'

He looked relieved. 'You'd do that?'

'You bet. I want to find the person who ripped up my car. I promise I'll call you if I find anything. Any good news?' I asked.

'I have your accident report.' He handed me the paperwork, blotched with sweat. 'Sorry about that. The heat's pretty bad.'

Ted finished his beer and snacks, then left. Dean took photos of Red for the insurance company. Then he and Rafael cleared out space in the lower level of the garage so my disfigured car could be stored inside. I couldn't bear to look at the remains while they put my poor car away.

I know I was carrying on over a hunk of metal, but to car nuts like me, cars have personalities. Wicked Red was a good car, fast and reliable. The one time he had serious trouble, he made sure he died in a parking lot a block from my home. A lesser car would have abandoned me on a dark country road. So yes, I mourned his injuries as if he was a real person.

Dean promised to call the restoration company in the morning. I called the insurance company and filed a claim.

Once that sad duty was out of the way, Calypso and I spent most of the night in my office, planning the reunion. We made reservations and I bought the plane tickets. All four cousins would be arriving in three days.

We shopped online for food. At two a.m. I wearily climbed the stairs to my apartment, relieved this day was finally done.

By nine the next morning, I was ready to visit the Crocus condo. I dressed formally for Florida – a crisp white shirt, black pants and black sandals – and left by the beachside door to avoid the press out front.

I heard the sound of heavy machinery in the Florodora parking lot, and saw Red being loaded on a flatbed tow truck. Dean was supervising. Bless him, he'd ordered a flatbed. Flatbeds were better for towing vintage cars than the old hook-and-chain wreckers.

This was no time to contemplate my wounded car. I had to get into the Crocus, and it was protected by a tall metal fence. I waited until an older man opened the condo's beachside gate and came up behind him. He smiled and let me through without a word.

I was over the first hurdle and inside the Crocus's manicured grounds. I passed a pickleball game in progress and a lively bocce game, and saw six seniors exercising in the heated pool.

The Crocus lobby was painted various shades of lavender, with small bouquets of silk crocuses (croci?) everywhere. The white-haired residents tottering around the lobby made me think of the irreverent Croak Us nickname. I followed a thin, older woman in pink capri pants through the lobby doors and almost made it to the elevator when I was stopped.

There was nothing old or feeble about the front-desk security guard, who looked carved out of solid mahogany. He had to be at least six-and-a-half-feet tall, with shoulders like a linebacker.

'May I help you?' His voice boomed through the lobby like the voice of God.

'Yes.' I wished my voice wasn't a mouselike squeak. 'I'd like to talk to a resident.'

'Which one?' He frowned at me. 'I can't let you inside unless you give me a name.' The older woman slipped inside an elevator, leaving me alone with the massive guard.

Now I was in trouble. I didn't know anyone in the Crocus. Think fast, I told myself, if you want to find out who ruined your car. 'Smith' popped into my mind. There had to be a Smith living here. It was the most popular surname in the States.

'Uh, Mr Smith,' I said.

'Which one?' The guard sounded irritated, like he'd toss me out at the slightest excuse.

I took another guess. 'Bob,' I said. 'I want to see Bob Smith.'

'And what's your name?'

'Norah McCarthy.'

'I'll call Mr Smith and see if he's available. Sit there.' He pointed to the purple couch with a finger as big as a bratwurst.

I sat. Two Smiths in one building. What a lucky guess. Maybe I should buy a lottery ticket.

I could hear the guard on the phone. 'Yes, sir,' he said. 'I'll open the boardroom for you, sir.'

Whoever this Smith was, he must be important. He really made the guard snap to.

'Mr Smith says he's not expecting you, but he'll come down and talk to you for five minutes before the board meeting.'

Gulp. What board meeting? What had I summoned from the depths of the Croak Us?

The guard glanced at a security monitor over his desk and said, 'That's him on the elevator.'

Bob Smith was a gray man, from his drab hair to his dust-colored tennis shoes. Pale bird legs poked out of baggy pigeon-colored shorts. Smith marched into the lobby and glared at me.

'I'm—' I started to introduce myself, but Smith interrupted me.

'I know who you are. You're the spawn of that senile showgirl who killed Alberta's only son. My friend hasn't been the same since Max disappeared.'

The man mountain of a guard stood next to Smith, glowering. I didn't care. I was furious.

'My grandmother wasn't crazy or senile and she didn't kill Max. In fact, Max killed both my parents and left me an orphan.'

Smith shrugged. 'That's no great loss.' I longed to wring his scrawny neck. 'Everyone knew your parents were cokeheads.'

I saw red. I didn't think that could be true, but I was so furious my vision dissolved into a blood-red rage. 'If my parents were – and that's a big if – they didn't deserve the death penalty. They didn't deserve to die alone, bleeding out on a road. Max did that. And everyone knew he was a drunk. Your buddy Alberta and her husband covered for their worthless son until he became a killer. So Alberta can blame herself – and follow Max straight to hell!'

I realized I was shouting. A cluster of frightened older people was staring at me from behind the safety of the glassed-in lobby.

Bob's face was no longer gray. It was brick red. The man looked like he'd stroke out any moment. At first he couldn't talk. Finally, he managed a three-letter word.

'Out!' he shouted. 'Right now. You are barred from this condo! Do you understand? Never set foot in here again. The guard will post your photo to make sure you can't come back. Now leave, before I call the police.'

Bob was breathing heavy now, and I scrammed, too afraid to look back. I kept running until I reached the Crocus's beachside gate, and was back inside the Florodora five minutes later. I found Calypso cleaning my office. She was wearing a lime green dress and singing a hymn I didn't recognize.

'Let's take a break,' I said. 'I need your help.'

The singing stopped. 'Anything wrong?' she asked.

'Not sure.' I fixed two cups of strong Colombian coffee in the Keurig, and we sat at the small table in the kitchen behind the office.

We both drank our coffee while I told her what happened.

'So I'm banned from the Crocus,' I said. 'Can you help?'

'Maybe,' Calypso said. 'But I'm going to need some help from you. After your parents died, a lot of people thought your grandma killed Max Clifford.'

'Why didn't I know about this?'

'You were a little thing, missing your mama and daddy. You didn't need to hear that. Anyway, those were just rumors.

'I think I can help you, but I'm going to need some help from you first. My friend Yolanda is a housekeeper who lives in the penthouse at the Crocus. We see each other sometimes on our days off. Yolanda and her lady, Mrs Upton, know everyone at the Crocus, and if there's a video of your car being damaged, Yolonda will find it for me.'

'What do you want me to do?' I took a long drink of coffee.

'Find out who killed Max Clifford.'

I nearly spit out the brew. 'What? Why?'

'Yolanda and Mrs Upton believe your grandmother killed Max. I've told them she was out of town visiting a sick friend, but they won't help unless I can prove she didn't do it.'

'Did you tell Detective DeMille that Grandma was out of town when Max was killed?'

'Of course not,' she said. 'If Yolanda won't believe me, do you think a cop would take my word?'

'How am I going to solve a crime that happened more than thirty years ago?'

'You can start by asking Lennox who he thinks killed Max.'

'You've known Lennox longer than I have, Calypso. Can't you ask him?'

She shook her head. 'Lennox won't talk to me the same way. I'm the housekeeper. You're the niece he never had. He loves you.'

'Do you think Grandma was a killer?'

'I don't believe so, honey,' Calypso said. She only called me that when she felt sorry for me. 'But I need proof. Get some answers for me and I'll try to get some for you.'

I glanced at the kitchen clock. It was only ten thirty. Lennox should be awake by now. I gulped the last of my cooling coffee and slowly climbed the stairs.

Was I going to discover the woman who raised me, the person I loved and admired most, was a killer?

TWENTY

I knew Lennox didn't leave for rehearsal for another hour or so, but I still hesitated to knock on his door. Since I was a little girl, he'd been my favorite honorary relative, fixing me warm milk when I couldn't sleep, tucking me into bed and reading me stories.

Finally I took a deep breath, and summoned my courage.

Lennox answered, dressed in a stylish but florid outfit of pink-striped linen. His gray hair was in a low ponytail. 'Good morning, dear,' he said. 'To what do I owe this honor?'

'I have some questions about my parents' deaths,' I said.

He hesitated just a moment – Lennox was too good an actor to show his surprise.

I pressed on. 'Do you have any time?' My voice had a slight wobble.

'Now? Right now? Of course. I've made some strong coffee. Come sit in the living room.'

I loved Lennox's apartment. I sank into an elegant black sofa and enjoyed the details of his living room. The floor was covered with a dramatic gold silk Persian rug and the walls were lined with framed posters from his theatrical performances. Tall book-cases held volumes on Shakespeare, piles of theater scripts, and theatrical biographies.

Props from plays were scattered about. Yorick's skull grinned from a shelf. Mounted on the wall was a prop sword with an elegant basket hilt, so called because the basket-shaped lattice protected the hand. Lennox had used that sword in *Henry IV, Part 2*.

Lennox fussed around in the kitchen and returned with a tray holding two gold-rimmed Wedgwood china cups and a plate of biscotti. He poured coffee from an exquisite bone china coffee pot and handed me a cup. His hand was shaking slightly.

'Now, why the sudden need to know about your parents?' he asked.

I told him about my car and why I needed the video.

'When my parents died,' I said, 'you hid things from me.'

He started to protest, but I patted his hand. 'It's OK. I know you did it out of kindness. I was too young to understand. But I'm grown now, Lennox, and I need to know everything.'

'Are you sure, dear? Sometimes it's better to keep to our illusions. Your parents were beautiful and charismatic. Isn't that enough?'

'No, Lennox. That's how I remember them, too, but I know there was more to them. They had a dark side and I need to hear about it. Let me tell you what I know. Maybe that will help you start.'

I took a long drink of strong coffee to bolster my courage, then began. 'I know my mother was a model and my father was a skilled woodworker. He had a shop in downtown Peerless Point.'

Lennox nodded agreement and dipped his biscotti in his coffee.

'I know my parents used cocaine. When I was a little girl, Mama called it her special medicine and told me never to touch it. She kept it in a silver box in her dresser. The box had a little mirror with scratches on it.

'I spent a lot of time at Grandma's. Most of my memories were of Mama coming into my room at night in a cloud of perfume, wearing pretty dresses with sequins on them. Daddy wore fancy clothes, too. He had a pink tux, and a black one with a crimson cummerbund, and even a sequin one.

'Then I heard the front doorbell ring late at night and Grandma screamed. I came out of my room and you put me to bed.' My voice wavered but I was determined to push on. 'My parents didn't come home any more and then I was at their funeral.'

A single tear slid down Lennox's face. He patted my hand and said, 'All that is true, my dear, but it's not everything. Are you sure you want to know?'

He hesitated, waiting for my answer. My heart was beating. I was afraid what I would hear, but I had to know. 'Yes,' I said.

Lennox looked sad as he told me their story. 'Your parents' beauty and charm were their downfall. It's how they were lured into using coke. In the Eighties, cocaine was the drug of choice. Let me tell you how drugs were *perceived* back then. Pot was for hippies, heroin was for degenerates, and coke was for the rich and pretty.'

I started to protest, and Lennox held up his hand. 'Just listen, darling. I'm talking about perception, not the truth. Thanks to the cartels, coke was fairly cheap, and it was everywhere. If you signed a major contract in the arts world, coke was brought out to celebrate the deal. Coke was chic. The TV show *Miami Vice* enforced that perception. Cocaine was also seen as the drug of rich, white people, and law enforcement tolerated it. Coke came out of the back rooms and bathroom stalls into public view at parties, expensive restaurants, clubs, wherever the beautiful people gathered.

'It seemed anyone – well, any white person – could carry coke and nothing would happen to them. Your father wore an antique silver coke spoon on a chain around his neck.'

'I asked him about that,' I said. 'It was very pretty. Daddy said it was a Georgian silver marrow bone scoop. I didn't know what that was.'

'Neither did he,' Lennox said. 'I doubt he ever used it to scoop the marrow out of beef bones. People rarely eat marrow bones any more.'

We drank our coffee in a sad silence. Lennox poured another round, and I dunked a chocolate biscotti in my coffee. It tasted like sawdust, but that wasn't the biscotti's fault. My mouth was dry with fear.

After a pause, Lennox began again. 'You have to understand that cocaine was marketed like any other product. The local dealers were smart enough to give away free samples to the beautiful people. And that's who your parents were. Selling coke became a normal business.'

'Except for the illegal part.' I took a long drink of my cooling coffee.

'Exactly,' he said. 'Your parents got sucked into the whole lifestyle. They lived large and loved champagne and cocaine. Then the free samples stopped and your parents started spending thousands on their habit. They were hooked. Your father quit working at his shop, creating his beautiful carvings. Your mother was too unreliable to model any more. She was still beautiful, but her drug-fueled late nights were taking their toll.

'At first, coke makes a person feel on top of the world,' he said. 'Then your personality starts to change. Your parents became short-tempered and violent. Before coke, they were never like that. Now they had terrible fights, throwing things and shouting at each other.

'Your grandmother could hear them screaming upstairs in her apartment. She would run down to their apartment, throw open the door, and find you cowering in a closet. She would tell them to stop fighting and carry you upstairs.'

'Grandma must have been worried sick,' I said.

'She was,' Lennox said. 'You were spending more time in your grandmother's apartment than with your parents. Soon your mother and father ran through their money. Then they squandered their savings. It all went up their nose. When they ran out of money, your mother forged her name on one of your grandmother's checks and helped herself to five thousand dollars.'

I felt like I'd been stabbed in the heart. 'Mama stole from Grandma?' I heard the tears in my voice. 'She stole from her own mother?'

Lennox patted my hand. He'd warned me.

'Addiction is a disease, Norah, and your parents were in its grip. They couldn't help themselves.'

I wanted to shout, 'Yes, they could,' but I didn't.

'Stealing that money was the last straw for your grandmother,' Lennox said. 'She knew they'd wind up in jail if she didn't stop them. She made plans to get custody of you and have your parents committed to a rehab center. She told them she was worried about them driving at night, and they promised to stay home.'

'Drug addicts don't keep their promises.' I sounded bitter.

'No, they don't. When your grandmother was asleep, your parents snuck out and went clubbing. The lure of cocaine was too strong. Your parents were probably high and drunk when Max crashed into their car. Max was guilty, but your parents weren't blameless. Their addiction led to their death.

'Your grandmother never forgave herself. She told me over and over, "I should have acted sooner. I should have taken their car keys so they couldn't go out."'

I started weeping. I couldn't help it. Lennox handed me his pocket handkerchief, and I wiped my eyes.

'I'm so sorry, my dear,' he said.

I sniffed back more tears and said, 'No, I asked for the full story, and you told me. It's bad enough that my parents were drug addicts, but my grandmother's regret tears my heart. She did everything to take care of me. She had nothing to feel sorry about.'

'That's not how guilt works, Norah,' he said. 'We both know your grandmother did a fine job caring for you, but her guilt was an infection that never healed.'

He waited patiently while I recovered. Finally, I said, 'Tell me what you know about Max.' I fortified myself with more coffee.

'He was a drunk, and because his rich parents coddled him, he was never held accountable for his bad behavior,' Lennox said. 'Alberta believed her only son could do no wrong. She let Max drop out of college when he complained it was too hard. He was supposed to work in the family construction business, but Max couldn't handle a nine-to-five job. Not even at his family's business.

'Max was a party animal, and soon he was a drunk with a string of DUIs. His parents used the best lawyers, and applied a little pressure on the judges to get him out of trouble. But when he killed your mom and dad, even his family's money couldn't keep him out of jail. They did get his sentence reduced to two years, but he still had to go to prison.'

'Good!' I said.

'Not necessarily. Max went to prison as a rich pretty boy. He was arrogant and had no street skills. In prison, he was attacked and his face badly scarred with a homemade shiv. So he suffered too.'

'Not nearly enough,' I said.

'Max blamed your family for his injuries,' Lennox said. 'When he got out of prison, he found that nitwit Priscilla, who used to live here, and convinced her he'd repented his sins. Priscilla was a sucker for redemption stories and promised to help him. As I told you, Priscilla was dumb enough to believe him. Your grandmother was no fool. She sent Max packing – along with Priscilla. Max returned every night after that to torment your grandmother. Each visit was more vile than the last. He'd shout terrible things under her window.'

'What did he say?' I asked.

'I stayed with her a couple of nights. I was there the night he told your grandmother how her son-in-law and daughter looked while they were dying. She called the police.

'They would lock Max up for a day or two, but he would always come back to torture her. I heard Max shout, "I touched your daughter's tits. They were still warm. She wasn't bad-looking for a coke whore."'

I winced at the sheer cruelty. 'Did Grandma kill him?'

What about Calypso, Rafael, or even you, Lennox? You all loved Grandma. Enough to kill for her? I didn't have the courage to ask that question.

'I don't know, sweetheart,' Lennox said. 'But the details may be in her diaries.'

'What diaries?' This was new information.

'Your grandmother kept a series of diaries,' Lennox said. 'One book for every year since 1920. Didn't you find them after she died?'

'No. Where do you think they are?'

'I'm not sure. I'll give you some suggestions. They could be in the attic. There's a closet on each landing of the secret staircase, the one that goes up to your room. Did you ever look in those?'

'No.'

'What about that portrait of your grandmother in the office?' Lennox asked. 'Did you look behind it?'

'No.'

'Check behind it for a hiding place.'

Lennox glanced discreetly at the clock on the shelf. It was time for me to leave. I thanked him, and he gave me an avuncular kiss on the cheek.

Grandma's diaries could answer one vital question: was she a killer?

TWENTY-ONE

I left Lennox's apartment, a woman on a mission. Calypso was dusting the office. I told her what Lennox said and she gave me her blessing to begin my quest.

'I can take care of what we need for the family reunion,' she said. 'Do your research and get those diaries before someone deletes the video of the car vandal.'

'Do you know where Grandma kept her diaries?'

'No, I knew your grandma kept them, but I have no idea where the diaries could be. Now, go. Find them.'

I was grateful for the search. I didn't want to dwell on the sad details of my parents' lives. So much talent and beauty, tossed away. So much heartbreak in the wake of their deaths. Lennox's story had opened another wound.

I shook my head. You don't have time to brood, I thought. Get moving.

My search started at the top, in the attic. I pulled down the attic staircase from the fourth-floor hallway ceiling and climbed the narrow stairs. At the top of the ladder, the attic was hot enough to bake bread.

I was hit with the stink of mold, and saw the leak in the corner. Because of the extreme heat, I didn't expect to find anything useful in the attic. A couple of broken picture frames were stacked against a wall, along with a three-legged chair and a lot of dust.

By the time I climbed down the attic stairs, I was sweating and dirt-streaked. I lived in my grandmother's old apartment, and I'd already been through everything she'd left there. I stopped at my home, washed the dust off my face and had a long cool drink of water.

Refreshed, I was ready for stage two, the storage spaces in the not-so-secret staircase. The first-floor door was hidden behind a huge Florodora poster. No closet there. The second floor door was behind the gold-framed *September Morn*, which didn't look like any September morning I'd ever seen. I was sure it had been painted by a perv with a paintbrush.

The closet on that landing was lined with thin shelves, filled with Twenties and Thirties knickknacks, including an art deco cat, a pale green bowl that had to be at least a hundred years old, and a graceful porcelain figurine of an art deco dancing lady. And last but not least were a pair of simpering Dutch boy and girl salt-and-pepper shakers.

The secret stairs were hot, and I wanted out of there as soon as possible. I shut the door to the second floor and moved up to the closet on the third-floor landing. It was guarded by a long, thin painting of flappers by the sea. Their lips were red and their swimsuits were scandalous for the time.

Inside the closet was a treasure trove of prints and paintings, including a gorgeous Twenties' Alberto Vargas print of an elegant woman in a burnt orange and sea-green gown. Behind it were several art deco paintings of flappers, and a framed photo of Rudolph Valentino and Vilma Bánky in *The Son of the Sheik*.

Did Grandma have the hots for the Latin Lover, with his slick hair and smoldering eyes? Why didn't I explore these treasures sooner?

Ridiculous as it sounded, I was stunned when Grandma died in her sleep at age ninety-eight. Yes, I know she was nearly a century old, but she seemed so much younger. She was a force of nature, and I was lost without her.

Inheriting the Florodora when I was twenty left me bewildered. After Grandma died, I was in a daze, until the daily chores of running the Florodora took all my time.

I had one more place to search in the apartment. Lennox said I should look behind the painting of Grandma in her showgirl glory in the office.

Downstairs, I tried to move the heavy framed painting but it wouldn't budge. Then I pulled on the right side of the frame, and it swung out like a door.

That's when I saw them. Shelves of small books. Old, lined notebooks, ledgers, and leather diaries with locks. Diaries! I'd found them. I counted eighty-four, one for each year since 1920, when Grandma had turned fourteen and joined the Florodora Girls.

When I talked to Lennox about my parents, I was Eve, itching to bite into that forbidden fruit, proud of how smart I was.

Now I knew. The forbidden fruit left a rotten tang that wouldn't go away. It filled my mind with fearful doubts: was my grandmother a murderer?

The answer was in those blasted diaries. I knew Grandma wouldn't lie – not even to herself.

TWENTY-TWO

I couldn't face those diaries. Not yet. I'd face them in the morning, when I felt fresher.

I spent a restless night, wondering if my grandmother was a killer.

When I woke up, the Florodora was alive with activity. Someone was clanking and banging on the ancient elevator, someone else was hammering, and a vacuum roared outside my door.

I peeked out and saw Willow vacuuming the hall carpet. Cheerfully. At the impossible hour (for her) of eight a.m.

Willow gave me a sunny smile. 'I've taken over Calypso's hall duties. Calypso is cooking for the reunion.'

After dressing and fortifying myself with coffee, I followed my nose to Calypso's apartment, and knocked on her door.

'Come in!' Calypso was working in her kitchen, wearing a flamingo pink dress, yellow apron, and a smudge of flour on her nose.

'What smells so good?' I asked.

'Rum cake,' she said.

'You're wearing some on your nose.'

She wiped the flour off with her apron and went back to stirring the batter with a wooden spoon in a blue mixing bowl.

'Why are you here wasting my time?' she asked. 'Have you read your grandma's diaries?' Her tone was impatient.

'Not yet. Everyone else is working.'

She looked at me closely. 'Norah McCarthy, you're avoiding those diaries.'

'Why do you think that?' I widened my eyes, hoping that made me look innocent. Or as innocent as I could look at forty-one.

Calypso didn't buy it. 'Don't give me that so-called innocent look. And don't answer a question with a question. Now, why don't you want to read those diaries?'

'I'm afraid I'll find out Grandma killed Max.'

Calypso snorted. 'Your grandma was eighty-five years old when that nasty man disappeared. Do you really think she was strong enough to murder Max – a man forty years younger?'

'She could have pushed him in that hole.' My voice trembled.

'And covered the body with several feet of dirt so the plumber didn't notice a body was down there? You ever dug anything with a shovel? Do you know how heavy dirt is when you're shoveling it?'

'What if Lennox helped her?' I asked.

'Lennox! So you think your Uncle Lennox is a killer, too?' Her scorn was withering. 'Do we even live in the same house?'

Now Calypso upped the scolding tone. 'You want to work? Those diaries are your work. I'm meeting my friend Yolanda this afternoon, and I need proof that your grandmother is innocent.'

'But you just said—'

She interrupted me. 'I said I didn't *believe* your grandmother or your uncle killed Max and buried him in that hole. But Yolanda and her lady won't take my word. You get me the proof from your grandmother's diaries. Something in writing that I can show them. Everything is under control here. All you have to do is sit down and read. Go!' She pointed the spoon at the door, an angry angel evicting me from the kitchen paradise.

I went.

As I pounded down the stairs, I wanted to believe Calypso, but I knew Grandma was strong. During spring cleaning, I'd seen her move the heavy furniture in the lounge like it was balsawood. She was in her eighties then. She could have shoveled dirt over Max.

I approached my grandmother's portrait with dread. It seemed surrounded by a dark, pulsing cloud.

What was I going to find in that hidden space? What if Grandma, the pretty, flossy, Florodora Girl, was a killer?

It would break my heart. I'd already lost my parents, and now their memories were tarnished by Lennox's revelations – and my insistence to know the so-called truth. What if Grandma's memory was also destroyed?

I gathered my courage, and pulled on the side of the portrait. It opened like a door.

I riffled though the diaries until I found the leather-bound volume stamped '1991' in gold.

I opened it to October, and paged through it. My grandmother's old-fashioned, flowery handwriting was fairly easy to read. To my delight, Grandma's diary was packed with salty language and Twenties slang.

I could almost hear her voice. I skimmed the pages until I saw the name Lemuel Sykes, the father of our two plumbers. Lem was working on the pool in 1991. Grandma had the same plumbing problem thirty-four years ago.

October 7, 1991
Lem Sykes showed up at ten this morning, completely sozzled. I was glad to see him, despite his state. He didn't show up yesterday at all. Lem is a drunk, and only works when he isn't too hungover.

I put up with Lem because he understands this building's old plumbing and tries to fix it, instead of ripping everything out like most plumbers. Lem and his brother, Luke, started Sykes Brothers, but when Luke keeled over from a heart attack and Lem's wife died in the same year, Lem ran the business alone – and took to the bottle.

Lem has two sons, Liam and Lester. Lem says they'll run the business after they graduate from high school. Those two have the personality of flat irons, but they're steady and hard-working. Meanwhile, I put up with their old man.

That's life in Florida. You have to make accommodations.

I was working in my downstairs office, when who came in but Priscilla the Pill, the worst resident here. I made a major mistake when I rented to her.

Priscilla was bumping her gums because she saw Basil, Calypso's boyfriend, coming out of our housekeeper's apartment at 6 a.m. Basil's a fine hunk of man.

'Mind your own business,' I told Priscilla.

'I'm only concerned for that young woman's immortal soul.'

What a phonus-bolonus. I bet Priscilla was drooling with envy – not that a man like Basil would notice her. She was

sour, skinny and pleasure bent. That's what the men in my
old neighborhood called bowlegged women. I also bet she'd
never wrap those scrawny legs around someone as muscular
as Basil.

Priscilla was still yammering about sin when I interrupted
her. 'Let she who is without sin cast the first stone.'

'What?' Priscilla looked surprised. I don't think she realized the devil (me) could quote scripture.

'Jesus was friends with Mary Magdalene, a so-called
sinner. Maybe you should follow his . . .'

Hey! The diary ended there. No fair! I needed more. I ran over
to the portrait, opened the door, and searched frantically for the
rest of the diary.

Finally, I found the missing pages, stuffed in the front of the
1992 diary, and read the rest of Grandma's sentence.

October 7, 1991 (continued)
'Jesus was friends with Mary Magdalene, a so-called sinner.
Maybe you should follow his example.'

Priscilla the Pill stomped all the way to her apartment,
and slammed the door. Peace at last.

My sweet little Norah came home from second grade.
With her dark curls, she looks so much like her mother, my
Dot. I just hope my Norah didn't inherit her mother's love
of fast men and bad drugs.

'Grandma!' she said. 'I'm in the Bluebird reading group.
That's the best one.'

Of course it was. Norah was a smart little sprout.

I'll summarize the rest of the month. I'm too embarrassed to
repeat it. According to Grandma, I was a budding genius, a
prodigy in a plaid parochial school uniform.

In between doting entries about me, Grandma complained
about drunken Lem, who showed up maybe every other day.
He kept working in that hole by the pool and claiming he'd
have the pipes fixed 'any day now.' Grandma was losing
patience.

November 1, 1991

To my surprise, Lem showed up today, and we had a heart-to-heart talk. He promised he'd have the pipes to the swimming pool fixed in two weeks.

Norah played with her Halloween candy haul, and I persuaded her to put some of it away for a while.

A quiet day, and then a quiet night. And so to bed.

November 2, 1991

I thought the day ended when I went to bed that night, but no such luck. I was awakened at one o'clock by the doorbell. I sat straight up in bed, my heart pounding. The last time I was awakened at that hour was when I lost my beautiful Dot and her husband, Joey.

As I slipped on my robe, I reminded myself maybe it wasn't news of a disaster. Maybe some drunk who wandered in from the beach was ringing the doorbell.

Downstairs, Priscilla was waiting by the front door. I glared at her. She seemed frightened, but regained her courage and said, 'Someone is outside, asking for your forgiveness.'

'Then why doesn't that person come here at a decent hour?' I was angry, and didn't bother hiding it.

'Please,' she said. 'It's important.' Priscilla opened the door and called, 'It's OK, Max, you can come inside.'

Max? Not Max Clifford. The man who killed my child. I was seething. The last time I'd seen Max was in court. He'd been handsome then. Prison had taken care of that. He had a long brutal cut on his face, from his right eye down to his mouth. The cut pulled down his eyelid and turned his mouth into a rictus. Now he looked as ugly and deformed as his soul.

'Go ahead,' Priscilla prompted Max. 'We've prayed together on this.'

Max looked at his feet and mumbled, 'I found God in prison and I've come to beg your forgiveness.' He knelt on my doorstep.

Hot anger flashed through me like lightning. 'Get that trash off my property, Priscilla. Now.'

Max began spouting Bible verses. He had the nerve to quote St Luke: 'If your brother or sister sins against you, rebuke them; and if they repent, forgive them.'

'You can't apologize for what you did, you sack of garbage,' I said.

Priscilla said, 'Max was washed in the blood of the Lord and God has forgiven him.'

My voice went hard and flat. I spoke very slowly. 'That worm is washed in the blood of my daughter. If God wants to forgive him, good for God. But I'm not God. Get the hell away from my house before I kick your sorry ass, Max.'

Priscilla was staring open-mouthed. I turned on her and said, 'Priscilla, I want you out of my house by morning. Got it?'

Priscilla said, 'Fine. I don't want to live in this godless place.'

I turned back to Max, who hadn't moved. 'You! Get the hell out of here. If I see you again, I'll kill you.'

TWENTY-THREE

I reread the last line in my grandmother's diary, when she shouted at Max, 'If I see you again, I'll kill you.'

Lennox never mentioned that threat. And neither did Calypso. My heart was frozen with fear. Was Grandma angry enough to kill Max?

I forced myself to keep reading Grandma's diary.

November 3, 1991
Priscilla moved out by eleven this morning. It was a Sunday, but she found two movers who piled her belongings in a rental truck. She took off without a backward look. Didn't even ask for her November rent back.

Absolutely no one in the Florodora said goodbye to her. I popped a bottle of bubbly to celebrate, and we toasted the departure of Priscilla the Pill.

Little Norah and I went to the beach. She insisted on taking the beach wagon, loaded with about two hundred pounds of her junk. What the hell, it makes her happy, so I dragged the heavy wagon through the sand. The sun and sea tired us out, and we went to bed early.

This entry was not good. Grandma was strong enough to pull a heavy beach wagon through the sand. She was strong enough to kill Max.

November 4, 1991
A busy day. Calypso and I cleaned Priscilla's old apartment, so I could advertise for another renter. My Norah came home from school at 3. She'd written a letter to Santa, telling him what she wants for Christmas.

She wants 'Lisa Simpson roller skates.' And 'lots of books.' No requests for dolls, clothes or girlie toys. My girl will be a smart, strong woman.

I figure this is about the last year she'll believe in Santa Claus, and I want her to enjoy Christmas. I gave her the usual spiel: If she's good, Santa might bring her what she wants.

I was awakened at midnight by someone shouting and throwing things at my living-room window. I looked out the window and there was Max Clifford, yelling unspeakable things about my daughter. He screamed that Dot would perform oral sex (only he didn't say it like that) for a line of coke. So much for his jailhouse conversion.

I opened the window and screamed at him like a fishwife.

Next thing I knew, Lennox was in my room. He insisted on calling the police, and had me file a complaint. Because this was Peerless Point, where Max's family is a big deal, the only thing the police would charge Max with was trespassing, but at least the cops took him away.

I knew his parents' lawyers would have that dirtbag out in a couple of hours, but for now, he was gone.

Lennox fixed me a hot toddy, and listened to me cry. When I was all cried out, he tucked me in like a child. He's such a good man.

From November fourth through November twelfth, Grandma's nights were the same: Max would wake her up shouting vile things about my mother. Lennox would call the cops, who would take Max away, and then sweet Lennox would let Grandma cry on his shoulder and tuck her in.

Truly, I don't know how she endured the harassment night after night. I needed proof she wasn't a killer, and everything I read made her sound guilty. No way anyone could see these diaries.

This was bad. On Wednesday the thirteenth, things changed. For the worst.

November 13, 1991
Lennox gave me unwelcome news: he and his friend Randy are flying to San Francisco this afternoon, and won't be back for a week. It's selfish, I know, but Lennox's departure leaves me alone with my tormentor. Max.

I don't know how long I can last without killing Max. I promised Lennox I will call the police when Max shows up.

I hope I can keep my promise.

Max was under my window again at midnight. This was his worst attack yet. He shouted, 'After she was dead, I touched your daughter's tits. They were still warm. She wasn't bad-looking for a coke whore.'

I screamed like my heart was ripped out, grabbed a marble bookend off the coffee table, and ran for the stairs. I wanted to beat Max to death, to shut his foul mouth. Calypso rushed out and stopped me. I fought to push past her so I could kill Max, but she was too strong.

I dropped the bookend, and it broke in a million pieces. Calypso forced me into her living room, and made me sit on her couch while she called the police about Max. Again.

Then she poured me a large shot of rum. And another. Soon I was drunk as a sailor on leave. I fell asleep (passed out was more like it) on Calypso's couch and she covered me with a blanket.

November 14, 1991
The next morning, I woke up about six when I heard Calypso clattering around in her kitchen. My head pounded. My mouth felt like an army had marched through it – with their boots on.

Calypso made me drink a big glass of water and a mug of hot coffee. Then she ordered me to eat a big, greasy breakfast of fried eggs, bacon and home fries. While I ate at her kitchen table, she scolded me. I knew Calypso was upset when she lapsed into Bahamian slang.

'You need to think of little Norah. She's already lost her mama and daddy. She'll be all alone if you go to jail for killing that "trapsy" Max. Dis ting go with sense. Ignore him.'

Translated, I thought that meant, Norah will be all alone if you go to jail for killing that troublemaker Max. You have to do things that make sense. Ignore him.

'How?' I asked.

Calypso handed me a box of earplugs. 'Next time Max starts yammering, call the police and stick these in your ears. Got it?'

My head ached. I winced. Calypso must have realized I was in pain, because she patted my shoulder and said, 'Finish your breakfast. Then go upstairs and sleep off that hangover.'

Some people would be shocked that I let myself be lectured by an employee. But Calypso was more than someone who worked for me. She helped me raise my granddaughter. Her mother, Zina, was Dot's nanny. Calypso was entitled to give me a dose of good sense.

I finished my breakfast and went upstairs to sleep. At noon, my phone rang. It was my old friend Millie. Her voice was so soft I could hardly hear her.

'Ellie,' she said. (I love the fact that she still calls me Ellie from when I was a Florodora Girl.) 'I'm afraid the end is coming. Will you stay with me for a while?'

'Of course, dear.' Millie had been battling cancer for years.

'Are you at home?' I asked.

'Yes, the hospital said they couldn't do anything more.'

'I'll be there tonight,' I said. 'I'll take the next train to Winter Park. See you soon.'

Winter Park, Florida is about six hours north of Peerless Point. I checked the timetable. The express train left at four this afternoon. I packed my suitcase with a week's worth of clothes, including a black dress, in case the worst happened.

I went downstairs to tell Calypso. She seemed relieved that I was leaving for a while, and promised to take care of Norah.

When Norah came home from school, I told her I'd be gone for a few days, because my friend Millie was very sick. Norah's lip trembled a little, but she quickly cheered up. She must have remembered the fun she had the last time Calypso babysat her.

I gave Norah a hug goodbye. My cab was waiting in the driveway.

On the way out the door, I saw the hole Lem had dug by the pool. It was even bigger. You could have dropped a

Toyota in it. Lem was lounging under a palm tree, drunk as a skunk.

'Lem!' I shouted.

Lem looked up, bleary-eyed. 'Huh? Wha?'

'What's that big hole doing in my yard? And why are you passed out?'

'I'm awake,' he said. 'I'm shele-celebratin'. Found the problem.' Lem held up a mud-crusted pipe. 'Doan' be mad, Miz Ellie,' he said. 'It's all fixed. I'll put the dirt back tomorrow.'

'Please put a barrier around that hole so nobody falls in,' I said.

'OK.' He hiccupped. 'I'm gonna do it now. Then I'll go home.' Lem stood up and staggered to his truck for the barriers.

The cab driver blasted his horn, and I left for the Amtrak station.

On the long trip north, I thought about Millie. We'd both joined the Florodora Girls in 1920. I was fourteen and she was a year older. Four of us Florodoras rented a room near the theater for a dollar a week. That was cheap for New York then, but unlike most boarding houses, Mrs Pasternak didn't provide meals.

I fell in love with Johnny when I was sixteen and we got married. Millie danced on Broadway until she was fifty, when she had enough money to hang up her dancing shoes and buy a cottage in Winter Park.

Millie and I stayed in touch. Five years ago, she was stricken with cancer. She fought hard, but now it seemed she was losing the battle.

My train pulled into Winter Park at 10:10 and I caught a taxi to Millie's Victorian cottage, a pretty place with a garden and a white picket fence. A sign taped on the door said, 'Come in, Ellie. I'm in the front bedroom.'

Millie was awake when I opened the bedroom door, but I barely recognized her. Millie had lost most of her hair. Her skin was gray and she had black circles under her eyes.

'You came,' she said.

'Of course. What can I get you?'

'Nothing.' Millie moved restlessly, wincing in pain. 'I've left you some notes about what to do when I die. They're on the dresser.'

'You're not going to die.' My voice trembled. I fluffed her pillow and straightened her covers.

'Ellie,' she said, 'quit fussing. Sit down and hold my hand.'

A big, comfortable armchair was next to her bed. I sat, reached over and held her hand, which was covered with dark bruises. To take Millie's mind off her pain, I sang a song we performed together in the musical, *Florodora*: 'Tell Me Pretty Maiden.' Millie quit twisting in pain, and soon fell asleep. And so did I.

When the sun came through the bedroom window next morning, I was still holding Millie's hand. It was ice cold.

Millie was dead.

TWENTY-FOUR

I was too frightened to turn the page in my grandmother's diary. If she went home that day – Friday, November fifteenth – that was the date Max Clifford disappeared. Lennox was in the clear. I was too afraid to ask about Calpso and Rafael. Calypso said Grandma was visiting a sick friend, but she could catch an early train and be home by nightfall, with more than enough time to murder Max.

Lord knows Grandma had good reasons to kill Max. Lots of them. He taunted her night after night. If he was murdered, he asked for it.

I sneaked upstairs for a soda when I was ambushed by a furious Calypso.

'What are you doing wandering around?' she said. 'I gave you one thing, and one thing only, to do and did you do it? No. I'm meeting Yolanda in thirty minutes. Get down to your office.'

'I—'

Calypso cut me off. That's when I noticed she was wearing one of her best dresses, a vibrant purple number, and a sunhat with a purple band. She must have wanted to impress Yolanda.

'Quit standing around with your mouth open like you're catching flies,' she said.

She followed me down to the office, sat in a chair across from my desk, and glared at me until I started reading.

I finally turned the page. Now I was too afraid not to. If Grandma was a killer, at least Calypso was here to help me survive the blow.

November 15, 1991
Millie was dead. One of the last people who knew me as a young girl was gone, and our shared memories died with her.

We'd had good times as Florodora Girls. We were young and pretty and full of hope. We used our youthful energy to dance and sing. And now my friend of seventy-one years was gone.

Oh, hell, who was I kidding? Yes, we were young and pretty, and we didn't have the aches and pains of getting older, but we had a lot of worries. We were almost always hungry, and sometimes it was hard to make the rent.

We were naïve, and the men we went out with could be brutal. They thought because we were Broadway dancers we were easy targets for rape, and back then the courts wouldn't believe a woman was innocent. They thought we 'led the man on.'

I carried a hat pin with me for protection. Stab an over-amorous man in his tallywacker with a hatpin, and the problem went away. Actually, it went down, and I bet he didn't get it up again for a while.

I laughed. I couldn't help it. Grandma was funny.

'Hey!' Calypso said. 'You don't have time to be laughing. Keep reading!'

November 15, 1991
The morning sun shone on Millie's face. Now, with the pain gone, I saw traces of her long-ago beauty. She looked younger and peaceful. I put my head down and cried for a long time.

Then it was time to get my rear in gear. I found the folder on the dresser. Inside was a copy of her will. Millie had left her small estate, including the proceeds from the sale of her house, to the local library.

The will said I could take whatever I wanted from her home, 'in memory of our long friendship.'

Millie wanted to be buried as soon as her body was released. She had a burial plot at a local cemetery, and a burial plan. The dress she wanted to wear was on a hanger on her closet door.

She also left the name of her family doctor, Kim Kingsley, 'who will start the ball rolling,' and her lawyer, William Butler.

I kissed Millie's forehead, then checked the time. It was eight o'clock. I fixed a cup of coffee and then called

Dr Kingsley, and gave her the news. She sounded genuinely sad.

'I'm so sorry. Millie was a fighter. She wanted to go home when the end was near. I'll call the police and let them know. Do you know the name of her funeral home?'

I gave Dr Kingsley the name.

'Will you be there with Millie for a while, Mrs Harriman?'

'Yes,' I said. 'I'm staying for her burial. I'll call her lawyer after the funeral home takes her away.'

'Thank you. I'm glad she has such a good friend.'

'Yes!' I shouted.

'Twenty-five minutes until I leave,' Calypso said. 'Did you find the proof yet?'

'Almost,' I said.

Now I was skimming. I quickly paged through the entries for November fifteenth through the eighteenth, and learned Grandma didn't come home until after Millie's funeral. Grandma's train got in Monday evening, November eighteenth.

'Twenty minutes,' Calypso said. 'You better get going.'

'Almost there.' I hoped that was the truth.

November 18, 1991

My train got in at eight that night. I called Calypso from the station, then grabbed a cab. Calypso and my little Norah were waiting at the door when the cab dropped me off, and I was so happy to see their smiling faces after my sad trip. The cab driver carried the pot with my moonflower vine to the courtyard near the pool.

I tipped him well. That plant was heavy.

'Grandma!' Norah ran toward me.

I wrapped her in a hug, and her words came tumbling out. 'I missed you, Grandma. Calypso and Rafael got hurt, and I got to stay with them in the hospital and eat red Jell-O and Mr Sykes was acting funny and Calypso sent him home.'

'Whoa, whoa,' I said. 'Give me a moment to take all this in.'

That's when I noticed Calypso was leaning on a cane, her face creased with pain.

'Norah,' Calypso said. 'Your grandma is tired. Go upstairs and set the table in my kitchen and I'll cook dinner.'

'You're not cooking,' I said. 'I'm ordering chicken dinners from the beach diner. They'll deliver. Norah, go upstairs, please. I want to talk to Calypso for a moment.'

'When's Uncle Lennox coming home, Grandma?' Norah asked.

'Wednesday,' I said. 'Now upstairs, please.'

'Norah asks that question every five minutes,' Calypso said.

'Calypso, come in and sit down, please, and tell me what's happened. What can I get you?' I asked.

'Nothing,' she said. 'I'll be fine. I just want to sit a minute.'

While Calypso limped to the lounge, I called the diner and ordered roast chicken dinners and apple pie for all of us, then went into the lounge to talk to Calypso. She was in one of the tall chairs, gripping the arms.

'Thank you, Calypso, for taking care of Norah. Now, why do you have a cane and how did Rafael get hurt? And what's this about the hospital?'

'That idiot Sykes left a tool lying in the grass,' she said. 'One of those giant pipe wrenches. Rafael didn't see it and fell over it. I pulled my back trying to get him in the cab so we could go to the hospital.'

'How badly hurt is Rafael?' I asked.

'He has a broken collarbone and a mild concussion. The hospital kept both of us overnight. Norah was with us and she slept on a cot next to my bed. She thought it was a big adventure.'

'Where is Rafael now?'

'He's staying in my guest room,' Calypso said. 'His arm is in a sling and he's in pain. He won't be able to work for at least two months.'

'And what about your back?'

'Just a pulled muscle. I'm sleeping with a heating pad and taking something the doctor gave me. I'll be fine in three or four weeks.'

'And why was Mr Sykes acting funny?'

Now Calypso looked angry. 'Lem Sykes started working at eight Friday morning,' she said. 'He was so drunk he could hardly stand. He had that noisy Bobcat and backed up and hit one of our palm trees. I went out and made him stop work. He'd left that hole wide open Thursday.'

'He did? I told him to put a barrier around it when I left for Winter Park.'

'Well, he didn't.' Calypso snapped at me. She was fed up. 'Lem passed out in his truck and I had to wake him up at six Thursday night and make him go home. He showed up Friday morning just long enough to kill our tree.'

I didn't ask Calypso if she remembered me asking Lem to cover the hole when I left on Thursday. She was feeling bad enough.

'After Lem left, Rafael and I did our usual work. Norah came home from school. She was having cookies and milk in the kitchen when we heard Rafael shout. I found him in the grass with his head all bloody. Rafael said he was fine, but I could tell he wasn't. He wouldn't let me call an ambulance, so I got a cab, the one driven by that lazy Sam Jance. Sam sat on his fat bum while I helped Rafael get into the taxi. Norah got my purse and she went with us to the ER.'

'We came home about ten o'clock Saturday morning and there was Lem, drunk again. At least Lem dumped enough dirt in the hole so nobody could fall in. I told him to leave and come back when he was sober.'

'And did he?'

'Yes. The next day. Sunday. He finished, put the pavers back and hauled off the dead tree. And he had the nerve to ask for more money because he worked on the weekend.'

Calypso shook her head. 'Can't we hire someone else? There must be some sober plumbers.'

'With any luck, we won't need him for a while,' I said. 'His son Liam will join the business when he graduates this spring.'

The doorbell rang. Our dinners had arrived.

'Fifteen minutes, Norah.' Calypso was impatient.

'I've got it!' I said. 'Grandma didn't kill Max.'

'Told you so,' Calypso said. Now she was just plain smug. 'What are the details?'

'Lennox and his friend left for San Francisco Wednesday, November thirteenth, and didn't come back for a week. So he's cleared. Grandma left for Winter Park to see her friend, as you thought, the next day, and didn't return until Monday, November eighteenth. So she couldn't have murdered Max. He disappeared November fifteenth.'

'And how did he die?' Calypso said. 'Hurry up. I have to leave in ten minutes.'

'Lem dug a big hole to fix the plumbing – in the same spot where his sons found Sammie's body. Lem was drunk. Grandma told him to barricade the hole on Thursday, but he passed out and didn't. On Friday, November fifteenth, Lem was drunk again. He started up the Bobcat, knocked down a tree, and you sent him home.

'The day Max disappeared, the hole was wide open. You, Rafael and I were at the hospital on that fatal Friday night. When we came home Saturday morning, a drunken Lem was back and started to fill in the hole. You sent him home. He finished the job on Sunday.

'I think Max, drunk as usual, came here Friday night to torment Grandma, fell in the hole, broke his neck and died. Drunken Lem didn't see the body and covered Max up in the hole.

'On Sunday Lem finished the job and put the pavers back. So Max's death is an accident, and Lem, the man who covered up the body, is long dead.'

Calypso heaved a sigh of relief. 'Thank the Lord.'

'I thought you were sure that Grandma was innocent.'

'I was, but there was no way I could prove it,' she said. 'I have to leave now. Give me that diary.'

I was relieved, too. The diary also proved Lennox, Rafael and Calypso were innocent. If they ever knew I suspected them of murder, it would break their hearts.

I handed Calypso the diary, bristling with yellow Post-it notes.

'Be careful what you show your friend,' I said. 'Lots of those passages make Grandma look really guilty. I've marked the safe parts.'

TWENTY-FIVE

Calypso took off in a purple blur, proof in hand. She'd barely shut the door when my phone rang.

Carl, from Peerless Point Auto Restoration, had news about my wounded Mustang.

'They really did a number on your car, Norah,' he said. 'I can fix everything for about six thousand bucks. And I guarantee your new ragtop won't leak like the last one. What's your insurance deductible?'

'A thousand dollars,' I said.

'Your car should be ready in about three weeks.'

I'd have my car back soon. That good news zipped right by me. All I could think was I owed a thousand bucks. Now I really hoped Calypso would come back with a video of the vandal.

Rafael knocked on my office door. The maintenance man's overalls were streaked with black grease. 'Do you want the good news or the bad?' he asked.

'Bad first. I'm sitting down.'

'The elevator repairs will cost twenty thousand dollars.'

'Whoa. That's a real wallop in the wallet. What's the good news?'

'They have the parts to fix it.'

'Do we really need an elevator, Rafael? The Florodora doesn't have a gym. Those steps are an in-house StairMaster. Free fitness. Walk to your room at your own pace and get a cardio and strength workout.'

Rafael didn't laugh. Now he was dead serious. 'What if someone sprains their ankle or breaks a leg? Are we going to carry them to their apartment?'

'I hadn't thought of that,' I said.

Rafael was just getting warmed up. 'What about Calypso, Norah? She'd brain me with a bleach bottle if she heard me say this, but she's sixty years old. She's dragging her vacuum and cleaning supplies up and down the stairs ten times a day. At the very least, buy her a vacuum cleaner that she can keep on each floor. She doesn't need more exercise.

'It's not my money, Norah, but yes, we need an elevator.'

Now I felt ashamed. 'I'm sorry, Rafael. Of course, we'll get the elevator fixed. And I'll ask Calypso to order more vacuums for herself.'

Dean was next. 'I hate to be the bearer of bad news,' he began.

'Too late,' I said. 'What's wrong? You were showing the electrician around.'

'You've got more problems than the outdated electrical box. Parts of this building still have the original wiring from the Twenties. It's a fire hazard. And speaking of fire hazards, Billie is running a TV, a computer, and a sound system off a two-dollar extension cord in his apartment. It's seriously overloaded.'

'Billie needs new outlets,' I said.

'So do Willow, Lennox, Calypso, and, well, everybody. The house needs rewiring.'

'We better do it before the place burns down,' I said.

'This inspection could be a blessing in disguise,' he said.

'Very disguised. What's the estimate?'

'Fifteen thousand dollars. If you're lucky.'

'I'm not feeling real lucky right now, Dean. Between the elevator repairs and the wiring, I'm now up to thirty-five thousand dollars. And we haven't even started the major work.'

'Can you handle that kind of money?'

'Yes. I'll have to talk with the bankers, but I can do it.' I'd have to dip into the money Grandma left me, and she'd often lectured me about the dangers of touching capital.

'You look a little shellshocked,' Dean said. 'Want to go for lunch?'

'I've eaten, thanks. I'm waiting for Calypso to return from lunch with her friend Yolanda, who just might have the video of my car vandal.'

'How long do those lunches take?'

'When those two get talking, two hours easy. Calypso may be back by three.'

'It's only one thirty,' he said. 'Come with me to the Egg-Zack-Lee-Rite on the Beachwalk. It's open till three. We'll have one of Zack's cinnamon rolls and coffee. Leave Calypso a note, if you're worried.'

He smiled winsomely. How could I refuse a cinnamon roll with a sun-burnished certified hunk?

It was hotter than blazes on the Beachwalk, but the sea air felt soft. Zack's diner was only two blocks away. On our walk, we heard the polyglot sounds of tourists: Germans here on package deals, French Canadians, and thrifty Midwestern families taking advantage of the cheaper rates this time of year.

Zack's was nearly empty at this hour. The breakfast diner had a funky beach vibe. The turquoise walls were covered with oddball items Zack found on the beach, including glass buoys, driftwood and rusty boat propellers. Strings of shells hung from the ceiling. Zack also liked offbeat signs. This green sign hung over the cash register: 'Beware of the dinosaur' with a raging T-Rex. Little kids loved that one.

The tables and booths were made of driftwood. Helen, a big, curvy woman, was rushing around, trying to bus some empty tables.

'Grab a clean table,' she said. The veteran server looked a bit frazzled this afternoon.

We took a table with a view of the ocean. Helen hurried over. 'What can I get you?'

'Do you have any chocolate cinnamon rolls?' Dean asked.

'You're in luck. I have two left.'

'We'll take them,' Dean said, 'and two black coffees.'

'You want the rolls heated?' Helen asked.

'We do,' I said.

'Zack's chocolate cinnamon rolls are better than sex,' Helen said.

'I wouldn't go that far,' I said. 'But they're pretty darn good.' I wondered why people said that. Did they even have sex? Or had it been a while?

Helen poured us both mugs of hot coffee. I watched the Kit-Cat Klock on the wall. It was only one thirty-seven.

Soon Helen plopped down two heated cinnamon rolls the size of hubcaps. I could see slivered almonds and chocolate chips in the filling, and smell the melted chocolate drizzled over the frosting.

I tried not to drool as I bit into my roll, and suppressed a small moan.

Dean was grinning. 'Looks to me like that is better than sex,' he said.

'Not with you,' I said, then wished I hadn't talked.

He laughed out loud. 'You're blushing.'

I was annoyed – at him and myself. Also desperate to change the subject. 'Look. Zack has a new sign.'

Posted on the wall by the door was: 'The fact that there's a highway to hell and only a stairway to heaven says a lot about the anticipated traffic.'

I checked the clock again. It was one fifty-one. Time had slowed to a crawl.

Dean reached across the table and squeezed my hand. 'Watching that clock won't make it go any faster,' he said. 'I'll help you pass the time until Calypso returns. Have you heard the latest Florida Man story?'

'Does it involve alcohol and alligators?'

'Nope. Satan in schools.'

'You got me,' I said.

Perversely, Dean took a big bite of his cinnamon roll and chewed slowly.

Finally, he started his story.

'Our very own elected Florida Man, Governor Ron DeSantis, wants more religion in the state's public schools. He signed a new law to have volunteer school chaplains.'

'Doesn't separation of church and state keep religion out of public schools?'

'It should. The governor says the chaplains can participate after school. At least one group responded quickly to his call: the Satanic Temple. They have an After School Satan program.'

'What are they going to do with the little devils? Sacrifice a goat?'

'According to reports, the After School Satan Club's activities include games, solving puzzles and promoting critical thinking. Also, the Satanists say they do not promote a "belief in a personal Satan."'

'Hah! They never had class with my geometry teacher,' I said. 'What did the governor say about the Satanists' offer?' I took a long drink of coffee.

'His communications director said, "HELL, NO."'

I nearly snorted coffee out my nose. 'Warn me when you do that again.' I was nearly choking with laughter.

Dean waited until I set down my coffee cup. 'The governor has said repeatedly that the Satanists are not a religion. However, the Satanists say they are recognized by the IRS.' Dean took a sip of his cooling coffee.

'The devil knows his own,' I said.

Now it was Dean's turn. He started choking. Helen rushed over and began pounding his back. 'You OK? Drink some water.'

Dean did, and gradually regained his breath. Helen was rubbing his back and then began massaging his shoulders.

'Ooh, a little lower,' he said.

I felt a quick flash of jealousy, and then realized I had no right to. Dean and I were just friends. Good friends. Weren't we?

Dean finally said, 'I'm fine, thank you, Helen.'

'Can I get you anything else?' The server eyed Dean like a starving woman contemplating a big, juicy steak.

With that my cell phone buzzed. 'I have a text from Calypso,' I said. 'She's home. With news.'

'Just the check, Helen,' he said.

We threw money on the table and were out the door. Despite the pounding afternoon heat, the two of us ran all the way to the Florodora.

Calypso was waiting in my office, with a big glass of ice water and a look of triumph.

'What?' I said. 'Did you find something?'

'Sit down. Both of you.'

I sat on the edge of my desk. Dean sat next to me.

'You're going to draw this out, aren't you?' I said.

'Don't be rude,' she said. 'Yolanda and I had a lovely lunch on the balcony of Mrs Upton's apartment. Chicken salad and key lime pie.'

I wanted to interrupt Calypso so she'd tell us what she'd found, but Dean squeezed my hand and I shut up.

'I'm glad you enjoyed your lunch,' he said. 'You deserved it. You've been working yourself to the bone for this reunion, and your family is coming in tomorrow.'

Strangely, Dean's comment spurred Calypso to tell more of her story.

'You won't believe this, but Mrs Upton had the answer all along. Her niece, Tina, has been staying with her this whole month, including while Mrs Upton was out of town. Tina was photographing a flock of pelicans from the condo balcony with her phone. Tina says the birds look like pterodactyls. You know, the flying dinosaurs?'

I nodded. Come on, Calypso, don't drag this out. Dean gave my hand another cautionary squeeze before I said anything.

Calypso took another long drink of water. 'Tina's camera was photographing a man flying a kite on the beach when a squadron of pelicans flew by. They skimmed right past the Florodora. That's when Tina saw a man ripping up your car top.

'She forgot about the pelicans and photographed the man who was tearing up your car. He ripped the top with some kind of knife, then slashed your seats and started carving words in the paint.'

'And she didn't call the police?' I asked.

'No,' Calypso said. 'Tina's from Iowa. She wasn't sure if that's how people in Florida were supposed to act.'

'We're crazy, but not that crazy,' I said.

Calypso finished her water and started to get up for another glass.

'I'll get it,' Dean said. 'You wait right there.'

He ran to the kitchen. I heard the fridge open, cubes clinking in a glass, and the glug of water from a pitcher. Calypso refused to talk until Dean returned with a fresh glass. The wait was agonizing.

When Dean was sitting next to me, Calypso said, 'Now, where was I?'

'Tina was photographing pelicans and saw a man tearing up Norah's Mustang.' Dean squeezed my hand again. He could sense my impatience.

'Right. First, Mrs Upton accepted your grandmother's alibi.'

Come on, Calypso, I wanted to scream. Tell the freakin' story. Dean squeezed my hand so hard I thought he'd break a bone.

'Tina heard her aunt calling around for videos of the car vandal and showed Mrs Upton the one she took. She sent a copy to me and another to you. I gave Tina your cell phone number, if that's OK?'

'Of course it is.' I barely disguised my impatience. Dean gave me a warning look.

I didn't realize I had a video. When did it come in? I grabbed my cell phone to call up the video and asked, 'Did you see it, Calypso?'

'I sure did. Tina caught the whole crime.'

'Do you recognize the guy?'

'Nope,' Calypso said. 'Never saw him in my life. Looks like some kind of overgrown frat boy.'

TWENTY-SIX

At last, I could see the video. Tina seemed to be on the penthouse balcony, videoing a man flying a kite on the beach. The kite was a pair of women's legs wearing fishnet stockings and garters.

No wonder Tina thought Floridians tore up cars for sport. Tina abandoned videoing the flying legs when a squadron of brown pelicans rounded her condo and headed north to the Florodora.

The lead pelican dropped about ten feet, and the other birds followed, flying right over Wicked Red, my Mustang.

And there was the evil man destroying my car. Live and in color.

He was still wearing the pink polo shirt and smug smile he'd had in his sleazy office. I watched him rip my beautiful car to shreds. I recognized him immediately.

'It's Vixen Tamer,' I shouted.

Dean looked at me like I had heat stroke. 'Who?'

'What kind of name is Vixen Tamer?' Calypso said. 'Was he baptized with that name?'

'I don't think there's a Saint Vixen,' I said.

'Isn't Vixen a girl's name?' Calypso asked.

'More like a stripper name,' Dean said.

'Close,' I said. 'Vixen Tamer is a local porn star agent with an office in downtown Peerless. He was Sammie Lant's agent and now he's repping her competition, the Countess Crawlie.'

'How do you know this trash?' Calypso asked.

'I went to his office because I wanted to know if he killed Sammie.'

'Why would he murder Sammie if he was representing her?' Calypso asked.

'Because Sammie was getting old. The countess is younger and fresher looking. That's what Vix told me, anyway. I reckon he wanted to add Countess Crawlie to his books but Sammie put her foot down. I bet she gathered a lot of dirt on Vix while working for him, and probably threatened to expose it if he tried to drop her for a younger client after *Sex on the Beach* came out. Plus he'll get her royalties for the film as she doesn't have any heirs. He'd bag a small fortune.'

Calypso groaned. 'Please tell me you aren't trying to solve Sammie's murder.'

'Somebody has to. The police haven't arrested anyone yet.'

'Hold on,' Dean said. 'Is that what you're going to say when you call Detective DeMille? Because you're going to have to tell him why you were at that sleazeball's office.'

'I had every right to be there.' I sounded indignant.

'Really? Were you looking for a job?' Dean asked. 'Curious about his name? Or stopping by to meet the merchants in downtown Peerless Point? The police are going to want to know why you were at his office.'

'I'll just tell the truth.'

'That you think the local police are incompetent?'

'No! Why are you carrying on like this?' I was furious, partly because Dean was right.

Calypso just stood there, staring at us. She never asked why Dean knew so much about police procedure. No one at the Florodora did. Maybe they assumed a certain kind of white guy was born with that knowledge.

'Enough,' I said. 'I'm calling Detective DeMille right now. He can write out a report and arrest that creep. I'll also tell him about Grandma's trip to Winter Park and solve a cold case for him. He'll be thrilled.'

'If he doesn't arrest you first,' Dean said.

'Oh, go . . .' I paused, and then carefully considered my words. 'Dean, don't you have some fishing to do?'

'I'll see if Rafael needs help.' Dean was gone, and from the way he slammed the front door, he was angry. Calypso said she had work to finish and drifted away.

I phoned DeMille with my news. 'I'll be there in ten,' he said.

While I waited for DeMille, I used my office machine to Xerox the crucial diary pages.

The detective must have driven over with lights and sirens. Seven minutes later, DeMille was sitting in my office. He turned down my offer of coffee or a cold drink, and didn't waste time with polite pleasantries.

'What's this proof you have that Max Clifford wasn't murdered?'

'It's right here.' I patted my grandmother's diary. 'I've made a copy so you can read it yourself.'

I quickly outlined the facts.

'Max Clifford was last heard from on Friday, November fifteenth, 1991, right?' I asked.

'Agreed,' DeMille said.

'After that date, he was presumed dead.'

'Yes,' DeMille said.

'Meanwhile, here at the Florodora, Lemuel Sykes, father of the current Sykes brothers, was trying to repair the plumbing by the pool. Grandma's diary said that Lennox and a friend flew to San Francisco Wednesday, November thirteenth. They were gone for a week, until November twentieth.'

'OK.' The detective nodded. I kept going.

'The next day, Grandma learned her old friend Millie was dying. Millie lived in Winter Park and Grandma took the train to be with Millie that same evening, November fourteenth. Millie died during the night. Grandma stayed in Winter Park for Millie's funeral. She was executor of Millie's estate and Grandma didn't come home until Monday, November eighteenth.'

DeMille looked a little bewildered.

'Are you following me so far?' I asked.

'I think so,' DeMille said.

'Grandma couldn't have murdered Max, since he disappeared November fifteenth.'

'So how did Max die?' DeMille asked.

'I'm getting to that. Let's go back to the repairs, which started all this. On Thursday, Lem the plumber dug a big hole in the same spot where his sons found Sammie's body. Lem was a drunk. According to Grandma's diary, Lem was supposed to put a barrier around the hole Thursday night. Instead, he passed out. Lem was too drunk to work Friday, November fifteenth, the last day Max was known to be alive. Lem came back to the Florodora on Saturday, and partially filled in the hole. He finished the job Sunday.

'Now, back to Max. If you read the diary, Max had a habit of coming to the Florodora every night and tormenting Grandma with the death of her daughter. You should have the police reports of his nightly visits. Max was a drunk and a rat.'

DeMille didn't argue with me.

'I think Max came here on Friday night to torment Grandma. He fell in the hole, and broke his neck.'

Now I went out on a limb and asked, 'That's how Max died, didn't he? Of a broken neck?'

'Yes,' DeMille said.

'So Max's death is an accident and Lem, the man who covered up the body, is long dead.'

'And I have to take the word of this diary?' DeMille asked.

'You can corroborate the important parts.' I handed the detective a sheet of paper.

'This has the airline Lennox and his friend took to San Francisco. The flight was in the afternoon. You should find their flight information in the government's Passenger Name Record. That will put Lennox in the clear. He didn't help Grandma dump the body in the hole.'

I gave DeMille a second sheet. 'I don't think you can get Amtrak records from '91, but Millie's doctor, Kim Kingsley, and Millie's lawyer, William Butler, are still practicing. They should have records to verify when Millie died and when they were in contact with Grandma. And finally, here's a copy of the pages of Grandma's diary.

'So,' I said. 'What do you think?' I expected him to smile and congratulate me.

Instead, DeMille said, 'I need to check this information.' He also asked for the original diary. I reluctantly turned it over after he gave me a receipt.

'Now, about the man who tore up my car.' I told DeMille the story of the video and he watched Vix Tamer destroy my car.

'I know this slimewad,' DeMille said. 'He's a pimp as well as a so-called agent to porn stars. What did you do to tick him off, Norah?'

'Well, I may have implied that he was short.'

'He is short, about five feet four, five-five at the most.'

'I mean short where it's important for a man to be . . . uh, long.' I could feel my face turning red.

DeMille leaned back in his chair. 'Why so coy, Norah? This isn't like you.' He was enjoying my discomfort. 'And how do you know Vix Tamer? Did you apply for a job?' He was grinning in an irritating way.

'Me? No!'

'Then why were you talking to him?'

'I don't have to tell you that.'

DeMille leaned in toward me. 'No, you don't. And I don't have to go see Vix Tamer. But I'm not walking into his office and getting blindsided. So tell me why you were there, or I will drop the subject. Permanently.'

He paused. I waited.

After a long moment, DeMille said, 'That means I won't arrest him for the damage to your car.'

'But he's guilty,' I said.

'Maybe so, but I want the whole story.'

I had a quick argument with myself. Was I going to tell DeMille or let Vix Tamer go free?

'OK, I went to see Vix Tamer because he was Sammie Lant's agent.'

'Oooh.' He drew out the word. 'So now you're Miss Marple.'

'I'm not a spinster and I don't knit.'

'Last I heard,' he said, 'a spinster is an unmarried woman, somewhat past the prime age for walking down the aisle.'

That hit close to home. 'Are you going to help or not?'

He stuck his finger in my face and sounded angry. 'You're playing detective, Norah, and that's a dangerous game with a man like Vix. Sammie isn't the only one of his clients who's suddenly disappeared. We haven't been able to catch that snake, but if I were you, I'd be careful laughing at his trouble tube.'

'Trouble tube?' Now I was laughing. 'Are you referring to his . . .?'

'Yes, I am,' he said.

'OK, can we be adults? I made fun of his penis. Vix Tamer bragged that he "road-tested" his clients. That disgusted me. So I said, "I bet you're short, too. And I'm not talking about your height. That's why you have to road-test your stars."'

'Good Lord, Norah, you're lucky you're still alive,' DeMille said. 'Men have killed over lesser insults. Especially from women. Vix clearly has a violent streak. Look what he did to your car.'

'I saw, thank you. In great detail.' My voice was crisp, maybe even spinsterish.

'I'll show this video to the city prosecutor and see what she wants to do.'

'Will you call me if she says yes?'

'I'll call one way or the other,' he said.

TWENTY-SEVEN

Next morning was Reunion Day, and the entire household was up early, even Willow. The apartment house gleamed. The furniture smelled of lemon polish. The floors were scrubbed. The windows were washed. We were ready to meet Calypso's cousins.

The newly restored courtyard was ready. Calypso swept the courtyard three times, then glared at the trees shading it, daring them to drop so much as a leaf.

Even when the work was done, Calypso kept fussing, fluffing pillows and straightening chairs. She issued the same instructions, over and over. Dean and Rafael were delegated to pick up the cousins at the airport.

For the third time, Calypso told Dean, 'Don't forget, Cousin Eric goes in the front seat of your Jeep. Don't make him ride in that raggedy-ass pickup, where he has to slap the air-conditioner to make it work.'

She glanced at Rafael and said, 'Sorry.'

Rafael shrugged. 'It is true. My truck is old but faithful.'

Calypso missed that mild reproof and kept giving orders. 'Godfrey can sit in the back seat of Dean's Jeep with Ian. Put Ozzie in the pickup with the luggage. He's the youngest.'

'Yes, Calypso,' Dean said, and winked at me. We'd never seen Calypso this excited.

'What time is it?' she asked.

'Ten o'clock,' Dean said.

'Their plane lands in an hour. Better leave now.'

'We're only ten minutes from the airport,' I said.

'What if there's traffic or road construction?' Calypso said. 'What if there's an accident?'

Or a meteor lands on Federal Highway, I thought.

Dean and Rafael knew they would have no peace unless they left now.

As they headed for the door, Calypso reminded them for the fourth time, 'Don't forget to call me if their plane is delayed. And come straight home.'

'We promise,' Dean called over his shoulder. Rafael waved goodbye.

What was I going to do with a nervous, excited Calypso for the next two hours?

'Norah, help me set the table for lunch,' she said. 'I'm going to serve the cousins mac and cheese with jalapenos, and coleslaw, then send them to work.'

'Shouldn't they rest up today?' I said.

'They don't have time to waste if they're going to make that deadline,' she said. 'They aren't here on vacation.'

Once the table was set to Calypso's satisfaction, she went to her room to change. She came back in a new dress, white splashed with blue flowers.

By that time, Dean and Rafael returned home with the guests. Calypso ran to greet her cousins. There were tears, hugs, and cries of delight. The Florodora residents began hauling the cousins' luggage to their apartment.

After about fifteen minutes, Calypso brought her cousins over and introduced them.

Eric, the oldest, was a short, barrel-chested man of about fifty with close-cropped graying hair and a Bahamas football shirt. He was a muscular man, his arms and shoulders shaped by years of hard labor. When Eric shook my hand, I could feel the calluses on his fingers.

Godfrey was almost a carbon-copy of Eric, except he wore a Bahamas Bowl Champions shirt.

Ian, tall and skinny with a basketball-sized gut, was the jokester of the group. His shirt said, 'My stomach is FLAT. The L is silent.'

He kissed my hand. 'Pleased to meet you, my lady.'

Oswald, the youngest, was in his mid-twenties. Calypso frowned at his T-shirt, which had a sailboat and this slogan: 'Time to get ship-faced.'

'I'm Oswald, Ozzie for short,' he said.

Calypso took over as straw boss. 'Time for lunch,' she said.

'Everyone take a seat at the courtyard table.' Dean and I followed her to the kitchen.

'We're going to eat by ourselves,' I said, 'so you can catch up with your family.'

'Dean, be back in an hour,' Calypso said. 'I'd like you to tell my cousins what work needs to be done. Both of you can help me get the food on the table and then you can go.'

Calypso led the way out to the courtyard with a bubbling casserole dish of mac and cheese. I followed with the giant bowl of coleslaw, and Dean brought out the homemade bread and butter.

The cousins were laughing, joking and talking so fast I could barely understand them. Calypso, in her new dress, looked radiant.

Dean and I slipped away. 'I'll make us pizza,' I told him.

I followed him upstairs to my apartment. Damn, that man was handsome. I wished Calypso's cousins weren't here and we could spend the afternoon romping in my apartment. Too bad we had to save the Florodora.

Instead, I popped a frozen pepperoni pizza in the oven and we talked about what the cousins needed to tackle first.

'I want Ian to remove the lead paint in the garage,' Dean said. 'Eric and Godfrey can fix the leak in the attic and work on the mold removal before we get more rain. Rafael and Ozzie can replace the gutters and downspouts, then work on the garage. I'll start working on the ramp for the beachside entrance.'

The timer dinged on my oven, and I brought out the pizza. It was OK, cheese and tomato sauce with a hint of cardboard.

Over slices, I asked, 'What can I do?'

'Order the parking lot landscaping from the Peerless Nursery. Here's a list of how many trees and shrubs you'll need.'

Dean handed me a list stained with tomato sauce, and reached for more pizza. 'Tell Jim – he's the owner – you want landscaping that can withstand hot sun, salt, and constant sea breezes. Beach conditions are hard on plants. Jim's crew should plant the land-scaping. It will cost a little more, but they'll do it right.'

'What's another couple hundred at this point,' I said.

'You can take my Jeep for the errand.'

This was a big offer. Dean didn't let anyone drive his beloved classic. 'I'll be careful,' I said.

We finished the last two pizza slices. Our lunch hour was up. I had my marching orders and Dean's keys. We were leaving my apartment when my cell phone rang.

Detective DeMille said, 'Norah, I have information about Vixen Tamer. I need you to come to the station.'

I didn't like how his voice sounded.

'The station downtown?'

'That's the only one we have.' DeMille sounded impatient and a little angry.

'I'm on my way.' I hung up. Now I was frightened. Something was wrong. I could feel it.

Dean was hovering nearby. 'Norah, who was that? What did he say? You're white as a sheet.'

'DeMille. He wants me to come to the station. That means I'm a suspect in Sammie's murder, doesn't it?'

'Not necessarily. Do you want me to go with you?'

I did, but I didn't want to be a coward. 'I'll be fine.'

'Remember my rules for how to treat the police, especially a detective,' Dean said.

'Be polite. Don't lie,' I said. 'Don't get angry.'

'Right. Treat him like he's a three-hundred-pound gorilla,' Dean said. 'If you don't like the direction of DeMille's questions, ask for a lawyer.'

'Won't DeMille think I'm guilty?'

'If it's gone that far, then he already thinks you're guilty.'

Now my stomach twisted.

'You need to protect yourself,' Dean said. 'Think before you answer DeMille's questions. Pause. Take your time.'

In my room, I changed into a fresh blouse, combed my hair and added lipstick. Dean walked me to his Jeep and kissed me.

'You'll be fine,' he said. 'I know it.'

I didn't. My record of dealing with the police was sketchy at best.

All too soon, I parked in front of the Peerless Point police station, a late Twenties two-story white stucco building with a red tile roof. Inside, the station still had the original wood floor, which creaked. I stopped at the desk and told the uniformed officer on duty that Detective DeMille wanted to see me.

'Take a seat over there.' She indicated an alcove with a long wooden bench. The seat was disfigured with initials and semi-obscene carvings of male anatomy. A gruesome 'DRUGS KILL' poster dominated the alcove. The skull had marijuana leaves stuffed in one eye socket, a bunch of needles stuck in the other, and broken pills for teeth. Blood dripped from its eye sockets.

I listened to the phones ring and the clack of computer keys for about fifteen minutes, before a uniform with blond hair and peach fuzz cheeks came down the stairs. 'I'll escort you to Detective DeMille's office,' he said.

I followed Peach Fuzz up the wide wooden stairs and down a tiled hall painted that peculiar shade of government green – some ugly mix of lime and pea green paint.

DeMille's office had a beat-up desk from the Forties, with an ancient computer, stacks of files and a prize collection of coffee rings. He was hunched at his desk in shirtsleeves, his jacket over the back of his chair.

'Norah,' he said. 'Have a seat.' No offer of coffee or water. This definitely wasn't a social visit.

I sat on a hard wooden chair. The detective said nothing. Dean told me that was a cop trick to make suspects blurt out something. I was determined not to talk until DeMille talked first. I didn't break eye contact, either.

After three long minutes by the clock on the wall, DeMille said, 'I arrested Vix Tamer this morning. He's going to prison. When he vandalized your car, he committed two felonies. I checked with Peerless Restoration. Carl said the repairs will cost six thousand dollars. That's good.'

'Not for me.'

'Not for Vix Tamer, either. Trashing your car was a third-degree felony. He's looking at up to five years in prison and a five-thousand-dollar fine.'

'Good,' I said.

'Carving "Die Bitch!" in your paint is a written threat. That's a second-degree felony, which could get him up to fifteen years in prison and a ten-thousand-dollar fine.'

'Even better,' I said. 'Where is he now?'

'In jail,' he said.

'Well, that's good news.' I stood up to leave.

'Wait,' he said. 'I have more questions. Do you know a Jack Grisham of Austin?'

'No. I've never heard the name.'

'So you didn't send Mr Grisham here and tell him this station was a front for a brothel?'

'What? No!'

'Well, someone did. Mr Grisham came in here waving seven thousand dollars in cash and demanding a preteen girl.'

'That's insane.' Willow's prank had worked. I started laughing. I couldn't help it.

'Officer Kendra Hoag didn't think so. She was working the desk that day and Mr Grisham said, "Let me see your tits. Are those real?" Officer Hoag hit him with her nightstick and knocked out three of his teeth.'

'Good.' My laughter was reduced to giggles.

'Mr Grisham kept shouting that he wanted "a preteen girl, untouched" and said, "I know the password. Detective DeMille sent me."'

DeMille gave me the cop glare, the one that could bore a hole into my forehead. 'You didn't mislead Mr Grisham, did you?'

'Of course not.' I said that with a clear conscience.

'Then how did he know to ask for me?' DeMille asked.

'Detective, you've been on TV almost every night since the two bodies were found at the Florodora. You're the most high-profile member of the Peerless force. I assume Grisham was charged with assault.'

'Among other things,' DeMille said. 'He won't be going home to Austin any time soon.'

'Why haven't I seen this story on the news?' I asked.

'Because we've been able to keep it quiet so far,' he said. 'Mr Grisham is a business associate of the Clifford family and the episode is embarrassing for them.'

I couldn't wait to tell Willow. I started to get up and he said, 'Not yet, Ms McCarthy. I have another question. Do you have a locket?'

'I do. It's a silver heart with photos of my parents inside.'

'Can I see it?'

DeMille seemed to be waiting for my reaction.

I felt tears sting my eyes. I fought them. I didn't want to cry in front of someone I didn't like.

'I lost it,' I said. 'It was a gift from my grandmother. The clasp broke and I haven't been able to find it.'

'When did you last see it?' DeMille asked.

'Back in April sometime,' I said.

'Where did you last see it?'

'In the courtyard. When it slipped off my neck, I caught it and put it on a table by the pool. I wanted to take it to a jeweler and have it fixed, but I couldn't find it. Calypso and I looked everywhere for that locket. It disappeared. Did you find it?'

He ignored the hope in my voice and changed the subject abruptly. 'When did you last see Sammie Lant?'

'Sammie? The dead porn star? Sometime in mid-April. Why are you asking me that again?'

'Never mind. Tell us about that again,' DeMille said.

I hesitated. Why did he want to know this? I remembered Dean's advice to treat the detective like a three-hundred-pound gorilla.

'It's like I told you before,' I said. 'Sammie came to the Florodora, trying to rent a vacant apartment. She insulted Calypso, and we had a disagreement. You have the police report. You escorted Sammie off my property and that's the last time I saw her.'

'Where were you on April nineteenth?'

Now I was confused. 'I don't know. At home, I guess. There's nothing special about the date.'

He unlocked a desk drawer and took out an evidence bag. Inside was my locket, open to the pictures of my parents.

'Do you recognize this?' he asked.

'Yes, those are photos of my parents. Where did you find my locket?'

'In a pocket in Sammie Lant's beach bag.'

'The one the techs found under her body? What took so long?'

'We couldn't get an ID on the photos. I asked around the station. You can thank Ben the beach cop. He recognized your parents' photos. That's why it's good to have an old-timer on staff.'

I reached for the locket, but DeMille put the evidence bag out of reach on his desk.

'Let me help your memory,' he said. 'On April nineteenth, the plumbers were still working in that hole by your pool.'

'Yes. The Sykes brothers closed it up the next day or so.'

'Did you go near the pool site after the workers were gone?' he asked.

'No.'

Now he leaned in, so close I caught a whiff of his aftershave. 'I have two witnesses who say after the plumbers left, they saw you at the pool site after dark. What were you doing?'

'Me? Nothing. Your witnesses must be wrong.'

My mind was spinning. Who were these witnesses? They couldn't be Florodora residents. They'd never make up a story like that. Was it a resident of the condos that flanked the Florodora? Probably not. They'd have a tough time seeing the pool area at night.

Wait! It didn't happen. Dean told me that the cops lied sometimes to trick people. They weren't required to tell the truth.

'Who are these witnesses, Detective?' I was polite and careful.

'I don't have to tell you that,' he said.

I took a deep breath and said carefully, 'There are no witnesses, are there, Detective?'

No answer.

'Are you going to charge me?' I asked.

'Not yet.'

'Then in that case, I'll say goodbye.'

I stood up, then stopped at the door. 'May I have my locket?'

'After I catch Sammie Lant's killer.' He slid the evidence bag into his desk drawer and locked it.

TWENTY-EIGHT

I was shaking so badly I could hardly walk to Dean's Jeep. As soon as I unlocked his ride, I sat in it for a moment to recover, then called Dean. He answered on the second ring.

'Norah! How did the interview go?' he asked.

'I don't know. Can you meet me at the Grass Shack?'

'Right away. What should I order?'

'A pitcher of mojitos. And whatever you want.'

'Sounds serious.'

'See you in ten,' I said.

The Grass Shack was my favorite beach bar. Their mojitos were a perfectly balanced mix of fresh lime and mint, as well as rum. Lots of rum. By the time I parked Dean's Jeep and hiked to the Grass Shack, I was feeling better.

I stood in the entrance and saw Dean had scored a comfortable loveseat with a view of the ocean. On the table beside it was a pitcher of icy mojitos. Our table held an array of bar bites, including lobster sliders and steak medallions on buttery baguette slices.

As soon as Dean saw me, he waved, then poured my drink. I kissed his tanned cheek and said, 'Thank you. You've saved my life.'

I slid on to the loveseat next to him, and took a long drink of the chilled mojito. My head spun a bit at the sudden infusion of alcohol, so I helped myself to a lobster slider and a steak medallion.

Dean let me put my feet up and sip my mojito. What a perfect day to drink at a beach bar. The soft, warm air was soothing. The ocean was a silky turquoise, shading to a deep purple.

I sighed with contentment. Life in Florida was crazy as a bucket of frogs, but just when I was fed up with the place, I'd be overwhelmed by its startling beauty.

'Norah,' Dean said softly. 'Are you awake?'

'Of course.' I sat up and poured myself another mojito. 'I don't know if I made things better or worse when I talked to DeMille.'

I told Dean the whole story. 'Detective DeMille claimed he had two witnesses who saw me hanging around the hole the plumbers dug the day Sammie disappeared. I asked him for their names and he refused to tell me. I didn't believe he had any witnesses and said so. Then I asked, "Are you going to charge me?" and DeMille said, "Not yet." That's when I stood up and walked out.'

'You walked out?' I heard the disbelief in Dean's voice, and knocked back the rest of my mojito.

'Yes. Was that OK?'

He kissed me again. 'Woman, you've got balls.'

'Guts,' I said. 'Don't measure me by men's standards.'

'You acted just the way an innocent, informed person should,' Dean said. 'I'm so proud of you. Let me buy you dinner. It's a little early, but the Shack has the best steaks.'

'Deal,' I said. Actually, I slurred the word a bit. I definitely needed food.

'OK if I order for us?' he asked.

'Yesh.'

Dean signaled for the server, and he appeared – a tall, bony man in shorts with knobby knees and a kind smile. Dean ordered steaks with mushrooms and roasted blue cheese potatoes.

I poured myself another mojito and realized I'd almost finished the whole pitcher.

'What can I get you to drink?' Dean asked.

'Water,' I said. I was drunk, but not *that* drunk. I set the mojito glass on the table.

The server quickly brought water and our meal, and Dean and I dug in. After several bites, Dean looked around and said, 'The place is nearly empty. What do you plan to do next?'

I took a long drink of water and said, 'Keep looking for the killer. I want my locket.'

'Let DeMille do that. He's supposed to find the killer.'

'He hasn't done anything so far,' I said. 'He's not any good at investigating.'

'How do you know?'

'His team insulted Sammie's landlady when they were searching her apartment, and the landlady gave me Sammie's things that were in storage.'

'And you didn't give them to DeMille?' Dean sounded outraged. 'How the hell is he supposed to investigate?'

'Don't yell at me!'

I was angry now, and concentrated on my food. We ate in an uncomfortable silence.

Finally Dean said, 'Norah, I'm sorry I yelled at you, but I've already warned you it's dangerous to investigate a murder if you're not law enforcement. You aren't trained and you don't have backup. I know I said you should prove your innocence before, but I wasn't expecting you to go straight after a killer, someone who strangled a woman and threw her body in a hole. This person is ruthless.'

'I don't care.' I took a big bite of steak, and realized I sounded childish.

When I finished chewing, I said, 'Dean, I have to find Sammie's killer. Our home – and everyone in it – is under suspicion until I do. As for backup, can't you go with me?'

'No,' he said. 'I'm not encouraging you to take this any further.'

'You don't get to play big strong male,' I said. 'If you won't go with me, then I'll go alone.'

He seemed to think this over.

'And I'll run everything I find past you,' I added. 'You can be my sounding board.'

'Maybe.'

Was he coming around? Not quite, but he was interested enough to ask a question. 'What did you find in Sammie's things that her landlady gave you?'

'Proof that her life was sad,' I said. 'I found the outfit she was probably going to wear to her movie premiere, a photo of her when she graduated high school, looking young and innocent, and a pack of roofies with four tablets missing.'

'Roofies?' he said.

'Ben the beach cop thought Chet had been drugged, but his blood tests didn't show anything.'

'Roofies disappear quickly in the bloodstream,' Dean said. 'That means Chet was probably raped.'

'I know that,' I said. 'Now.'

'Well, it's too damn late,' Dean said. 'The chain of custody is broken. Those roofies can't be used as evidence to help Chet.'

'I realize that.' I sounded contrite, but Dean was riled up, and rightly so.

'Men get raped, too, you know.'

'Yes,' I said. 'I'm sorry.'

'Sorry doesn't cut it. Do you know how many men get raped every year in the US? Thirteen thousand. And those are just the reported rapes. This is an underreported crime.'

'You sound like you've made a study of it.'

'I have. When I was in high school, my friend Jonah had a fling with one of his teachers. He was underage, and she was a sweet little blonde who drove Jonah home in her convertible. We thought he was lucky. The rest of us were looking at centerfolds and he had the real deal. She dumped him when he went to college.

'That fling was rape. Statutory rape. And Jonah paid for it, with two busted marriages and a drug problem. Rape victims are more likely to use drugs and have problems with stable relationships.'

'Jonah wasn't so lucky after all,' I said.

'If you'd checked with me when you got Sammie's things, I could have helped you give them to DeMille. See, that's why amateurs—'

'Don't,' I said. 'I'm sick of hearing that. You have to admit, I can be pretty good at finding things. So are we going to join forces?'

I could tell he was starting to change his mind.

'I can go with you sometimes,' he said, 'but I'm helping Calypso's family finish the Florodora repairs by the deadline.'

'When you can't go, what about my temporary roommate, Mickey?' I asked. 'She's taken self-defense training. I'll be safe with her.'

'Well . . .' Dean was still reluctant.

'And I'll call you before we leave and when we return.'

'That's a little better.' Dean still wasn't convinced.

'Before we interview the person, I'll turn on my cell phone so you can monitor what we're saying.'

'I still don't like it,' Dean said.

'Don't be sexist. You can't say that I'm investigating on my own. I'll either have you or Mickey with me, and you'll hear every word that's said. You can call nine-one-one if you think the situation is turning dangerous. It will be your judgment call.'

'OK, but you have to keep your promise.'

'I will.' Suddenly, I was alert and sober. 'I want to start with Chet Parker's football coach.'

'Why?'

'He lost a lot when Chet lost his football scholarship. The coach invested his time and reputation training Chet for the big leagues, and then his star lost everything because of an aging porn actress's terrible stunt.'

Dean gave an exasperated sigh. 'Date rape is a bit more than a stunt,' he said.

'I know. Sammie likely drugged and raped that young man.'

'The coach is a possibility,' Dean said. 'But what about Chet himself?'

'He won't talk to me.'

'He doesn't have to,' Dean said. 'Nobody does. That's the problem with being an—'

'Stop right there,' I said. 'What about Vix Tamer? He has a motive. He gets Sammie's royalties because she doesn't have any heirs. We already know he's a nasty piece of work. If he tried to add the countess to his books and Sammie threatened him . . .'

'True. And Countess Crawlie is younger and a potential big moneymaker. But there's nothing to link him directly to her death. I'm not convinced it's a slam-dunk yet.'

'Then who else do you think I should look into?'

'What about Chet's sweet old mother?' Dean asked. 'How does she feel about the woman who ruined her son's life? Sammie embarrassed Chet's mother, smeared her son's name, and was responsible for him losing a scholarship. How do you know Chet's mother didn't kill Sammie?'

'Because I saw her on TV,' I said. 'She was in a wheelchair.'

'Oh, and she wouldn't sit in a wheelchair to get sympathy for that interview?'

'She looks old and she weighs about eighty-five pounds,' I said. 'I hate the term, but she's a little old lady. Too frail to do any damage.'

Dean laughed so hard he choked on his potato. I pounded his back, extra hard.

'Ow,' he said. 'I'm fine.'

Our server came over. 'Everything OK, folks?'

'Yes, my friend just choked on his food, but he's recovered.' I smiled at the server until he went away.

'What's so funny about Chet's mom being old?' I asked.

'Back when I was a cop, one of the most vicious murders I've ever seen was committed by a so-called little old lady. I was the uniform who answered the call. Agnes was seventy-five and married to the neighborhood drunk. We all knew Bud spent his wife's Social Security check on booze and constantly criticized her.

'Bud complained about her cooking while he got drunk with her money. "Pork chops," he'd say. "Whenever my old lady doesn't feel like putting a decent meal on the table, she makes those damned pork chops."

'None of us understood how Agnes put up with him for fifty years. One evening Bud came home drunk and Agnes was at the kitchen stove, wearing a flowered apron.

'"What's for dinner?" Bud asked.

'"Pork chops."

'"Again?"

'That was Bud's last word. The long-suffering Agnes turned around and hit him in the head with the cast-iron frying pan, pork chops, grease and all. And she kept hitting him.

'The neighbors heard Bud screaming and called the police. By the time I got there, that "sweet old lady" had pounded her husband's head nearly flat.

'That's why I never, ever underestimate any woman, even the old ones. Especially the old ones.'

'Point taken.' If I'd had a frying pan, I would have slammed it in Dean's smug face. I took a long drink of water. I was becoming a mean drunk.

Dean changed the subject and asked, 'Who else was affected by Chet's fall from grace, besides his coach and his mother?'

'His ex-fiancée, Katie, who now lives at the Florodora.'

'I know. I've met her,' Dean said. 'What about Katie as the killer?'

'I don't think so. Katie broke off the engagement before his encounter with Sammie because she realized he wasn't the one; they're just friends now.'

'Some "just friends" relationships can hide a lot of secret passion,' Dean said.

'And sometimes, they're just friends with benefits.' I was sorry I'd said that. It hit too close to home. 'Anyway, Calypso and Chet's own mother vouched for her. Katie goes to their church.'

Dean spoke slowly. 'So you're taking the word of that frail, sick woman. And Calypso, who only sees Katie in church. That's not a recommendation, Norah. You do know that charmer, Dennis Rader, the BTK serial killer, went to church every Sunday. And he killed at least ten people. And what about Peter Tobin, a Glasgow serial killer? He may have murdered forty-eight people. He was only caught when he hid a body *under* a church. So being in church doesn't clear anyone.

'How often have you talked to Katie?' he asked. 'Besides when you interviewed her?'

'After the meeting about the Florodora citations, Katie offered me money for the repairs. We talked about her relationship with Chet. She said they're best friends, but he needs some space – he blames himself for what happened.'

'Did he confide in her about being drugged?'

'I don't know . . . she looked so sad about it all. I didn't want to upset her further.'

'Have another conversation. Take her out for drinks and get her talking.'

'She has acting classes most nights.'

'Then take her out for breakfast.'

'Good idea. I should start investigating right now.' I stood up and the room spun. 'Whoa.' I sat back down.

'Better wait till tomorrow for any investigating,' Dean said. 'I think that pitcher of mojitos hit you hard.'

Dean called for the check and paid it. I downed the last of the mojitos.

This time, I stood up carefully, and held on to Dean's arm. Outside the cool restaurant, the heat hit me hard. I told Dean where I parked the Jeep. I was a bit wobbly on the walk, and he helped me inside. I fell asleep on the short drive home.

Dean carried me inside the Florodora, where Calypso met us. 'What's the matter with Norah?' I heard her ask.

'Norah's had a little too much sun,' Dean said.

Aw, I thought, he lied for me. That's sweet.

'Must have been liquid sunshine,' Calypso said, 'because I smell rum.'

The last thing I heard as Dean carried me upstairs was Calypso's laugh.

TWENTY-NINE

When I woke up the next morning, the sun blistered my eyelids. I quickly clamped my eyes shut, but couldn't go back to sleep. I heard men laughing and cracking jokes, and a terrible pounding, like hammers on concrete.

Wait. The pounding was in my head. Now I remembered. I was monumentally hungover from that pitcher of mojitos. And the noisy men were Calypso's family, working on the Florodora.

I sat up, slowly and carefully, so my head wouldn't roll off. Everything hurt, even my toenails.

'How are we this morning?' A cheery voice assaulted my aching ears.

'Huh?' One word – more like a croak – was all I could manage.

Mickey, my temporary roommate, brought me a lifesaving flagon of coffee.

'Thank you.' There, I said two words.

'Would you like breakfast?' Mickey asked. 'Maybe bacon and eggs?'

My stomach rumbled ominously. 'Maybe some oatmeal a little later.'

I carried the coffee into my too-bright dining room and sat down. Mickey was also bright, in a caftan of pink-and-orange stripes, with a matching turban. She sat down at the table and asked, 'So, what are you doing today?'

I told her about my visit to DeMille yesterday, my quest for my silver locket, and Dean's objections to me investigating.

'Men,' she said. 'They carry on like we're so fragile. I'll go with you.'

'I told him you'd had self-defense training.'

'I took a class with the Peerless Point police,' Mickey said. 'Graduated first in my class.'

While she talked, I nuked a bowl of instant oatmeal. Something neutral for my stomach.

'And I have this.' Mickey showed me a black flip-top canister. 'Pepper spray. So we're armed and dangerous.'

I was perking up, thanks to the heavily sugared oatmeal. After I showered and dressed, I felt even better.

When I emerged from my room, Mickey asked, 'Where should we go first?'

'The Peerless Nursery, to order the parking lot landscaping.'

'At your service,' Mickey said. 'We can take my car, if you want.'

I did.

'I also want to talk to Chet Parker's mother, Nettie.'

Mickey gave me a blank look.

'The football star caught on the beach with Sammie.'

'Oh, right,' Mickey said.

'Calypso knows his mother, Nettie. I'll ask her for an introduction.'

'I'll be waiting at my car,' Mickey said.

Calypso was in her kitchen, stirring chopped onions, garlic, and thyme in a big pot. The hot oil sizzled and cracked.

'Mm. Smells good. What are you making?'

'Peas and rice for the crew's lunch.' She held up a can of pigeon peas.

'The work is up to schedule,' she said. 'My cousins are working like dogs. The electrician is ripping things out right and left and mumbling. The elevator repairman is banging away on that old machine like it insulted his mama.'

I laughed, and said, 'I'm ordering the landscaping for the parking lot. Mickey's going with me. Do you need anything?'

'No, thanks,' she said.

'May I ask a favor?'

'What?' Calypso dumped the can of pigeon peas into the pot and stirred with a big wooden spoon.

'Would you ask your church lady friend, Nettie, to talk to me?'

'About what?' She was still stirring.

'Her son, Chet.'

Calypso looked wary. 'And why do you want to talk to Nettie about her son?'

'Uh.' I tried to think of a quick, harmless reason, but Calypso was too smart.

'You're investigating Sammie's murder, aren't you?'

'Yes.'

'You're trying to trap a sick woman into incriminating her own son.'

'Not if he's innocent.'

'Why don't you ask Chet?' she asked.

'I tried. He wouldn't talk to me.'

'Hah! Nettie always brags her son is smart. Guess she's right.'

'Come on, Calypso. Please?'

'All right. Don't you dare upset her. Remember, she's getting chemotherapy.'

Calypso pointed her spoon, dripping hot oil, at me. 'Go on. I'll call Nettie. And if I hear you caused that poor woman any grief, I'll boil you in oil.'

Calypso handed me Nettie's address and a square box wrapped in ribbons. 'That's guava pound cake,' she said. 'I was going to give it to Nettie at church, but you can deliver it for me.'

Mickey and I were off, the guava pound cake balanced on my lap, her little blue VW Bug chugging along, to the Peerless Nursery. Jim, the owner, showed me a selection of what he called 'salt-tolerant' plants. I made some choices and wrote a whopping down payment.

Next, Mickey and I headed for Nettie's home in Orchid Heights.

'What are you trying to find out when you talk to Nettie?' Mickey asked.

'I want to prove that Chet's mother really is a frail woman who uses a wheelchair. I need proof she couldn't kill Sammie. Also, I want to ask Nettie about Chet without upsetting her. If I upset Nettie, Chet will track me down and break my neck. Calypso threatened to boil me in oil.'

'Better dust off your diplomacy,' Mickey said. 'We're almost at Nettie's house.'

Orchid Heights is in an older section of Peerless Point with Spanish-style homes. Orchids bloomed everywhere: splashes of purple and white in trees draped with Spanish moss, and magenta or yellow orchids in pots on porches.

Mickey drove slowly down Tiger Orchid Drive. 'That's Nettie Parker's house,' I said. 'The two-story stucco with the tiger orchids on the porch.'

'And the wheelchair ramp,' Mickey said.

'It could have been built for a previous owner,' I said. 'I'm not taking anything for granted.'

I didn't bother to call Dean this time. Mickey and I were a match for a sick, older woman. At least, I hoped so.

I carried the guava pound cake and Mickey pressed the doorbell.

A small, brown woman with white hair, matchstick limbs, and an old-fashioned lace-collared dress answered the door, looked at the ribbon-wrapped cake box and said, 'Oh!'

I introduced us and said, 'We're hoping to talk to Mrs Nettie Parker. Calypso sent this guava pound cake for her.'

The white-haired woman seemed flustered. 'Oh, my. I'm Ann, Nettie's sister. Do come in, dears.'

Mickey and I trooped into a living room time-warped from the Seventies: an orange velour couch preserved by plastic slip-covers, orange-flowered chairs that matched the curtains, and an orange shag rug.

'Nettie's coming down now for lunch,' Ann said. 'She loves cake.'

I put the beribboned box on the coffee table.

We heard a mechanical noise, and an elevator opened into the living room. Nettie was in a wheelchair, pushed by a large woman in a nurse's uniform.

No doubt now. I could see Nettie was too frail to attack anyone. Nettie unwrapped the pound cake with shaking hands. All three women oohed and aahed over it.

The cake had been baked in a round Bundt pan, and topped with a snowfall of powdered sugar. 'Would you like some, dears?' Nettie asked.

'No, thank you,' we said. I wanted to devour the whole thing.

'This is the texture of cake I like,' Nettie said. 'Not like those soft cakes they sell in the store. This is homemade.'

'Calypso is the best cook,' I said. Nettie smiled her agreement.

Ann and the nurse went off to the kitchen, bearing the cake. Mickey and I each sat in a flowered chair. Nettie stayed in her wheelchair.

'I'm so glad Katie is renting an apartment at your place, Norah. Even though she broke off the engagement, I still love that girl. She's the daughter I never had.'

'Everyone likes Katie,' Mickey said.

Nettie wanted to get down to business. 'Now, while my lunch is being heated, how can I help you?'

I hoped my diplomacy would get me through this. 'I'm sure Calypso told you Sammie Lant's body was found in my yard.'

'Yes,' Nettie said. 'That terrible woman led my poor son astray.'

'It wasn't Chet's fault,' I said. 'I think Sammie drugged him. I found roofies in Sammie's things. She slipped them in his drink.'

'He was drugged and raped,' Mickey said.

Nettie gave us a sweet smile. 'Oh, no, dears,' she said. 'Men can't be . . . raped.'

She hesitated before she said that last word and patted my hand. 'My boy doesn't like to talk about what happened, but he said what happened was his fault. He shouldn't have been drinking. I don't know the exact details, but I know that Sammie woman was pure evil.'

'Yes, she was,' I said. 'On that we can agree.' I needed crucial information, and hoped it wouldn't upset Nettie.

'The police said Sammie disappeared April nineteenth.' I left that line hanging there, hoping it would prompt Nettie to talk.

'That's what that police detective said when he interviewed me,' Nettie said. 'Everyone was blaming my boy, but I knew it wasn't true. Chet would never act in such a disgraceful way. As soon as that nasty talk started, I sent my boy to his grandparents' home in Atlanta. He stayed there April third through the twenty-ninth. I wanted him out of town. That detective wouldn't believe me when I said Chet wasn't home. I had to show him Chet's airplane ticket.'

'That was a smart move, keeping Chet out of the spotlight,' I said.

'You should have seen the TV reporters camped out in front of my home,' Nettie said. 'I finally went out and gave them a piece of my mind. Ran them right off my property.'

Now I saw a flash of the fierce, determined woman who'd defended her son on television.

'You're a fighter,' I said.

'I am.' Nettie sat up straighter. 'My mother taught me how to be one. If you were a black person growing up when she was a girl, you learned not to trust authority. My family knew your grandmother, Eleanor, and trusted her. She was a friend to our people. We helped her when she wanted her baby girl.'

'Really?' I wanted to know about my mother, but I couldn't get distracted. Not now.

'What did you know about Chet's felony assault charge?' I asked.

Ann was back in the living room. She'd heard that last question and frowned at us. 'Nettie, it's time to eat your lunch. Your soup will get cold.'

One last chance. 'Nettie, why did Chet beat up his teammate? Did Chet serve time? Is he on probation?'

'I'm afraid Nettie must eat, dear.' Ann undid the brakes on the wheelchair and firmly pushed Nettie toward the dining room.

'Please close the door on your way out.'

THIRTY

'Wow, did we get the bum's rush,' Mickey said, as the VW headed home.

'Yes, but we learned some important information,' I said. 'Nettie couldn't possibly have killed Sammie. And Chet was in Atlanta during the time that Sammie disappeared.'

'If Chet stayed in Atlanta the whole time,' Mickey said. 'It's a nine-hour drive from Atlanta to Peerless Point. He could have driven here, killed Sammie, and drove back.'

'Possible,' I said. 'I want to find out more about Chet. How am I going to do that?'

'Let me think,' Mickey said.

We rode home in silence, both of us cogitating. Upstairs in my apartment, Mickey said, 'Let's take a look at that wedding website again.'

I fired up my computer and found the site.

'Look at this,' I said. 'The website has an attendants' page. Katie has five bridesmaids and one maid of honor. Each has their own bio. Two bridesmaids are from New York, one lives down in Miami and one lives up in Palm Beach. Wait – the maid of honor is local.'

'How local?' Mickey asked.

'She's the manager of Beach Sweets on the Beachwalk. Her name is Ashleigh Harris. It's a ten-minute walk. Want to go with me when I talk to her?'

'Yes! I can eat candy in the line of duty.'

On the Beachwalk, the salt air was soft and warm. Mickey and I passed beachgoers playing volleyball or sunbathing under bright-colored umbrellas.

Beach Sweets sold old-school penny candy from the days when those treats really did cost a penny. The white stucco building was painted with red candy-cane stripes.

Inside, the store had floor to ceiling clear plastic bins of colorful candies, from Pop Rocks to Tootsie Pops. A young pony-tailed mom was talking on her cell phone while two tow-headed boys gleefully destroyed the store.

The older boy, who seemed about six, was overturning chairs. The younger one, who looked about four, was dipping his hands in a glass of water and painting the display cases with grape Lik-M-Aid.

A harried blonde employee in a striped jumper was following the older boy around, saying, 'Don't do that, dear. You could hurt yourself.' The kid ignored her.

Mickey observed the mayhem, then went up to the boy painting the candy cases purple. 'Hey! You! Stop that!'

The kid stared at her and went back to smearing the display cases.

'Give me that.' Mickey took the Lik-M-Aid out of the kid's hand and he started bawling.

Mom put down the cell phone and said, 'Don't you dare touch my boy.'

'Your kids are tearing this store apart,' Mickey said.

'I don't have to listen to this,' the woman said. 'Caleb, Colton, come with Mommy.'

She took their hands, and just like that, the mom and kids were gone.

The employee said, 'Hi, I'm Ashleigh. Thank you for your help. Those kids were damaging the store.' She took a deep breath and said, 'Now, how may I help you?'

'I'd like the Big Box of Fun,' I said.

Mickey raised a questioning eyebrow.

'For the workers,' I told her.

'Terrific,' Ashleigh said. She handed me a card with the candy choices. 'You can have a mix of three hundred pieces of any of these candies.'

The list was a mouth-watering selection of childhood favorites including Bit-O-Honey, candy buttons, Mary Janes, wax lips, jaw breakers, candy cigarettes, Lik-M-Aid, root beer barrels, Tootsie Pops, Tootsie Rolls, and Circus Peanuts.

'Everything but the Circus Peanuts,' I said.

'What are those?' Mickey asked.

'They're marshmallow candy shaped like peanuts. They taste like banana-flavored sponges.' I shuddered at a distant memory of eating one.

'No, thanks,' Mickey said.

'They're not my favorite,' Ashleigh said, as she began filling my order, digging into the candy bins with deft, practiced scoops. 'Still, Circus Peanuts have been around more than a hundred years. And you'd be surprised how many people eat them for breakfast.'

'They do?' Mickey and I were a startled chorus.

'In the Sixties, a General Mills employee chopped pieces of Circus Peanuts into a bowl of Cheerios. That discovery led to Lucky Charms cereal.'

Ashleigh finished scooping the candies into a striped hat box. 'All done. What would you like? Any treat, on the house.'

'Candy cigarettes,' I said. 'As a little girl, I used to wear Aunt Tillie's old beaded dresses and "smoke" cigarettes. I thought I was so sophisticated.'

Ashleigh laughed and asked Mickey, 'How may I help you?'

'I'd like the Taste of Nostalgia, with five strips of candy buttons.' Candy buttons were colorful sugar dabs on strips of white paper.

'Even though you'll wind up eating paper?' I asked.

'No calories in paper.' Mickey winked.

Ashleigh handed her the bag of candy and Mickey gave Ashleigh a ten-dollar bill.

'Your money is no good here,' Ashleigh said. 'You saved my store.'

Mickey dropped the ten in the tip jar when Ashleigh's back was turned.

'Anything else I can get you, ladies?' she asked.

'Yes, I need your help,' I said. 'You were supposed to be Katie Penrod's maid of honor. What can you tell me about Katie and Chet's engagement?'

Ashleigh looked wary. 'Why should I talk to you?'

'Sammie Lant, the porn star,' I said, 'was buried on my property and I need to clear my name.'

Ashleigh shook her head. 'That worthless woman caused more trouble.'

'Tell me about it,' I said. 'I had the cops and the press crawling all over my place for weeks.'

Ashleigh still hesitated.

'Don't forget, we helped you,' Mickey said. 'And anything you tell us stays with us.'

'OK,' Ashleigh said. 'Help me put the store back together while I talk. I'm expecting another customer rush at five, when people start going home from the beach.'

Mickey and I arranged the chairs around the tables, then wiped sticky fingerprints off the plastic menus. While we worked, Ashleigh struggled to remove purple swirls of Lik-M-Aid from the candy cases.

'I was Katie's maid of honor because we went to Miss Vivian's Academy in Miami.'

Both of us must have looked surprised. Miss Vivian's is a pricey girls prep school. It was cheaper to go to Harvard than graduate from Miss V's.

Ashleigh noticed our startled look. 'My family had a bit of a setback in the stock market,' she said. 'I have a scholarship to Hallandale Beach College, but I work here for extra money. Katie and I were close friends in school. You've seen photos of Katie, right?'

'Yes,' I said. 'She lives at the Florodora now. Katie seems fragile and ethereal.'

'She's definitely tougher than she looks. When one of our friends, a petite girl like Katie, was assaulted, Katie said that would never happen to her. She took self-defense classes and strength training. Katie has a steel backbone and a hot temper. She's also charming, smart and funny. And she can be terribly generous.'

I remembered Katie offering me money to help with the Florodora's repairs.

Ashleigh scrubbed at the stubborn purple mess on the case while Mickey and I worked on restoring the room. No one spoke.

Finally, Ashleigh broke her silence. 'Katie was ambitious, but not the way most Miss Vivian's girls were. She didn't want to be a lawyer or a doctor or a professor. She wanted to marry well.'

'She's taking acting lessons,' I said.

'Another good way to meet the right kind of man,' Ashleigh said. 'When Katie saw Chet Parker at a local game, she thought he was the answer. You've met Chet, haven't you?'

'Yes,' I said.

'Then you know he's incredibly handsome. He didn't seem that interested in football. His real love was computers. But Chet had natural talent and his mother and his coach pushed him. Hard. Pro scouts were circling. Married to Chet, Katie would have instant fame. She'd be splashed all over magazines in one of those "Hot Wives of the NFL" features. She'd be on TV at the games and go to Super Bowl parties. It would boost her acting career, too.

'It was easy for someone as dazzling as Katie to meet Chet, and before Chet knew what was happening, they were engaged.'

'Did Chet love her?' I asked.

'I think so. But I don't think Chet ever had a serious girlfriend before Katie. He had no idea how handsome he was.'

Ashleigh kept scrubbing the cases. The purple mess was starting to yield.

'What do you know about Chet's felony arrest?' I asked.

'I know it was unfair,' Ashleigh said. 'And the charges were reduced. Chet and Katie announced their engagement at one of his football practices. She was flashing her ring and everyone was congratulating them and slapping Chet on the back. Everyone except Travis. He was angry and jealous. Travis insulted Katie and Chet in front of the whole team, using the N-word. Then he told Katie the children she'd have with Chet would be "mud bloods."

'Katie burst into tears. Chet walloped Travis, leaving him bruised and breaking a rib. Chet was charged with felony assault.'

'That's not fair,' Mickey said.

'Exactly,' Ashleigh said. 'Florida has something called the "fighting words law." The charges were reduced to misdemeanor assault.'

'Do you think Chet could kill someone?' I asked.

Ashleigh shrugged. 'I doubt it. Travis really provoked Chet, but he only hit back when Travis insulted Chet's fiancée.'

'Why did Katie call off the wedding?' I asked.

'Once Katie got used to the idea of being engaged and the excitement was over, she realized she loved Chet – as a brother. She couldn't go through with the marriage.

'I give her credit for that. Some women would have married Chet anyway, but Katie wanted real love. Katie called it quits long before the Sammie scandal.'

'Katie says they're best friends,' I said.

'Oh, they are,' Ashleigh said. 'Chet was deeply wounded by Sammie and cried on Katie's shoulder. She was always there for him. Katie knew how badly Chet was hurt and embarrassed.'

'One last question,' I said. 'After the Sammie episode, Chet's mother sent him to Atlanta to stay with his grandparents?'

'Smart move,' Ashleigh said. 'Chet used to spend summers with his Atlanta grandparents. He has lots of friends there.'

Ashleigh stood back and admired the store. The candy counters sparkled, and the tables and chairs were in place.

'Don't get me wrong,' Ashleigh said. 'I like Katie. I just don't think she was a good match for Chet. But she had the character to break off the engagement when she realized the spark wasn't there long term, and she loves him like a brother. I hope Chet meets a woman who falls *in love* with him.'

The bell over the door rang, and a horde of sandy, shouting kids rushed into the store.

THIRTY-ONE

The next day, Mickey, my temporary roommate, was drinking her morning coffee in the dining room. She wore a magnificent peacock-patterned caftan. I whistled when I saw her.

'Love the outfit,' I said.

'Thanks. I have an interview with the Hallandale Beach College art department's search committee at nine. They're looking for someone to teach a semester as a visiting artist. Pays well, too.'

'At a college?' I didn't hide my surprise. 'Colleges are notoriously stingy when it comes to paying part-time help.'

'This post has a grant. I have to look like an artist – like I couldn't hold a serious job.'

Mickey put her coffee mug in the dishwasher, poured me a cup and handed it to me.

'Gotta run. Wish me luck.'

She was out the door before I could say anything. So much for asking Mickey to go with me when I talked to Chet's coach, Tuck Sullivan.

This morning, I thought I'd invite Katie to breakfast for that next conversation. I finished my coffee, showered, dressed, and knocked on Katie's door. Dressed in a long pink robe, a sleepy Katie answered. She looked like she'd just got out of bed.

'I'd love to,' she said, trying to hide a yawn. 'But I got in late last night. Could we make it tomorrow at nine thirty?'

That chore out of way, I decided to track down Dean. Maybe he could go with me when I interviewed Chet's former coach.

I found Dean outside helping Rafael at the garage. The humid heat was like a slap in the face with a hot, damp towel.

Eric and Godfrey were working on the Florodora roof. Ozzie was stripping paint off doors in front of the garage. Dean was taking a break in the shade by the garage, chugging a frosty bottle of water. I could hear hammering inside the garage, and guessed that was Rafael and Ian at work.

'On break?' I asked.

'For a while.' Dean looked tired and sweaty, and it was only nine thirty.

'Want to go with me when I talk with my next suspect, Chet's coach, Tuck Sullivan?'

'You mean *the* Tuck Sullivan?' he asked.

'He's famous?'

Dean groaned at my ignorance. 'Tuck Sullivan is a legend. He was a star college quarterback in the Eighties. He won the Heisman Trophy.' Dean said those last two words with religious reverence.

'That's a big deal, right?'

'A big deal?' Dean sounded shocked. 'It's the most important award in college football. It's given to the outstanding player of the year. Tuck signed on to the NFL after college. A torn ACL destroyed his career after one incredible season.'

At least I knew an ACL was the anterior cruciate ligament. For athletes, an ACL tear could be a career-ending injury.

'And you're just going to stop at his gym and talk to him?' Dean reacted as if I'd decided to pop by the Vatican to have tea with the pope.

'Sure? Why not?'

Dean insisted on showering before he met his hero. He drove us to John W. Sewell College. On the way, he regaled me with Coach Sullivan's history.

'After that first spectacular year, Tuck Sullivan had surgery and came back to the team. It had taken him eight months to recover. At first, it seemed Tuck was back in fighting form. Then, at his second practice, he blew out his knee. Again. This time, the damage was permanent. Doctors had warned Tuck to be careful or he could reinjure his knee, but he was young, and didn't believe bad things could happen to him.'

'Did Tuck have more surgery?' I asked.

'Yes. He can walk, but he can't play football any more. His career was over. Tuck went through a bad period where he drank too much and made the front pages. Finally, Tuck went into rehab and recovered. But after his very public history of alcoholism, the best he could do was coach mediocre teams at mediocre colleges. It was a stroke of luck when he discovered Chet Parker. They say Sullivan pinned his hopes on Chet's career.'

'It must have been a blow when Chet lost his scholarship,' I said.

'That's what I heard. Coach Sullivan has had enough bad luck for a lifetime.' Dean shook his head.

We'd reached John Sewell College, named after an early mayor of Miami. The school was fairly new and the architecture was undistinguished – state school sterile. The buildings were a series of drab concrete boxes surrounded by asphalt parking lots. The buildings were labeled with huge, painted white letters, starting with A. Fortunately, G Building was the gym.

Dean parked the car and we went inside. The place smelled like a locker room: a combination of sweat, damp towels, and industrial cleaners. Lucky for us, the secretary's cubicle had an 'On Break' sign.

We walked right into the coach's office. In the far corner was a small shrine to his glory days, with the Heisman Trophy, photos of Sullivan on the field, and a clutch of DVDs.

Even sitting down, Coach Sullivan was a massive man, with muscular arms and broad shoulders. His white hair was cropped short. His skin was dark and his brown eyes seemed kind.

'May I help you?' His voice was deep.

'Is that a real Heisman Trophy?' Dean's voice was reverent. He fanboyed the coach and they began talking a strange language I assumed was footballese.

I could pick out individual words like yards, receivers, rushers, fumbles, and punt returns, but combined, they didn't make much sense. At least not to me.

As Dean and the coach talked, I gathered Tuck Sullivan was reliving his glory days and enjoying it. He had a new sparkle in his eyes.

Dean looked almost as happy worshipping his idol. After fifteen minutes, Dean had talked the coach into letting him watch the DVDs of Tuck Sullivan on the gridiron. Coach Sullivan showed Dean to a small conference room and said, 'You can watch the DVDs in here. You know how to work the machine?'

'Yes, sir.' Dean did everything but salute.

The coach shut the door and said, 'Now, how can I help you, miss?'

The coach and I wandered into the empty gym. He had a slight limp and wore a knee brace.

We settled on the bleachers. 'I'd like to ask you about Chet Parker.'

The coach's face lit up. 'Chet's a fine young man. And so talented. Why do you want to know?'

'Because Sammie Lant was found buried in my yard.'

Sullivan's face darkened and his eyes flashed fire. 'That woman.' He spat the word. 'That woman is a snake in female form. She seduced that innocent young man and ruined his career.'

'It wasn't seduction,' I said. 'I believe she roofied his drink and date-raped him.'

'She deserved to die,' Sullivan said. 'I'm sorry she was found at your apartment house, but her burial was fitting. She was found with a gold Gucci bag. Fake. Just like she was.'

'How did you know about the fake gold bag?' I asked.

'What do you mean?' His voice was wary.

'I said, how did you know about the fake gold bag?' Suddenly my every nerve was alert. Something was off here.

'I think it was on TV,' the coach said.

'No, it wasn't,' I said. 'And I didn't tell you I lived in an apartment house. To know that information you would have to be—'

The coach interrupted me with a roar. 'Are you accusing me of murder?'

I stood up and backed toward the door. 'No, no. I just wanted to know how you—'

'Get out!' he screamed, and rose to his full height, which seemed like seven feet of fury. He pointed his finger toward the door. 'Out! I said out! Before I personally throw you out!'

I grabbed my purse and ran toward the conference room where Dean was reliving the coach's past glories.

'Dean! We've got to go,' I said.

'Now?'

'Right now. The coach is really mad.' I grabbed Dean's hand and pulled him out of the room.

The coach was still raging. 'I can't believe you're accusing me of being a killer.'

Dean picked up on the coach's anger and we both ran. Coach Sullivan limped to the door, shouting, 'Get out! And don't come back!'

On the way home, I told Dean what had happened. 'You accused Coach Sullivan of being a killer?' He sounded horrified.

'How else would he know those details?'

'Lots of ways. A cop or a tech could have told him, wanting to impress the coach. Or he really could have heard those details on TV.'

'I don't think so,' I said.

'Now I can't ever see the coach again,' Dean said.

From the way Dean said it, you would have thought he'd been barred from paradise.

'Can I buy you lunch?' I asked. 'For driving me.'

'Not hungry.' His voice was sulky.

On the long, slow drive home, I had time to think about what Dean said. Maybe he was right. I hadn't seen every TV story about Sammie. And Coach Sullivan had a lot of connections to Peerless Point. Anyone working the case could have told him.

I still thought the coach had reacted like a guilty man, but I couldn't have Dean angry at me. Time to swallow my pride.

'Dean, I'm sorry,' I said. 'I shouldn't have insulted Coach Sullivan. I promise to write him a letter of apology.'

I didn't mention when I'd write the letter. If someone else killed Sammie, the coach would definitely get a heartfelt apology. Otherwise, forget it.

'You realize your amateur meddling could ruin this case, don't you?'

'Yes.' I sounded contrite. 'But you're being unfair. You agreed to go with me and encouraged me. And I've found out things that DeMille didn't. I'm not that bad.'

'No, you're not,' he said. 'But clumsy moves can undo lots of good work. When I was a cop, I had a case where a woman was assaulted. She was so traumatized she couldn't remember what her attacker looked like. One of her friends decided to "help." She suspected – like I did – that the neighborhood handyman had attacked her friend, and showed the victim a photo of the man.

'Now, if that ID had been handled by a professional like me, I would have shown the victim a "six-pack" – six photos of similar men. If she picked out her attacker from that, her ID would have meant something. The interfering amateur made it harder to solve the case.'

I listened quietly while Dean lectured me. 'Dean, I am sorry,' I said. 'But I haven't done anything like that. I just talk to people – and the police didn't even talk to some of them. I only have one more interview.'

'Who's that?' he asked.

'I invited Katie Penrod, my new renter, to breakfast tomorrow. After I ask her a couple of questions, that's it.'

I continued making my case. 'She's been a good resident of the Florodora and she volunteers five mornings a week at Hope Blooms, the charity plant shop. Its proceeds go to needy children. I'm taking her to breakfast at Egg-Zack-Lee-Rite on the beach.'

'Well, I guess you can't get in too much trouble.' Dean metaphorically patted me on the head.

I ignored his condescending manner.

'Can't Mickey go with you tomorrow?' he asked.

'I don't know. She's applying for a job and may not be available. I may want to follow Katie to her job at the florist shop. If that happens, may I borrow your Jeep tomorrow?'

'OK,' he said, 'but only if you call me before you go in the florist shop and keep your phone on so you're not alone. I'll be listening for any sign of trouble.'

We were home, and greeted by the sounds of nail guns, electric saws, clanging, banging and the smell of fresh paint.

Dean kissed me lightly on the cheek. 'I have to go back to work,' he said. 'Here are my Jeep keys.'

He looked me in the eye. 'Promise me you won't talk to that woman alone.'

'We'll be surrounded by people in the restaurant,' I said. 'It's nine thirty in the morning. A peak time.'

'I'm talking about if you go to the flower shop. Make sure you call me before you go into the building and leave your phone on. That way, if anything goes wrong, I'll be there in five minutes.'

'I promise.' I kissed him back.

'I mean it,' he said. 'I'm worried.'

'You worry too much,' I said.

'I have good reason. I'm an ex-cop.'

'There's nothing to worry about,' I said. 'She's short, skinny, and wears pink. What's Katie going to do? Bop me with a begonia?'

THIRTY-TWO

Mickey greeted me in my apartment with a dazzling smile. 'They liked me,' she said. 'The search committee was impressed with my credentials and my portfolio. I have to meet the department chair tomorrow and if she says yes, I get the job.'

'Hooray!' I said. 'Let's have white wine to celebrate.'

'Just a glass,' she said. 'I have another appointment at nine tomorrow.'

I poured us both a generous glass and put a bowl of pretzels on the coffee table in the living room. We both took a drink of wine and crunched some pretzels.

I told her about my encounter with Coach Sullivan. 'I think he could have killed Sammie from the way he overreacted.'

'Maybe.' Mickey took another sip. 'Except an innocent man would be justly angry. If someone said you were a killer, you'd be furious.'

We thoughtfully sipped wine until Mickey asked, 'Who else do you think could have killed Sammie, besides Coach Sullivan?'

'Vix Tamer,' I said. 'The porn star agent. He got rid of Sammie the aging actress and signed on a younger, hotter client.'

'Guys like Vix have easier ways of getting rid of clients than murder,' Mickey said.

'But Sammie has no heirs, so he gets her royalites. And Vix has a violent streak. He destroyed my car.'

'What about Chet, the former football hero?' Mickey asked.

'He's the most likely possibility. He has a temper. He was so angry at me, he threatened my life. He beat up one of his team mates.'

'A man who insulted Chet's fiancée and made racist remarks,' Mickey said. 'That's extreme provocation.' Mickey reached for another handful of pretzels. 'And Chet was in Atlanta when Sammie disappeared.' She crunched a pretzel to enforce her point.

'But Ashleigh says Chet had a lot of friends in Atlanta,' I said. 'He could have told his grandparents he was staying with a friend overnight, and driven to Peerless Point, strangled Sammie, and drove home. Heck, the friend could have done the driving.'

'My gut says he didn't do it,' Mickey said.

'Now there's iron-clad evidence.'

Mickey's only response was another pretzel crunch.

'Chet's mom is too frail to hurt anyone,' I said. 'You saw her. She can barely walk.'

'What about Chet's ex-fiancée?' Mickey asked.

'Katie? Our new resident? You've seen her, too. That woman's a ninety-eight-pound weakling. I'm taking her to breakfast tomorrow.'

'What happens after you talk to Katie? Any other suspects?' Mickey asked.

'That's it. When I wrap up the last interview, I'll ask Calypso for help. If she'll go to lunch again with her friend Yolanda, the one who lives at the Crocus, she could find some video proof. Someone at the Crocus should have some video from when Sammie was buried in the Florodora yard.'

'Do you really think someone will keep a random video from six months ago?' Mickey asked.

'It's worth a try.'

I could tell she wasn't impressed with this plan.

Mickey changed the subject. 'Sorry I can't go with you tomorrow. Can Dean make it?'

'No, he has to work. I'm taking Katie to the Egg-Zack-Lee-Rite, and the restaurant will be packed. It's perfectly safe.'

'Careful,' Mickey said. 'That's what the family of the deceased always tells the police: "She said it was perfectly safe."'

'The biggest danger at that restaurant is high cholesterol,' I said. 'After breakfast, Katie will go work at the flower shop. Dean and I have a plan. If I decide to tag along with her, Dean wants me to call him when I get to the shop and keep my cell phone on. Dean can listen in case something goes wrong. If it does, he can be at the flower shop in five minutes.'

'OK,' Mickey said, drawing out the word. 'Just be careful.'

'Come on. I'm going to a flower shop. It's no big deal. I'll pick up a bouquet for Calypso.'

THIRTY-THREE

The next morning, the sun was smiling and the waves danced on the beach. It was a cool seventy degrees. I knocked on Katie's apartment door. She answered with a smile. As usual, Katie was wearing pink, from her hot pink designer dress to her matching flats and teeny purse. We were heading for breakfast on the beach.

We watched the sun sparkling on the water, and Katie said, 'I love living right at the beach. And the Florodora has such an interesting bunch of residents.'

'That's for sure.'

As we picked our way around piles of old wood, paint cans, and sawhorses at the Florodora, we had to shout over the sounds of the power tools.

'When will the work here be finished?' Katie asked.

'The city says it has to be done by the end of the month, so just under three weeks. So far, we're on schedule. When it's over, I promise it will be quieter.'

Soon we were on the Beachwalk and then at the Egg-Zack-Lee-Rite restaurant. We arrived at just the right time. All the customers were seated. Helen, the veteran server, found an empty table for us by the window.

Like everyone who saw the restaurant for the first time, Katie seemed delighted by its quirky touches. 'I love that sign by the window,' she said. It said, 'Whatever you do today, do it with the confidence of a four-year-old in a Batman T-shirt.'

'Words to live by,' I said.

Helen, our server, brought mugs of hot coffee and asked, 'What will you have, ladies? The chocolate-chip cinnamon rolls are the house special.'

'I'll take a cinnamon roll, Helen,' I said. 'Warmed up.'

'I'd like one egg, scrambled, and one piece of wheat toast, no butter,' Katie said.

'That's all?' I asked.

'Yes,' Katie said.

'OK,' Helen said. 'But remember, skinny people are easier to kidnap.'

I laughed. Katie didn't.

Our breakfasts arrived quickly. Katie's single egg and dry toast looked pathetic next to my roll, fat with chocolate and fragrant with cinnamon. I wolfed down my cinnamon roll and Katie picked at her egg and dry toast. We said little while we ate.

After we'd finished and Helen had taken away our plates, we sipped coffee and continued our conversation.

'I'm still getting to know the residents of the Florodora,' Katie said. 'What can you tell me about the woman with the long blonde hair? Kind of hippie-looking?' Katie took a long drink of her coffee.

'That's Willow,' I said.

'She's beautiful,' Katie said.

'Willow used to be a New York model. She got tired of the rat race and materialism and now devotes her time to Eastern mysticism.'

'I've met Billie, the movie critic. Is he successful?'

'Very,' I said. 'His last book was a *New York Times* bestseller.'

'What about your neighbor, Dean? Is he dating anyone?' Katie asked.

'Me. But it's not exclusive.'

'Good,' Katie said. 'I'd like to know him better.'

I changed the subject. 'Have you seen the hunky detective who's been around here for the investigations? Detective DeMille is definitely a hottie, and he's single.'

'Does DeMille know who killed Sammie Lant?'

I must have looked startled because Katie said, 'Sorry. Shouldn't I have mentioned her name? The woman who was buried at your place?'

'If DeMille does know who killed Sammie, he's sure not telling me,' I said. 'Believe it or not, Sammie tried to rent your apartment.' I sipped more coffee.

'You're kidding,' Katie said. 'You didn't rent to her, obviously.'

'Of course not. Especially after she insulted Calypso.'

'The cleaning lady?'

'Housekeeper,' I said. 'I was so furious with Sammie that I yelled at her to get out. Someone must have heard the argument and called nine-one-one, because DeMille had to escort Sammie off my property. That was the last day she was seen alive.'

'Really?' Katie was wide-eyed. 'Was she dressed like a porn star?'

'Not exactly,' I said. 'But she wouldn't make the cover of *Vogue*. She wore a black pleather skirt and a red blouse that showed her assets. On her feet were red heels with big rhinestone butterflies on them.'

'And what about that clunky rhinestone butterfly pin on her chest?' Katie said. 'How trashy was that?'

'Somebody call the fashion police,' I said.

Katie giggled. 'Well, I'm so glad you rented the apartment to me. It's perfect.'

'You're a welcome addition to the Florodora.' I toasted her with my coffee mug.

Katie glanced at the Kit-Cat Klock on the wall. 'Oops. It's ten thirty,' she said. 'I have to open the plant shop. Must dash.' She started to open her purse to pay.

'This is my treat. I'll take care of the bill. You go to work.' I waved her away. Katie thanked me and ran out of the restaurant.

Helen came by and refilled my mug. I slowly sipped my coffee. Something about our conversation was nagging at me. I didn't like that Katie seemed interested in Dean, even though we weren't a couple.

But more than jealousy was bothering me about our breakfast conversation. Was it our catty remarks about Sammie? I wasn't proud of that, but something else was off. I thought back over what we said.

I described Sammie's clothes, the skirt, the blouse and the butterflies on her shoes. Butterflies. I took a long bracing drink and the coffee woke up my brain.

Katie mentioned the clunky butterfly pin on Sammie's chest. That was the information DeMille was holding back. Information only the killer would know. And Katie said she'd never met Sammie.

Katie strangled Sammie and shoved that butterfly down her throat.

THIRTY-FOUR

I threw some money on the table and dashed back home for Dean's car. I didn't see him anywhere. Since I had the keys to his Jeep, I headed straight to the charity flower shop downtown, Hope Blooms.

I felt a tingle of excitement. My quest was almost finished. Did Katie kill Sammie? I'd ask her right to her face. If she gave me a plausible denial, then with Calypso's help, I'd soon have an answer.

Mickey thought it was a long shot that anyone would keep the video on their phone for six months, but people didn't always kill off the videos on their cell phones.

The plant shop was a former service station, a riot of color among downtown's dull, flat-faced buildings. The shop was painted pink and decorated with giant flowers. The courtyard was crowded with containers of palms and outdoor flowering plants. The canopy over the entrance was a jungle of hanging plants. Both service bays of the former station were teeming with more plants.

The florist section was in the main part of the building. I parked Dean's Jeep and called him. After he answered I said, 'I'm going in the plant shop. I'll leave my phone on so you can hear.'

'I'm here and I'll be listening,' he said.

I sure hoped he could hear. I could barely hear him over the loud construction noises at the Florodora.

'And turn on the record button on your phone just in case,' he said.

In case of what? I wondered, but I turned it on anyway.

'Don't step in any poison ivy,' he said.

I turned up the sound and slipped my phone in my shirt pocket.

Inside, the shop had a huge glass-doored cooler along one wall, filled with flowers. On either side of the counter's cash register were bins and barrels of lethal-looking gardening tools:

rakes, garden forks, garden shears and more, many in pastel colors. Behind the counter were racks of ribbons, stacks of tissue paper and shelves of vases.

Katie was behind the cash register, watering orchid plants in a pink beach wagon. She was so pale, she seemed made of porcelain, and looked so delicate I wondered how she lifted the heavy water jug.

'Well, hey there, Norah,' she said. 'What brings you here?'

'I wanted to get a bouquet for Calypso.'

'That's really nice. But you didn't have to come here. You could have called and I would have brought it home.'

'I wanted to see your shop and ask a question.'

'About the bouquet?' Katie said. 'We have lovely fresh flowers, delivered this morning.' She opened the cooler and brought out a container. 'These are star gazer lilies,' she said. 'Don't they smell wonderful?'

I nodded.

'These tea roses are sweet, and the blush carnations have a spicy smell.' As expected, Katie was pushing pink.

'They're pretty,' I said, 'but Calypso likes purple.'

'No problem. We have amazing purple options.' Katie suggested a bouquet of purple anemones, peonies, orchids, and carnations.

'I like that.'

'Do you want this delivered?' she asked.

'No, I'll take it with me.'

'How about a vase?'

I chose a purple glass vase, and Katie began deftly arranging the flowers.

'Now, what was your question?' she asked.

'Something you mentioned at breakfast. About Sammie Lant.'

'What about her?' Katie's hands were trembling, and a fat purple peony slipped from her fingers. Was her voice slightly higher? Of course not. Must be the acoustics.

'How did you know she wore a butterfly pin?'

Katie dropped two stems of peonies. They fell on the concrete floor behind the counter and the petals splattered everywhere.

'Oops!' Katie tossed the denuded blooms into the trash.

'Plenty more where those came from.' Her laugh was shaky, but she managed to assemble a stunning bouquet.

'There,' she said. 'Let me add a bow. Do you want a dark purple or lavender ribbon?'

'Lavender,' I said.

I waited a moment and asked her again, 'How did you know that Sammie wore a big butterfly pin?'

Katie's milk-pale skin turned deep pink. She began stammering. 'Y-you told me. At breakfast. You said she wore a b-black skirt, red blouse, and red heels with b-butterflies.'

Her voice sounded high and thin.

'I said Sammie had butterflies on her shoes. I didn't mention the butterfly pin.'

'Then I must have seen it on TV.'

'No, you didn't. DeMille held back that information. Only the killer knows that.'

'How can you call me a killer?' Her eyes were wide and angry.

'Because you had good reason to hate Sammie. She drugged him, didn't she? Chet wasn't able to stop her, he was so out of it. I think he told you everything that happened that night.'

'She ruined Chet,' she said, glaring at me. 'She drugged his drink and date-raped him. She destroyed his career, ruined his reputation and broke his spirit. Chet will never be the same, thanks to her. And he couldn't go to the police. He was a joke. Many people think only women are date-rape victims. Chet would be laughed at. He was already laughed at. You can't believe the comments he had to listen to. He couldn't face telling anyone. Especially not his mother.'

'So you killed Sammie,' I said.

'No. Look at me. I weigh ninety-eight pounds. How could I kill that woman?'

'Easy. You've had self-defense and strength training. You strangled Sammie on the beach, and probably left her there until around five o'clock, when people start leaving. She was too heavy to drag, but I bet you put her in that cute pink plant wagon.'

Katie stepped away from the wagon, as if it was contaminated.

'You did, didn't you? The police will find Sammie's DNA in that wagon, and maybe her hair. That wagon will convict you.'

'No!'

'Yes!' I said. 'You killed Sammie because she was a predator.

She'd keep drugging other young men. Innocent young men like Chet.'

'I had to stop her,' Katie said. 'I did it to protect them and because she ruined Chet. It wasn't fair.'

Katie threw the vase of flowers at me. I ducked between a barrel of rakes and a bin of cultivators.

When I lifted my head up over the barrel, Katie had a gun pointed at me. A Walther PK380. Pink. It matched her dress.

Katie flicked what looked like a lever on the side. Was that the safety?

'Gun!' I shouted. 'Dean, she has a gun. Help. Dean! Are you listening?'

No answer.

Dammit. I wasn't going to be killed with a pink gun.

'Don't move.' Katie was snarling like a furious cat. I grabbed a cultivator, a three-pronged garden tool with a blasted pink handle, and swung at the gun. The weapon went flying out of her hand and landed on the floor, all the way over by the flower coolers.

I scuttled across the concrete floor for the gun while Katie threw glass vases at me. I kept my head down to avoid the flying glass. I was inches away from the gun when Katie ran up behind me and slipped a wide satin ribbon around my neck.

She was strong. So strong, I could hardly breathe. I tried twisting to grab her, but she was too far away. Darkness was closing in. She was strangling me.

My strength was going. Then I saw the ribbon.

It was pink.

No!

Using all my strength, I lunged forward. My fingers found the gun. I pointed the gun toward Katie, pulled the trigger, and fired.

THIRTY-FIVE

After the gun went off close to my right ear, I was dazed. I sat on the floor, trying to catch my breath. I couldn't hear and it hurt to breathe. I tried to take in deep lungsful of air, but kept coughing.

Where was Katie?

And what happened to Dean? Why had he deserted me? I thought I could count on him.

The silence was thick and oppressive. I felt trapped behind a glass wall.

After a while, I tried to stand, but was too shaky. I grabbed the handle of the cooler and pulled myself up. Slowly.

That's when I saw Katie on the floor. Blood was flowing from a head wound and her eyes were closed.

Good Lord. I'd killed her. If Dean had been paying attention, this wouldn't have happened. His inattention made me a killer.

I needed to call the police. I needed my purse to get my phone.

I made it across the floor by holding on to shelves, barrels and bins. I could feel broken glass crunching under my feet, but I still couldn't hear it. I saw the trampled remains of Calypso's bouquet, and shards of the purple vase. More pointless destruction.

Finally, I saw my purse on the counter. That's when I realized my phone was in my shirt pocket. I really was rattled.

Before I could dial 911, I heard a distant siren. Flashing police lights danced through the shop windows. The police were here.

A uniformed officer rushed inside. I recognized Ted Jameson, the helpful police officer who'd devoured Calypso's French toast and guarded the dig in the Florodora yard.

His lips were moving, but I couldn't hear him. I pointed to my ear and shook my head.

Ted handed me a pen and pad of paper from the counter. I wrote:

Just shot gun at woman on floor. She was trying to strangle
me. She killed Sammie Lant. Needs ambulance.

I pointed to the pink ribbon and the pink gun by the cooler. Ted
nodded and spoke into his shoulder mic.

Suddenly, Katie sat up and screamed. My hearing was starting
to come back slightly, because I heard her, but from a great
distance. I was so relieved she wasn't dead, I started to sway. I
quickly grabbed the edge of the closest bin.

Katie pointed at me and shouted, 'That woman shot me in the
head. She was trying to rob the store.'

'No!' My voice was a distant croak.

With that, Detective DeMille burst into the shop. 'Norah, are
you OK?'

'That woman – Katie Penrod – tried to shoot me and strangle
me,' I said. 'She killed Sammie Lant.'

'She's lying,' Katie howled. 'She shot me in the head.' Katie
was sitting on the concrete floor, leaning against a stack of potting
soil bags. She looked like a discarded Halloween decoration.
Blood painted her white-blonde hair, her neck and her pink dress.
Her eyes were wild.

DeMille checked her head wound. 'Looks like a graze,' he
said.

'The ambulances are on the way,' Officer Ted said. 'Two.'

'Who's the other one for?' My voice sounded full of broken
glass.

'You need to be checked out, Norah.' Ted's voice was still
muffled, but I could hear him a little better.

I expected the paramedics to arrive next. Instead Dean rushed
through the door. Mickey came flying after him. Hah! Too little,
too late, Dean.

'Norah! Thank God you weren't shot.' Dean wrapped his arms
around me. I realized I was shaking. I wanted to punch him.

'Officer,' Dean pointed to Katie. 'That woman killed Sammie
Lant.'

'No, I didn't,' Katie said. She turned to Dean with venomous
eyes. 'Prove it.'

This was my cue. 'I recorded her confession on my cell phone.
She attacked me.' I handed the phone to DeMille.

'You'll want your experts to check that pink wagon behind the counter.' I was still croaking like a raven. 'I think Katie moved Sammie's body in it after she strangled her on the beach.'

Both ambulances arrived. Katie had the most dramatic-looking injuries. She was carried out first. I was next.

Dean insisted on staying with me. He told Mickey to go home and tell everyone I was OK, and he would update them by phone. On the ride to the hospital, he tried to hold my hand, but I pulled it away.

Once there, we waited in the ER for about half an hour. I was stuck with Dean, and damn angry. 'What were you doing?' I asked. 'Did you hear what was going on?'

'Of course,' he said. 'When the gun went off, I didn't know who was shot. I didn't answer you because I didn't know how close the killer was to you. I called nine-one-one and said you were in extreme danger. I also told them to call Detective DeMille. Then, I tried to start Rafael's old truck, but I flooded it. That's when Mickey showed up in her Bug, and we took off. It's not the fastest car on the road, but we got there.'

'And that's your explanation?' I was still angry.

'I'm so sorry,' he said. 'But that's why amateurs shouldn't—'

'Stop right there,' I said. 'Don't you dare finish that sentence.'

Fortunately for Dean, a Dr Ethan Finley came in. He was tall and thin, with an egg-shaped head, tired brown eyes, and a short red beard. I liked his smile. Dr Finley poked and prodded me. I didn't realize my arms and hands were so bloody. The doctor picked glass out of several cuts with tweezers and closed the larger ones with medicinal glue.

A nurse put a washcloth on my neck and a cold pack on top of that. Her name was Sandy. Sturdy and businesslike, Sandy had a practiced touch. Dean turned on the charm for the nurse. 'You're really busy, Sandy,' he said. 'How can I help?'

'The knife and gun club has been active,' Sandy said. 'It's a full moon. Would you watch Ms McCarthy for me? If you see any swelling or if she has difficulty breathing, call me immediately.'

Dr Finley called in specialists, and sent me for assorted scans and tests. I'm sure he ran the bill up an impressive amount. Sandy checked on me periodically.

In the middle of the testing a police photographer showed up and took pictures of my wounds. Especially my neck, which was a lurid purple-red.

Finally, when all the testing was finished, my gurney was parked back in an ER cubicle. Dean sat in a hard plastic chair, which looked as comfortable as a rock. I hoped it murdered his back.

Even with ice on my neck, I managed to sleep on the gurney. It wasn't comfortable, but it had to be better than that chair Dean was sitting on.

Around eight o'clock, Dr Finley came back and woke me up. 'Huh?' I said.

'The results of your tests and scans are good, Ms McCarthy,' Dr Finley said. 'You don't seem to have any noise-induced hearing loss that could be permanent. Does your throat hurt?'

I nodded.

'There doesn't seem to be any damage to your voice box, windpipe or the arteries to your neck. You'll have some bruising on your neck, which will fade eventually. Continue with the cold packs and take Tylenol or Advil for the pain. Stick to soup and soft food until the pain goes away.

'If you have any bleeding, choking or vomiting, come back to the ER immediately. See your family doctor in two or three days for a check-up.'

'Can I go home tonight?' I asked.

'Yes,' the doctor said. 'But take it easy tomorrow. Expect to be tired and a little sore. I recommend you stay in bed and sleep for two or three days.'

While we waited for the discharge papers, Dean called Mickey with the good news. She insisted on driving over to pick us up.

Dean kept apologizing. 'I am so sorry, Norah. I thought I was doing the right thing. Obviously, I wasn't. You must have been scared to death.' Soon he was groveling. I let him continue for a bit before I forgave him.

I fell asleep in the car on the way home. Dean carried me upstairs, with Mickey trailing behind.

Mickey undressed me and put me to bed. Dean came in to say goodnight.

He whispered in my ear, 'I love you.'

At least, I think that's what he said. My hearing still wasn't working quite right.

THIRTY-SIX

I woke up about ten the next morning. My throat hurt and the dozens of small cuts itched and throbbed. I started to get up and the room spun.

'Whoa! What are you doing?' Mickey grabbed my shoulders. 'You're supposed to be in bed.'

'I need to use the bathroom.'

Mickey guided me there and waited outside the door, then helped me back to bed. 'Would you like breakfast?' she asked.

'Yes, please. Let me get dressed.'

Mickey barred the way to my closet. 'Oh, no. You're staying in bed.'

Calypso arrived with tea and scrambled eggs. I was hungry, but it was hard to swallow with my bruised throat. I fell back asleep after breakfast and woke up at dinnertime.

Calypso still wouldn't let me come downstairs. Mickey came up with a bowl of Calypso's homemade chicken soup and two heavily buttered slices of fresh baked bread. That meal was easier to eat than the scrambled eggs.

The second morning after the attack, I felt much better. Mickey checked on me and I told her I was making real progress. I proved it by getting dressed. I even braved a look in the mirror. The bruises around my neck were livid and my arms and hands were speckled with cuts and decorated with splotches of orange Betadine.

I managed a breakfast of tea and oatmeal, when there was a knock on my door. Dean came running in, stopped and said, 'Wow. Do you feel as bad as you look?'

Mickey glared at Dean.

'I'm much better, thanks. I'm going downstairs to my office.'

'Be careful,' he said. 'You still look shaky.'

Dean guided me down the steps, holding on to my arm. I sat at my desk and sighed with contentment. Much better.

Calypso came in. 'I'm sorry I recommended that woman.'
'It's not your fault. She fooled us all,' I said. 'I told Katie she
was a good addition to the Florodora.'

'Nettie feels bad, too. She wants to come by tomorrow afternoon and apologize.'

'She doesn't have to do that,' I said.

'I'm making guava pound cake,' Calypso said.

Even that temptation made me hesitate. 'Nettie is a sick woman.
Is she well enough to make the trip?'

'She says yes,' Calypso said. 'She also wants to tell you about
your mother.'

'Well, in that case, I look forward to seeing her.'

Finally, I would learn who my mother really was, a mystery
that had haunted me for most of my life.

After lunch, I dragged myself upstairs for a nap. A nap that
lasted until the next morning. Now I almost felt like my old
self.

I was up and dressed when Detective DeMille came pounding
up the stairs, Calypso following him. 'I don't think Norah's well
enough for visitors,' she said.

'She'll talk to me here or down at the station,' he said with a
snarl. 'If she has to be carried out on a stretcher.'

I opened the door. 'You wanted to see me, Detective?'

My voice didn't shake, a sure sign I was recovering. DeMille
had fire in his eyes. He kept running his hands through his hair,
until it stood up like he'd stuck his finger in a light socket.

'See you? See you? I want to lock you up and throw away
the damn key. What the hell were you doing confronting a killer?
You could have been killed.'

I pasted a smile on my face and said, 'Sit down, please,
Detective. I'm fine. May I make you some coffee? Or how about
some cold water?'

'Water,' he said. He sat in the beer baron's chair and gripped
the arms so tightly I thought he'd rip them off. I brought DeMille
water and some of Calypso's homemade chocolate-chip cookies
so he'd quit strangling the chair arms.

Cold water and four cookies calmed DeMille down enough
that he could talk without shouting.

'Now, explain to me why you went to see Ms Penrod alone.'

'I wasn't alone. Dean was listening on my cell phone the whole time.'

'He was across town,' DeMille said. I was afraid steam would shoot out of his ears if I kept trying to justify myself.

'I took Katie out to breakfast that morning,' I said. 'She'd rented the empty apartment in my building and she seemed to be working out fine. We all liked her. Katie and I went to the Egg-Zack-Lee-Rite. She had to go to work after breakfast. Katie asked me if you knew who killed Sammie Lant. I said if you did, you sure wouldn't tell me.'

DeMille snorted.

'We talked about Sammie Lant and what she wore the last time I saw her. I mentioned her skirt, blouse and red heels with the rhinestone butterflies on them. That's when Katie asked, "And what about that clunky rhinestone butterfly pin on her chest? How trashy was that?"'

'Shortly after that, Katie left to open the plant shop. I was finishing my coffee when I remembered you said the information about the butterfly pin had been withheld from the public. Also, Katie told me she'd never met Sammie. I realized Katie had killed Sammie and shoved that pin down her throat. I followed Katie to the shop to get her to confess.'

'I heard the recording,' DeMille said.

'So you knew she was guilty and I wasn't trying to rob the shop,' I said. 'And I bet you did your research and found many ways to tie Katie to the murder.' Yes, it was shameless flattery, but I wasn't too proud to use it.

DeMille jumped in, saying, 'I found out that Ms Penrod had lunch at the same restaurant as Sammie Lant on the last day she was seen alive. Katie Penrod's credit card receipt said she paid and left the restaurant two minutes after Sammie.'

'What about the beach wagon?' I asked. 'The hot pink one at the flower shop?'

'Ms Penrod's credit card receipts showed she bought the beach wagon at a Peerless Point Beachwalk store the same day that Sammie was last seen.

'I had a CSI team go over it,' DeMille said. 'The team made

some promising finds, including skin and hair in the wagon. It's being tested for DNA. I put a rush on the results.

'Also, Ms Penrod had a ticket for parking illegally on Surf Road near the Florodora at eleven forty-seven the night Ms Lant disappeared.'

'So Katie was near the Florodora around midnight,' I said. 'She could have dumped Sammie's body into the hole made by the plumbers and shoveled enough dirt to cover it.

'I can prove Katie was strong enough to lift a shovel. Look what she did to me.' I pointed to the purple-red-and-green bruises decorating my neck.

DeMille winced. 'Ms Penrod is also charged with your attempted murder,' he said. 'That's another felony.'

'Who is representing Katie?' I asked. 'Her mother, the hotshot lawyer?'

'Yes. Along with the firm's senior partner. I believe he's taking the lead.'

'Was Katie seriously injured?'

'Nope, just a graze. The docs did have to shave off all her hair on one side.'

DeMille smiled for the first time. He started to leave, then pulled his Columbo act again.

'One more thing,' he said, standing by my door. 'I accepted your explanation for Max Clifford's death, as established by your grandmother's diary. The medical examiner has ruled Clifford's death an accident. I'll make a statement to the media today. I expect the Clifford family to kick up a fuss.'

'Will they cause problems for you?'

'No,' he said. 'Facts are facts. That cold case is closed.'

DeMille returned Grandma's diary as well as my locket with the photos of my parents. 'Now get that clasp fixed,' he said.

THIRTY-SEVEN

Nettie Parker arrived at the Florodora at two that same afternoon, accompanied by her sister, Ann, and her caregiver. The frail woman with the snow-white hair was wearing a soft blue dress. Thanks to the Florodora's new ramp, Nettie's wheelchair had no problem getting in the building.

I met her at the door. I wore long sleeves and covered my bruised throat with a scarf so I didn't look so battered.

Calypso had set a tea service for us at a round table in the lounge, using Grandma's best silver and rose-patterned china. The centerpiece was Calypso's guava pound cake.

Nettie and Ann admired the lounge and the table setting. The women seemed pleased at the attention paid to this occasion.

Everyone sat at the table. Calypso poured the tea and handed round slices of pound cake.

Nettie said, 'Miss Norah, I owe you an apology. I should have never asked you to rent to that woman.' She sounded so apologetic I felt embarrassed.

'No need to apologize,' I said.

'Look at your throat. That scarf doesn't hide a thing. She nearly killed you.'

'It all worked out,' I said. 'Sammie's killer has been caught and Detective DeMille gave me back my necklace, a gift from my grandmother. Sammie stole it.'

'I'm just thankful that woman called off the engagement to my son,' Nettie said.

'That was a blessing,' Ann said.

'Let's enjoy our cake and tea and forget about that woman,' Calypso said.

For a while, the only sounds were delicate sips of tea and murmurs of appreciation for Calypso's cake. It was a knockout.

After we finished our first round of cake, Calypso cut us all another slice. 'I promised I'd tell you about your mother,' Nettie said.

Now my heart was pounding. Who was my mother? The product of a one-night stand? Or worse? The daughter of a crook or a bootlegger? There were plenty of them in south Florida. I needed to woman up.

'I'm ready,' I said, and took a long drink of tea.

'You know about segregation, right, dear?' Nettie asked.

'I know it was bad in the South.'

'And the North,' Nettie said.

'Segregation was all over the country. We went to separate schools, rode in the back of the buses, even drank out of "special" water fountains. There were "sundown towns" where black people had to be gone by sundown. They didn't call us black people, either. They weren't that polite.'

Nettie took a small bite of cake, as if the sweet taste would take away the bitter words that were commonly used. I knew exactly what they were.

'That's terrible,' I said. I fortified myself with a big bite of cake. 'Yes, it is.'

Nettie pointed at me with her cake fork. 'I'm not here to give you a lecture on racism. I want you to understand what the times were like for my grandmother, Irene, and Zina, Calypso's mother. Both ladies went to my church. Churches were our mainstay.

'Back to Ellie. When your grandmother hired a black person, she paid them the same money as a white one. Most black people did not get equal pay. Your grandmother helped support black families during the Depression.'

I'd always been proud of Grandma, but I was pleased to know this side of her.

'So when your grandma Ellie got into trouble, we helped her.'

'What happened?' I asked.

'Ellie was devastated when her husband died. She said her heart was broken.'

'That's what Grandma told me,' I said.

'Ellie didn't date for almost fifteen years after Johnny Harriman died,' Nettie said. 'Around Valentine's Day, 1941, Ellie started going out with a Miami lawyer named Danny Oliver.'

Calypso poured us all more tea.

'They had a whirlwind romance. Ellie was the happiest anyone had ever seen her. My mother believed they were in love. Then in late March, Danny's law firm sent him on a case to Tallahassee, almost five hundred miles north. It was a big promotion for the young lawyer, and he wouldn't be back here for months. After Danny left, Ellie discovered she was pregnant. Now she was in a real pickle.'

'Because she was unmarried?'

'Yes. Unwed mothers were shamed as Jezebels.'

'No one ever said anything about unwed fathers,' Ann said.

'You can't believe the way so-called Christians treated a woman who was pregnant and unmarried,' Nettie said. 'She was treated as a tramp and shunned by polite society. She was the subject of ugly gossip. That was bad enough, but they also took it out on the innocent baby. Some "nice" people wouldn't let their children play with the child of an unmarried mother. The baby would be talked about and tormented when she went to school.

'Zina figured out what was going on when she found your grandmother throwing up every morning and unable to keep food down. Zina asked Ellie if she wanted to keep the child.

'Ellie did, but she didn't want to go to a home for unwed mothers. Zina and Ellie put their heads together and figured out what Ellie should do. First, she went to a doctor in Miami and found she was eight weeks gone.

'Zina and Ellie decided that your grandmother should tell everyone she had to leave town because she had a cousin in upstate New York. This country cousin was a naïve young woman who got pregnant. Ellie called this made-up cousin Mary. Almost everyone had a cousin like that. Your grandmother said she'd go to New York to be with Cousin Mary and then adopt her baby.'

This was the story Grandma told me and everyone else. 'What about my mother's birth certificate?' I said. 'Wouldn't it have Cousin Mary's name on it?'

I ate another big bite of cake.

'It was a privately arranged adoption,' Nettie said. 'The birth certificate had your grandmother's name on it. Ellie liked that plan, but she had to move quickly. She was starting to show. She found a nice rooming house in the seaside town of Cape May, New Jersey, run by a widow lady, Rose Day, and stayed there. Your grandmother said she was a widow. Mrs Day, the landlady, assumed the baby was your late grandfather's child.

'During her pregnancy, Ellie and Mrs Day became good friends. Mrs Day treated Ellie like the daughter she never had. 'The baby was born November seventh, 1941. She weighed seven pounds, three ounces.'

'November seventh was my mother's birthday,' I said. 'The date she used.'

Nettie ignored the interruption and said, 'Your grandmother called her baby Dot. Ellie planned to stay in Cape May until January, 1942. Then the Japanese bombed Pearl Harbor on December seventh, and we were in World War Two.

'Ellie felt she'd better come home to Peerless Point. Mrs Day found a baby nurse to travel with Ellie and Dot on the train, a woman who wanted to move to Miami. They arrived safely home. Zina became Dot's nanny, and no one asked any questions about her origins. Zina and my mother, Irene, kept your grandmother's secret. And Ellie repaid us during World War Two.

'Florida officials issued "Work or Fight" orders. If a man wasn't in uniform, then he had to have a job. Roundups of so-called "loafers" almost always included black men. Your grandmother hired as many black men as she could to keep them out of jail.

'And that's it,' Nettie said. 'That's the story of your grandmother and mother.'

She surveyed the table with satisfaction: the remains of the cake, the pretty rose-patterned cups now drained of tea, and the shining silver teapot.

'Any other questions, Norah?'

'Did your mother ever meet my grandfather, Danny Oliver?'

'Yes, she did,' Nettie said. 'She said Danny was a fine figure of a man, tall and broad-shouldered, with thick dark hair and deep blue eyes. He was a good dancer, too. And he had a good personality.'

'Did he marry my grandmother?'

'He wanted to, but he'd enlisted in the US Army Air Corps to fight for his country right after Pearl Harbor. He didn't know about the baby, but he asked Ellie to marry him when he came home on leave.'

'What happened?'

'Like a lot of our boys, Danny was killed in action. He was shot down over Germany. He was awarded some kind of medal.'

'My grandfather was a war hero,' I said. 'I wished I'd known him, even for a day.'

'I know, dear.' Nettie patted my hand.

After the tea party broke up, Calypso returned to the kitchen behind the office, to fry chicken for that night's dinner. I cleaned up the lounge, and carried the tea party things into the kitchen.

I wrapped the remains of the guava cake and asked, 'Where do you want this cake?'

'Might as well take it,' she said. 'You and Dean can eat it.'

I was hoping she'd say that. I carefully washed the delicate cups and dessert plates, and dried them with a fresh towel, keeping the china far away from the spitting, sputtering chicken pan.

'Calypso, did you know that Dot was my grandmother's child?'

'I had my suspicions.' Calypso turned a chicken thigh with a fork. 'I knew lots of women had inconvenient children during the war years. Mama told me about so-called "premature babies" that weighed nine pounds. Babies who didn't resemble their daddy one little bit. "War widows" who showed up in town with cheap gold wedding rings and a baby carriage.

'It was nobody's business. As long as your grandma was happy and that baby was healthy, that's all that was important.

'You know my mama didn't marry my daddy, don't you?' Calypso asked.

'No.'

'Zina had been married back in 1938. Her husband and baby died of a fever, and Zina was broken-hearted. She came to the States in 1940 and started working for your grandma.

'I was born in 1965 right here in Peerless Point,' Calypso said. 'I was a souvenir from one of Mama's island vacations. When I was six months old, Mama sent me home to be raised by my nana. I came back when I was sixteen and too much of a handful for Nana. I helped Mama for a little more than a year, and then she up and died of a stroke.

'Did you know I was married?' Calypso asked.

'No.'

'It was before you were born. Mama was still alive. Nana sent me here when I turned sixteen because the island boys were way too interested in me – and vice versa. I was a bit wild until I met Thomas, a fine island man who lived here in Peerless. Thomas asked me to marry him, and I said yes.

'At our wedding, we celebrated with too much champagne. On the drive home, Thomas tried to beat a freight train.'

She stopped. Her brown eyes were brimming with sorrow. I could read what happened.

'I'm so sorry,' I said. 'I can't imagine what that was like.'

'I hope you never know,' she said.

'After Thomas passed, I was in the hospital a long time,' she said. 'The pastor of the Methodist church helped me through that dark time. Now I sing in the church choir and only lift my voice in song to praise the Lord.

'Your grandma, my mama and I, we have a lot in common. We were all crazy about our men, and when they passed, we never married again. But we also never stopped being women. You know what I mean?'

'Yes,' I said.

After I put away the last dish, I went upstairs and opened my computer. A quick online search revealed lists of airmen killed in World War Two.

And there was my grandfather. 'Daniel Edison Oliver, age thirty-five, Miami, Florida,' the list said. 'Killed in action April third, 1942, when the B-17 Flying Fortress he was co-piloting was struck by anti-aircraft fire during a bombing raid on a German aircraft factory.' The end of Danny's short life was summed up in one convoluted sentence. The bomber crew received the Air Medal with Valor retroactively.

I kept searching until I found an old black-and-white portrait photo of Danny in uniform, looking at the camera with a young man's pride and confident courage. My mother had Danny's smile and long-lashed eyes.

I hoped Danny's courage had been passed down to me.

THIRTY-EIGHT

Three weeks later, the work on the Florodora was finished, one day ahead of the deadline. I woke at sunrise, and slipped out the back door. I wanted to admire my newly restored home.

Outside, the air was warm and comforting and the ocean was soft as silk. The morning sun gave the walls a faint peach glow.

On the beach side, the new ramp was hidden by flowering bushes that added a touch of color. The new gutters gleamed. The roof had been repaired. Eric and Godfrey had carefully preserved the old roof tiles, so I couldn't tell where the repairs had been.

I walked around front to the courtyard. The pavers had been power-washed. In the pool, the flirtatious bathing beauty looked at home. We'd added more landscaping. Palm trees for extra shade and bursts of colorful flowers, including gerbera daisies, purple bougainvillea, and orange hibiscus.

The renovated garage looked new. The parking lot was the star. Fresh black asphalt was edged by tall palms, green shrubs and more flowers.

I went back to the pool, and sat in one of the new blue-striped deckchairs. I could smell traces of the sweet perfume of my grandmother's moonflower vine. I seemed to sense her with me.

'Well, Grandma,' I said. 'What do you think? Does your home look as good as it used to? I know you told me to be careful with capital, but maybe I was too careful. Rest easy, Grandma. I'll take care of your legacy.'

Maybe it was the palms sighing in the wind, or maybe it was her spirit, but I thought my grandmother was content.

I sensed the residents stirring in the Florodora and went inside to dress for the official inspection this morning.

Upstairs, I put on my good jeans, a fresh white blouse, and a sheer scarf to cover my bruised neck. Most of the pain was gone, but my neck was an ugly yellow.

The doorbell rang at eight forty-five and I ran downstairs to meet my lawyer, Judson Greer. I wanted him present when Elwin Sandford, the Peerless Point city code enforcement officer, showed up. I didn't trust that man.

Jud was a round, jolly Santa of a man, but behind that smiling face was one of the sharpest legal minds in south Florida. Jud's presence was a silent threat that the lawyer would sue the socks off whoever tried something funny.

Elwin arrived at precisely nine o'clock with a smirk on his rodent face. It disappeared when Jud greeted Elwin on the front steps.

'Mr Gre-greer.' Elwin was stammering. 'I-I didn't expect you here.'

'But here I am,' Jud said, and gave Elwin such a hearty slap on the back the inspector nearly fell down the stairs. 'Let's begin, shall we? I have Ms McCarthy's list, the one you signed. Where would you like to start?'

Elwin consulted the list. 'How about the elevator?' he asked. 'It was cited for "unusual noises, malfunctioning doors and erratic movements and stops."'

As we walked to the elevator, Jud said, 'Ms McCarthy was lucky to find replacement parts for this vintage conveyance. It's part of Peerless Point's historic heritage.'

Much to Elwin's surprise, the elevator performed flawlessly.

The inspector took more than an hour to go over the Florodora, with a smiling Jud at his side. The inspection ended at the new parking lot.

'Very nice, Ms McCarthy,' Elwin said. 'I have no idea how you did this so quickly.'

'But she did, didn't she, Elwin? Ready to sign off on the work?'

Elwin signed and nearly ran to his car.

'Thanks, Jud,' I said. 'I'm glad you were here.'

'I'm glad you kept the original papers, Norah. That little worm likes to create another set and claim people didn't finish everything. And I like to nail him.' Jud's smile stretched across his round face.

Inside, the Florodora seemed unnaturally quiet. For the first time, there were no construction sounds. Calypso's crew had the day off. Dean, Billie and Rafael were giving them a tour of the beach.

Calypso was out with Mickey, buying the items the crew's wives and girlfriends wanted from the States, and getting them shipped to the islands.

The two women came back about five o'clock. 'Calypso, are you going to fix dinner? If you're tired of cooking, I can order in.'

'Hah!' Calypso said. 'The men aren't eating tonight. Dean, Billie and Rafael volunteered to give my cousins a tour of the beach. Do you think they've been looking at the sights all day? Building sandcastles? Hell, no, they're hitting the bars.'

'But they left before nine,' I said.

Mickey giggled.

'The beach bars open early.' Calypso looked at me with pity, possibly for my ignorance. 'Those boys are going to be hurting when I wake them up at five thirty tomorrow morning to catch their plane home.'

Calypso, Mickey and I spent the evening in my apartment. I ordered in steaks and blue cheese potatoes from the Grass Shack, and we ate our meal with wine.

About midnight, our party was breaking up when we heard the men staggering back home.

'Ooh, boy,' Calypso said. 'This is gonna be fun tomorrow morning.'

The next morning at six o'clock, Calypso's crew was picking at their breakfast in the courtyard when Dean and Rafael arrived to drive them to the airport.

Calypso greeted them with a hearty, 'Good morning, gentlemen.'

The whole table winced. 'Not so loud,' Dean said.

Calypso couldn't stop laughing. 'I've seen better looking corpses.'

'Check the obituaries and see if they mention me,' Dean said.

I handed the crew their pay and bonus envelopes and thanked them for their hard work. After hugs and heartfelt goodbyes, the men headed for the vehicles. Calypso and I loaded the luggage in the truck. The men had a hard enough time loading themselves in the truck and the Jeep.

We waved goodbye until they disappeared.

'I'm gonna miss them,' Calypso said.

'Me, too.'

I'd promised Grandma I'd take care of her creation. She'd left me well-provided-for and lectured me about the dangers of touching capital. But this qualified as an emergency. I sold stocks and liquidated accounts to save the Florodora.

Once again, my family had saved me. The Florodora was my legacy, the only home I'd known, and the residents were my chosen family.

EPILOGUE

Renovating the Florodora changed me, too. I will be dealing with the fallout for a long time.

As for Katie, the woman who tried to kill me with a pink gun. The DNA found in the pink beach wagon definitely belonged to Sammie Lant. Together with credit card statements for the wagon and her lunch at the same restaurant as Sammie, plus the parking ticket that put her at the beach, Katie was in trouble.

For my attempted murder, Katie was looking at forty years to life in prison, and if she was convicted of murdering Sammie, well, Florida is a death penalty state.

Katie didn't want to chance the death penalty. She pleaded guilty to both felony charges and got life without parole.

She won't be wearing pink ever again.

The downstairs apartment is empty again, and it's going to stay that way for a while.

Chet, Katie's former fiancé, and another classmate at Hallandale Beach College created a successful IT startup. He's now worth fifty million dollars. Chet and his new wife formed their own foundation. The handsome couple are media darlings.

Sammie's father died a month after his daughter's body was found. Sammie's Cousin Betty claimed the porn star's body. She knew Sammie didn't want to be buried next to her father. She also knew Sammie loved the ocean. Betty had Sammie cremated and scattered her ashes in the sea.

Betty also claimed Sammie's royalties for her porn movies – the ones Vixen Tamer expected to live off. By the time Vix got out of the slammer after ten years for the damage and death threat carved into my car, his client, the Countess Crawlie had moved on to another agent.

Mickey has moved back downstairs to her place, and Dean and I are friends again. Very good friends. In fact, we're almost inseparable. I haven't said the L-word yet, but it's on my mind. As for love, I've been given a lot of it. I may be an orphan, but I do have a family, the residents of the Florodora. I learned my mother wasn't adopted. She was my grandmother's child. My parents' deaths were tragic, but the Eighties were a wild time when temptation abounded. I was sorry they couldn't resist it.

I found my grandfather and discovered he was a war hero. I learned my grandmother was a hero, too, in her way. I've always envied Grandma because she loved so passionately. Maybe I'll have a chance, too.

Dean stayed with me again tonight. I woke up at moonrise and stood at my grandmother's bedroom window, the one she'd gazed out of a century ago.

The moon made a path on the silver sea. Tonight, it seemed bright with possibility.